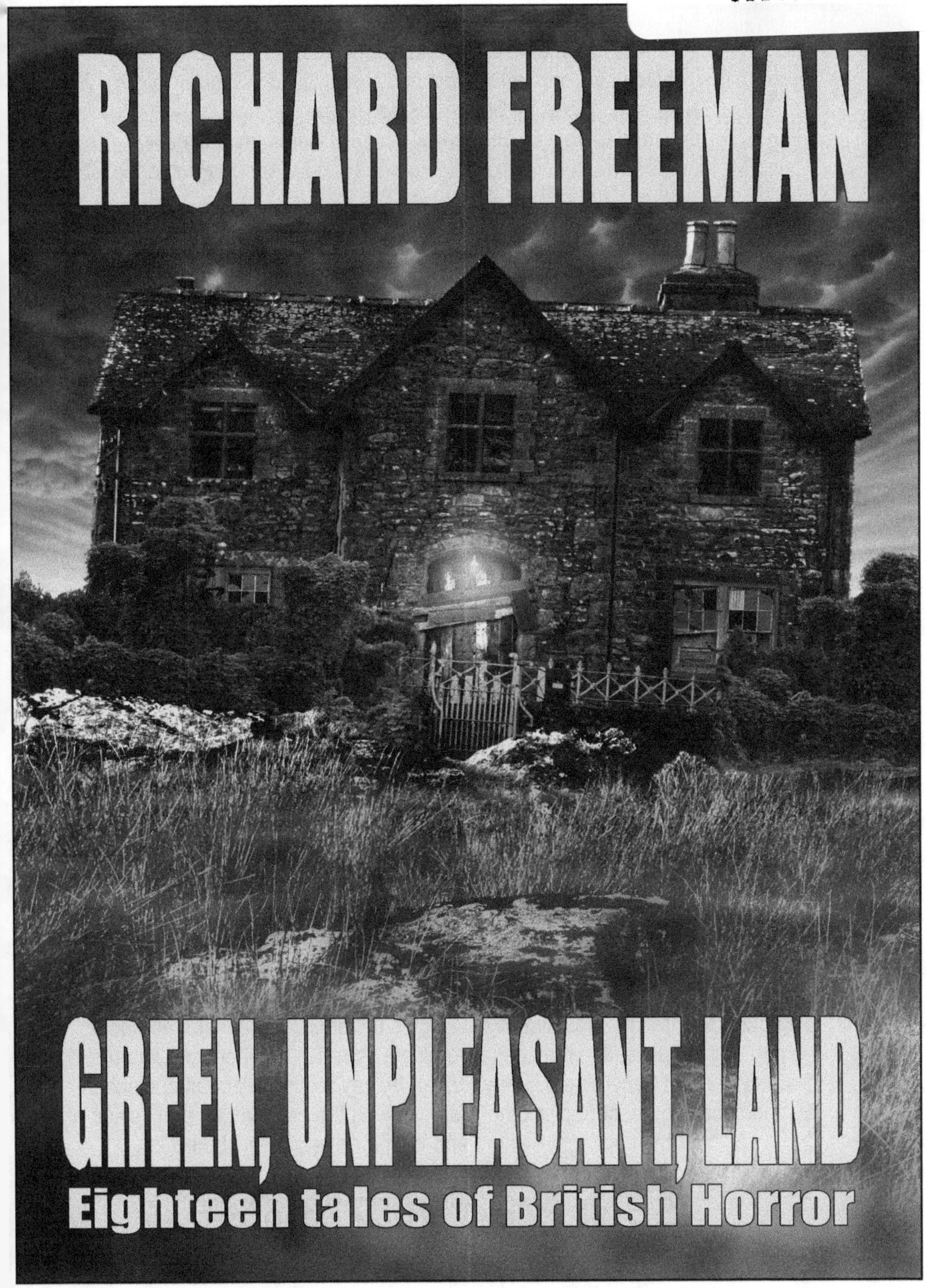

RICHARD FREEMAN

GREEN, UNPLEASANT, LAND

Eighteen tales of British Horror

Typeset by Jonathan Downes,
Edited by Corinna Downes and Gavin Lloyd Wilson
Art by Shaun Histead-Todd
Cover and Layout by SPiderKaT for CFZ Communications
Using Microsoft Word 2000, Microsoft , Publisher 2000, Adobe Photoshop CS.

First published in Great Britain by Fortean Words

CFZ Press
Myrtle Cottage
Woolsery
Bideford
North Devon
EX39 5QR

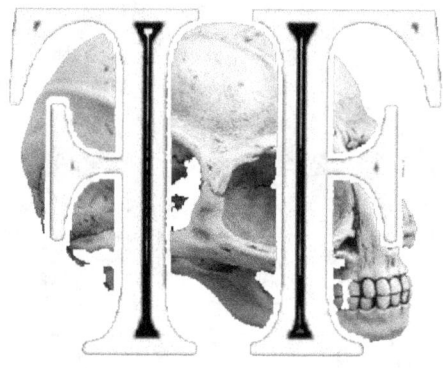

ISBN: 978-1-905723-85-0

For China Miéville,
whom I believe to be the greatest living writer

INTRODUCTION

I grew up with horror. I was weaned on *Hammer* movies and classic 1970s *Doctor Who*. As a lad, I found that the tactic of being very quiet as bedtime approached often meant that I could get to stay up later as my presence would be forgotten. Some of my earliest exposure to horror was experienced by this method; the wonderful Vincent Price playing the homicidal Shakespearian actor Edward Lionheart in *Theatre of Blood,* and Christopher Lee lurching through the swamps in pursuit of Peter Cushing in *The Mummy.* Adding to the mix was the immortal Ray Harryhausen and his wonderful stop-motion creations. These amazing films were shown in the summer holidays and never failed to inspire and fire the imagination: *Valley of Gwangi, The Seventh Voyage of Sinbad, Jason and the Argonauts*. Ray's creations were, and still are, worth a million of the dull, lifeless CGI creations that pollute films of today. In

later years, Ray's technique was used by others in such classic films as *Q: The Winged Serpent* and *Jack the Giant Killer.*

From Japan, Godzilla lumbered onto our screens. A 400-foot tall, radioactive, fire-breathing mutant dinosaur doing battle with alien behemoths, monsters made from solidi-fied pollution, three-headed cosmic dragons and giant robot replicas of himself, Godzilla is the definition of entertainment.

At the other end of the effects spectrum were the 1950s B-Movies. These amazing flicks brought us giant ants, gill-men, monster psychic crabs, killer shrews and a legion of mad scientists.

Then, of course, there was *that* TV show; the one that mesmerised millions of children and adults across the UK every Saturday evening. The one whose theme tune made the hairs on the back of your neck stand up. It was usually sandwiched in between Alan Tower's 'round up of the regional news and sport' and some light entertainment show like *The Generation Game*. I ended up owing my career to this programme. I refer, of course, to *Doctor Who*. For half an hour each week I was whisked away on some weird, dark adventure.

There were shop room dummies, and children's dolls that jerked into homicidal life. There were giant venomous maggots oozing from Welsh slag heaps, and super-evolved dinosaurs rising up out of the ocean, or awakening from an aeon's long slumber. Plus giant rats in Victorian sewers, ancient Egyptian gods with robot mummies as servants, and parasitic alien plants that infect and transform human victims. All this and so very, very much more. No wonder I grew up to be a cryptozoologist and hunt real life monsters. I owe an awful lot to Jon Pertwee and Tom Baker.

My book collection was just as weird. Aside from the *Dr. Who* Target novelisations, I collected any book about monsters or horror I could get my paws on. Usborne's *Mysteries of the Unexplained; Monster, Ghosts and UFOs, The Hamlyn Book of Horror,* and all those wonderful anthologies edited by the likes of R Chetwynd-Hayes.

I generally write non-fiction. This is my first work of fiction of any length, which I decided to write for a couple of reasons. The first is my own personal anger at the way the genre has been treated in recent years. The rot really began with the god-awful *Buffy the Vampire Slayer*. This vacuous series was an irritating teen soap opera dressed up in the trappings of horror.

A case in point was an episode when an ancient god was awakened, but was there a Lovecraftian horror in sight? Oh dear me, no. The god was realised in the form of a petulant teenage girl! Abysmally written and acted, it remains my least favourite TV show ever (and I'm including *Big Break* with Jim Davidson in that equation!). I've always maintained that its writer Joss Whedon wouldn't know what true horror was if it came up and bit him in the face.

I for one will scream if I see another film, TV show or book about good-looking teenaged vampires. After *Buffy,* horror fans have had to suffer *Angel, Twilight, First Blood, Vampire Diaries* and God knows how many more. Horror today seems to be dominated by soap opera-ish, unimaginative plots and tired hack writers.

There is some light at the end of the tunnel though. In recent years we saw the triumphant return of *Doctor Who*. As it was back in the 1960s and 1970s, *Doctor Who* is once again the BBC's flagship show. It has also kicked open the door for other programmes such as *Primeval, Life on Mars, Ashes to Ashes* and *Merlin*.

On the big screen dross still dominates, but we do see occasional gems such as *Cloverfield, Trollhunter* and *Let the Right One In*.

This book represents my own kicking back at the poor excuse for horror we have had to endure for so long. But my second reason for writing it was to showcase some odd and overlooked pieces of

British folklore. Too often horror is stuck in the rut of using the same subjects and monsters, when in folklore there is a wealth of concepts and creatures that are rarely tapped into. My favourite era of *Dr Who* was that of the third doctor, played by Jon Pertwee, and I think that one of the reasons I liked it so much was that for much of Pertwee's tenure in the title role, The Doctor was confined to earth, mostly Britain. So that is what I have done here: these eighteen stories are all set in Britain, either in the present day, or within living memory.

Herein you will find dragons and hellhounds, goblins and killer rodents, unicorns and basilisks. There is a vampire story, but the creature in it bears scant resemblance to the popular, and totally wrong, public perception of them. I hope this book will open your eyes to the potential of horror. It is more than just teenaged vampires hanging around schools.

Richard Freeman,
Exeter, December, 2011.

DRAKE'S BRIER

They looked like an army; the police in their helmets, armed with batons, crouching behind riot shields. They looked like Nazi Stormtroopers. Behind them loomed the diggers and bulldozers, their headlamps falling down like spotlights on the scene. They *were* an army, and this was a battle in a very real war, and we were ready to take the fight to them.

I was crouching low in one of the lookout posts on the edge of Elf Land. That's what we called it, Elf Land, the rambling network of tree houses and rope bridges that had been my home for the last six months. I glanced around taking in some of the faces I knew from the crowds of Elf Landers now amassed to fight for their homes and for the survival of Drake's Brier Woods; Kingsley Evans, the six-foot punk with a pink Mohawk and an absurd voice like a cartoon mouse; Crazy Lil with her shaven head and extensive tattoos; Billy the Troll, a hairy little Scotsman so-called for his ability to dig and live in tunnels. Oddest of all was Mrs. Parkhurst, Elf Land's oldest resident. A 70-year-old widow from the little town of Drake's End, she had hated the proposed relief road, and had fought for the survival of the woods from the outset. She had been living in the ragged conglomeration of arboreal shanties longer than I had.

I clutched the cricket bat to my chest and tensed myself for the police charge. Beside me were several petrol bombs and canisters of homemade napalm, a nasty mixture of Vaseline, polystyrene, and petrol. I always knew it would come down to this. The final battle. But the reality of being there; the thick pendulous atmosphere made my stomach turn over. Then from behind our ranks came a voice.

> *"And when he'd eaten all he could*
> *And when he'd had his fill*
> *He crawled away and wound his tail*
> *Nine times about the hill."*

He stepped out of the shadows and pushed his way towards the frontline. Walking forwards into "no-man's land" he stood before the police and work crew as bold as brass. It was Goatface.

Goatface had always been a part of Drake's Brier as far as I was concerned. A semi-legendary character.

I played in the woods as a boy. My friends and I would dare each other to go deeper. Into where the light didn't shine. Into where the mad tramp lived. He would come scuttling out of the shadows, muttering under his breath. Or sometimes loom from behind an ancient oak or yew silent as a ghost. I guess he must have looked pretty much like the average tramp. He wore a fading black trench coat, even in the middle of summer. About it was tied a piece of hairy string in lieu of a belt. He had shabby grey trousers and hobnail boots. He had a long unkempt beard that gave him his name, always flecked with spittle, filth and crumbs. It was almost as if he was cultivating something in it. His weather-beaten face had a Faginesque hooked nose and two mad pallid eyes that shone out through the grime. He looked like some ungodly cross between Old Father Time and Albert Steptoe.

And the woods themselves were equally as odd. According to the maps Drake's Brier covered around 300 acres. Yet it seemed so much bigger. Perhaps it just looked that way through a child's eyes, but the odd effect still struck me when I returned as an adult. Even at the edges very little light penetrated. It was filtered through the dense canopy of herbage above. This gave the woods an odd sort of constant verdant twilight. Everything seemed tinted green. In Drake's Brier you could think yourself in the middle of the Siberian Taiga. It seemed so distant, so far from civilisation. And at its centre stood Worm Hill.

Worm Hill rose several hundred feet out of the middle of the woods. Visible for miles around it was a well-known local landmark. No sheep ever grazed there. It was encircled by rings that formed tiers up its sides. The local legend was that they were formed by the coils of a dragon that laired in the hollow hill and came out to wrap itself about the mound.

We climbed up it on a number of occasions. We were always out of puff by the time we reached the top but it was worth it for the view. Miles of the North Yorkshire Moors were visible. On a clear day you could just make out Whitby on the coast to the east. We would run down the spiral coils in the hill imagining what size of beast would have made them.

My Dad told me that Worm Hill was actually an Iron Age fort and the circles were its ramparts. Apparently, in the early 1960s a team of archaeologists from Leeds University excavated the area, but the dig only lasted a week and then closed down abruptly. Apparently, nothing of note was found. The team's leader, a Professor Amos Hartley, retired afterwards. The hill had been left undisturbed ever since.

As we got older, our fear of Goatface lessened. He never actually did anything to us. He was never aggressive or unkind; he was just there. You would see him in the woods, he might stare briefly, but then he would go away into the trees, like an animal. He lived deep in the centre of the woods. I only saw his home a couple of times. It was in a thick tangled strand of blackthorn. I stumbled on it quite by accident. He had woven the thorny branches together to form tunnels running to a central dome of woven thicket and corrugated iron, with old bits of tarpaulin strung across it. A makeshift chimney rose from it, black and sooty.

It wasn't us who gave him his name. It was an older boy, Keith "Beefy" Johnson. Beefy Johnson was the bully of Drake's End Middle School, though he was quite a coward on his own. Beefy usually had an entourage of henchmen, the Beefy Johnson Gang. They took to hanging around the woods. They gave the old man the name of Goatface. They would torment him screaming *"Goatface, Goatface"* over and over, throwing stones and then running when he hobbled after them, swinging the gnarled old walking stick he always carried. He wheezed horribly and dribbled phlegm down his beard. He mumbled and hissed, but I could never make out the words. They sounded foreign.

Sometimes he would play strange music on a set of carved black pipes. The eerie, disturbing sound would float down through the woods sounding more like a piping language than music.

I was amazed when my Granddad said he knew him.

"Abner Skinner were his real name," he said. *"His family came from up Northumbria way. I knew 'im when I were at University down in Leeds."*

My Granddad had done three years at the university, rare for a working class bloke in those days. He studied farming and agriculture. It was not long after the war. He had been a bright lad and won a scholarship. He went on to farm rapeseed just outside Wakefield.

"Wouldn't credit it would yer, lad? He were bloody clever once, best in the year. He wouldn't have just been a farmer. He would have got a job down the Old Smoke with the agriculture department or somethin'. I couldn't believe it were same bloke, me."

"What happened, Granddad? If he were so clever like, what happened to him?" I asked.

"Went mad, son. Mad as a bag of spoons! He got a dose of religion. Don't ask me which one. Some crackpot foreign rubbish I think. Anyways he found this old book in one of them creaky old bookshops up Hebdon Bridge way. Said it told him how to grow crops really fast and no matter how poor the soil was. Somethin' to do with old gods and earth fertility. The more he read the loonier he got. He would wander up onto the moors and in the woods for days on end. Miss lectures, never wash, come back to his digs covered in dirt and blood. Some of the other students said he was sacrificin' cats and chickens to somethin' up in Drake's Brier but I can't say if it were true or not.

He said he had a theory that would revolutionise farming. Said there would be no hunger ever again. Now this was just after the war. People was still being rationed. Happen as that's why his tomfoolery was tolerated up at the university, to a point. He could have made it big. I think he could have really done somethin' special, groundbreaking. But then one night he was caught wandering through campus covered in mud and blood, screamin' his ruddy head off. He was thrown off the course and kicked out his lodgings. He just upped and left for the woods. Lived there ever since. Never been right in the head since. He's a wrong un, that bloke."

I often wondered what the old man lived off. I supposed he must pick berries and grow his own food. I thought he must have some livestock because on several occasions I heard him mention "feedin' it". It seemed to be the only words he said that were not gibberish.

The Beefy Johnson gang continued to torment "Goatface" for a couple of years. Then Beefy disappeared. No body was ever found despite a massive police search. No one was ever charged. I supposed they would have questioned old Abner Skinner but I never heard anything about it. The Johnsons moved away down south. Some of the people in the village suspected 'that mad old bastard up the woods' had done Beefy in. They spoke darkly about him but no one ever did anything. My Mum wouldn't let me play in those woods after that. My mates' Mums all did the same thing. That was in the summer of 1977. I didn't see Goatface again for years.

I grew up, left school, attended college, and finally moved away to study ecology at Cardiff University. I joined Greenpeace there and went on several protest marches and rallies. It was just after my graduation that I heard of the government plans to run a road straight through my childhood playground.

There were bee orchids in Drake's Brier, there were red squirrels, some said there were even mouse eared bats. Stuff that you rarely find elsewhere. The woods were like a little national park. The plan was to run a relief road through the woods and skirt around Worm Hill. It would destroy many acres and bisect the forest. The danger the heavy traffic would pose to wildlife was obvious.

I left immediately to join the direct action protest. The thought of another piece of green stripped away forever made my blood boil. The fact that it was 'my' piece of green made me all the more angry.

The group grew over the weeks and months, as did Elf Land. I was surprised to find Goatface was still alive and well. We didn't see him that often. Usually we would hear his unsettling music rising through the woods when the moon was fat. A wet, reedy, piping, pregnant with strangeness. When we did bump into him on some deep woodland path he would never speak but gave us a nod as if he knew what we were doing and was grateful. I almost got to like him. Almost.

We had cost the government hundreds of thousands of pounds and had put their nasty little project back months. Roadblocks, iron spikes in tyres and caterpillar tracks, sand in engines. We tried all the tricks. Now it looked like it was all over. We were well entrenched, but vastly outnumbered. All that stood between the police and the diggers and us was Abner Skinner, old Goatface.

The sun was crawling behind the horizon, throwing the whole scene into the ethereal cloak of twilight. The old man cast off the huge trench coat and stood bare chested. His scrawny body was a network of scars. Strange symbols carved into his flesh. I had an unpleasant feeling that they were self-inflicted.

He threw back his head and bellowed. An animalistic primal scream that I found hard to equate with such a frail-looking old man. Then he began his jabbering. If they were words then they were not in any language known to me. They sounded more like guttural snorts, high-pitched whines, and horrid chitterings. Perhaps they were vestiges of the original, primal, uber language rising up from the old man's subconscious. Who knows? The police must have been slightly taken aback as they didn't do anything. At the height of his maniacal ravings he threw back his head and whipped a black bladed knife out of his malodorous pocket. Quick as a flash he was cutting sigils in his own flesh, opening up swirls and curves of flesh that wept tears of blood. His hands moved fast across his pigeon chest whilst his face seemed lost in a ghastly expression of almost orgasmic ecstasy. As the rills of gore fell into the dust he shrieked something that I think must have been an invocation, a calling, the name of... something.

"IA! IA! LLOIGOR!"

There was a dry rustling from the woods behind us. Something stirred the treetops and made the dead leaves dance tiny waltzes. The ground began to tremble as if something were stirring beneath our feet. A murmur broke out among the ranks, then someone noticed that the police were staring not at us but behind us.

As one, the crowd turned and looked up at Worm Hill. There seemed to be an odd kind of nimbus about it, like a heat haze. It seemed to trace a path down the ruts that encircled the hill. The effect seemed to move with an ophidian grace. It ran like water down the tracks forming coils about the hill. As I watched, trying to work out what was causing the strange sight, I noticed that it seemed to be solidifying. The haze was becoming more like a greenish light.

The front end of the phenomena reached the foot of the hill and seemed to slide into the trees. There was a rustling in the woods that began to grow as coil after coil of the green light slithered down from the hill and entered the woods.

None of us knew what it was. I think we were all imagining it to be some kind of trick Skinner had engineered. I recall being impressed at that point and wondering how the old bugger had pulled it off. None of us were ready for what came next.

Out of the woods came a sound. It was like nothing I'd ever heard. I could try to explain it as being bird-like, a sort of thundering screech. But that would not do it justice. It had more bass. It was almost as if the sound was inside my head rather than external, but I know that can't be right as I saw the others react to it. The noise seemed to stir something deep in my memory.

Something bad.

There was another sound accompanying the screech. It was like the sails of an old-fashioned ship unfurling or huge carpets being beaten. I realised with shock that I was listening to the beating of huge wings.

We didn't scream, not at first. We couldn't even move. What came crashing out of those woods, half slithering, half flapping, burnt itself onto the mind of everyone that saw it, together with one word: *Dragon*.

It was huge, hundreds of feet long. It rose from the shadows of Drake's Brier Wood, its titan bat wings half open. Armoured scales glistened an iridescent green, the sheen making rainbow patterns like oil on water. Four tree trunk thick legs terminated in clutching scythe talons. The tail seemed to trail on endlessly into the woods with an unceasing writhing and coiling. At the end of the long neck was a horned head, a reptilian nightmare. I saw row upon row of curved white teeth, strong as steel, sharp as razors. A great forked tongue flickered in and out of the scimitar-lined jaws tasting the air. Caustic saliva dripped from the maw hissing like water on a hot plate.

It wasn't the teeth that scared me the most. It was the eyes. Vast orbs of golden fire with black slits. They looked so old, so very, very old, and as it turned to glance down at the Elf Landers it regarded them with a vile understanding.

The wings opened and beat once. It was up and over the crowd landing with uncanny agility in 'no-man's land'. The jaws opened and it spat forth a white fire. Bulldozers exploded, cartwheeling high in the air and crashing down in charred ruin. The police caught in the blinding, white-hot blast were dead before they hit the floor. The heat boiled their innards, sending them vomiting from their own mouths as flaming liquid flesh. They danced briefly like ghastly marionettes before becoming wisps of carbon.

Those who escaped the blast ran, bowels emptying. The dragon fell upon them and the jaws flashed down and seized a victim. It hoisted him aloft and shook him in the manner a bull terrier might shake a rat. Again and again the jaws flashed as it snapped up human prey with a lurid wet crunching.

A handful of the men had escaped, running madly into the night. The beast could have easily caught them or struck them down with a jet of flame. I think it wanted them to escape. It wanted them to tell their masters what they had seen at Drake's Brier. I was doubled up retching, as were most of the other protesters around me. Some had fouled themselves. I saw Billy the Troll scoop up a prone Mrs. Parkhurst and run for cover.

It screeched again and some dark memory rose inside me. I was a frightened ape running across a plain under a hot sun, running for my life. A puny mammal that shat and pissed as it scampered for cover with other mewling members of its kind. A massive black shadow fell across the land as an airborne predator whirled above us. The screech came again, echoing through the ages, through the countless generations, across species and into the present day. The race memory faded leaving me in spasms. I heard a human voice and my mind clutched at it like a drowning man grabbing a branch.

"I knew he'd come, the old Wyrm. He'd come alright if he thought his home was getting messed with," I heard Abner hiss. *"Him's like an adder, hibernates but as an adder sleeps*

months he can sleep aeons. There's loads of 'em all over the world. Just not time for 'em to wake up yet."

He began to laugh, almost doubling up as much as I did in my sickness. The monstrous creature folded its titan wings and slithered back into the woods. As it went it seemed to be losing form again, becoming more ethereal. I turned my head up towards the hill and saw the shimmering coils slipping ghost like into the side of the hill itself. Goatface, his wounds now quite healed, calmly picked up his coat and followed it. I wondered about his words, about just when would be the right time for them to wake up.

I never went back to Drake's Brier. The government abandoned its plans for the relief road. An enquiry into what happened stated that one of the bulldozers had exploded due to a serious electrical fault. The flames had engulfed several more machines and ignited their petrol tanks. The men were killed in the ensuing explosion. I have not seen any of my old friends from Elf Land. I think that, like me, they have given up direct action. I now live in central London, as far as I can from any wood. Still, when the wind whips up the trees in the park, making the branches sway, or clouds send big shadows sweeping across the land, I shake. And the ancient screech of the dragon still reaches down through time to haunt what little sleep I have.

THE PATTER OF TINY FEET

Why has Robyn got silver hair?" The question would have sounded odd if it came from any other boy. But Benjamin Ramsey was not any other boy. He was staring out across Bodmin Moor, the third storey window affording him an excellent view of the autumnal landscape as it began to turn misty.

"I think I've told you before, Ramsey, you're a little too old for imaginary friends."

Father Andrew Grice would have normally been annoyed at one of his pupils ignoring his Latin lesson and gazing absent-mindedly out of the window. But there was something he liked about the boy. Small, pale, slightly built and quiet, Benjamin was a solitary child; he seemed to have no friends beside the one in his head.

"He's not imaginary, Sir. He lives on the Moor with his family. We play together sometimes. He brings me things. It's not right that he has silver hair is it, Sir? Only old people get that, don't they, Sir?"

Some of the other boys sniggered at Benjamin talking about an imaginary friend at the age of ten. Grice silenced them with a scowl.

"Since when are we studying biology, young man? What about Latin verbs?"

"Yes Sir, sorry Sir." The boy reluctantly pulled his gaze away from the darkening countryside outside the window and back to the long dead language on the page in front of him.

One of the older priests might have got angry, but Grice was still a young man. He wanted the boys to think of him as a friend. Boarding schools, especially one as religious as Saint Michael's could be daunting, if not downright scary, for boys. He flinched as he recalled his own unhappy schooldays. Why in the name of the Almighty was he here after what he had gone through? He suddenly felt guilty, part of a vicious circle, an accomplice.

He pushed these uncomfortable thoughts away and turned them to what he knew of Benjamin and his past. He was a bright boy, very bright when he could be persuaded to concentrate. But he was such a daydreamer; his thoughts never on what he was doing at the time. He still bore a bruise on his fair forehead where a football had smashed into it during a PE lesson. He had been gazing out across the moor again instead of following the game.

He knew Benjamin had been born out of wedlock, still a cause of shame in a remote corner of the country such as this. His grandparents had raised the boy and paid for him to come to Saint Michael's. They had been a very well-off family in one of the larger villages skirting the moor. All the more shame when their sixteen-year-old daughter fell pregnant. Grice had never heard of what had become of the father, or even if his identity had ever been discovered.

Benjamin's mother had been sent away just after he had been born, and he never knew her. She had suffered some mental problems. The headmaster Father Dougherty, an old fashioned Catholic conservative, had been horrified at the prospect of a bastard entering the school, but Saint Michael's had fallen on hard times. Fewer and fewer pupils through its doors each year meant that they needed every penny they could lay their hands on. Grice hated Dougherty and his attitude. The boy had enough on his plate without the headmaster's pig ignorant prejudice.

Saint Michael's was an anachronism in stone and mortar. The Victorian building stood defiant against the 21st Century and illumination seldom fell on it.

The shrill bell denoting the end of the lesson jerked him from his thoughts. The boys began packing their books and pens into bags and filing out of the room.

Grice held Benjamin back for a moment. *"You really must try to pay more attention; some of the other Fathers might not be as lenient as I am."*

"Sorry Sir, it's just that I haven't got many friends and Robyn is…"

"And you won't get many if you persist in this silly fantasy. Remember what the Bible tells us? When I was a child, I spake as a child, I understood as a child, I thought as a child: but when I became a man I put away childish things."

Benjamin looked up and smiled. *"Corinthians, chapter 13, verse 1."*

"Well done," Grice said patting the child's head, *"now get going"*. Benjamin scampered off down the corridor.

The school kept a small farm in its grounds, which was nothing more than a modest vegetable patch and a few chickens in a run. They were tended by Mr. Harding, an elderly man from Bodmin who headed a skeleton staff of groundsmen.

One morning Harding came to check on his charges and found a gaping hole in the chicken wire and no chickens. Grice saw him standing by the chicken run, surrounded by children and walked over.

"What's happened to all the chickens, Mr. Harding?" one boy asked.

Before he could answer another piped up, *"It must have been a fox. My Dad says a fox will kill every chicken in a coop even though it will only eat one."*

"This ain't no fox boy," Harding muttered. *"Fox causes one hell of a mess. He bites the heads off chickens and there's blood and feathers all over the gaff. Fox takes one chicken and leaves the others dead. And look at that wire; you think a fox is strong enough to do that? No boy, this were no fox."*

"So what do you think it was, Mr. Harding?" Grice pushed through the boys.

"This has 'Beast' written all over it."

"What, the Beast of Bodmin Moor? Are you pull…"

Grice stopped dead when he saw the look the old man was giving him.

"The Beast ain't no fairy story," he snapped. *"It ripped the throat right out of my niece's goat down Redruth way. Hauled the carcass fifteen foot up a tree. And I've seen the bloody thing twice. Once back in '97 and another time just last May. It ran out in front of my car at night. I saw it in the headlights. A black panther like you sees on them there wildlife shows. Big as a bull mastiff. God only knows how many of them are running round on the moor."*

"Really, Mr. Harding, you'll frighten the boys."

"Well maybes they should be frightened. I'd keep an eye on them if I were you."

The old man sauntered off to his tool shed, cursing under his breath.

"Do you think a panther ate our chickens, Sir?" one of the boys asked.

"No, no, it was probably a fox that got in and ate one. The others must have escaped," Grice lied. As the boys dissipated, he bent to look more closely at the wire. It looked as if it had been cut rather than torn.

A few days later Mrs. Mullany, the school cook, found the kitchen door unlocked and ajar. Inside she found what looked like a riot. Tables overturned and cupboards open. Much of the food was gone - packets of biscuits and loaves of bread, apples, bananas. The fridge door was open; a pool of foul-smelling water was widening across the tiles. Meat, both cooked and raw, had been pilfered from the fridge as had cakes and cheese. Canned and powdered foods had been ignored.

She looked at the windows; they were shut from the inside. This was no burglary. Then, in the crumbs from a packet of shattered chocolate digestives, she saw the unmistakable outline of a boy's footprint.

"Those little heathens!..." her rage made her gag and cut of further expletives as she turned and stalked towards the headmaster's office.

Outside Mr. Harding found every remaining vegetable uprooted and stolen.

Father Dougherty looked more dour than usual at assembly. A scowl played across his florid toad-like face. *"Boys, it is my very sad duty to inform you all that we have a thief in our midst, probably several. The school kitchens and the vegetable garden were raided in the early hours of this morning and a large amount of food taken. The windows were secure so we know it had to have been boys sneaking down and stealing from their own friends. Now midnight feasts might seem fun between the pages of the* Beano *or the* Magnet *but they will not be tolerated here, especially when it is the school's larder that is raided."*

He span round with an evil look on his face. *"We will be searching all the dormitories and lockers of every single pupil in this school. The culprits will be expelled."*

The headmaster's search revealed nothing. Still unsatisfied, he demanded at the next day's assembly that the culprits own up or the whole school would suffer. No one did own up and the boys went without dinner.

Father Dougherty arranged a night watch around the school and especially the kitchens. Each of the Fathers took turns. A new rumour grew among the boys that gypsies had raided the school.

Grice took his turn on watch, wandering the dark, empty corridors. Even in the short time he had been at St Michael's he had seen the drop-off in attendance. Most people could just not afford to send their children to a boarding school anymore. That, added to the lack of interest in the church, meant the school's days were numbered. All the staff knew it but no one said anything. He wondered what he would do when the inevitable happened.

As he wandered into the chapel, he stopped. Something caught his ear. It was right on the very limit of his hearing, almost too quiet to discern. It was a kind of furtive scratching, as a rat might make. It seemed to come from outside the chapel. Then it was joined by another noise. It was a low, queer sound almost like birdsong, if birds could whisper. It sounded like a voice, like language. What kind of animal made a noise like that? The low twittering was joined by a second as if it were answering the first. The windows were too high for him to look through. He thought of standing on one of the pews but most of the panes had stained glass. Breathlessly he slipped the keys from his pocket and approached the chapel's side door.

He twisted the key in the lock, painfully aware of the squeaking every turn made and how the still of the moonless night magnified them. He slipped out of the door and ran around the side of the building to where the noises had been coming from. He swept up his torch and played it over the wall and then the bushes. Nothing. Perhaps it was some animal. He knew vixens were supposed to make truly blood-curdling sounds when they were in season. He was about to turn in when something caught his eye. Small scratches on the wall of the chapel, about three feet off the ground. He brought the beam to bear and bent to look closer.

The scratches were new; they stood out against the sandstone. It appeared to be some kind of writing or code. An odd little script in symbols, seemingly gibberish. Just three lines of crudely scratched shapes. Grice shivered as he stood up. He looked briefly over his shoulder and went back inside, locking the door behind him.

After breakfast, he borrowed some paper and a wax crayon from the art room and made a rubbing. That evening he spent hours poring over historic and linguistic books in the school library without finding anything that came close to the strange little shapes. He locked the paper in his deck and decided to keep quiet.

The headmaster frowned on Hallowe'en but met Grice and some of the other Fathers half way in letting the boys have a party. There was to be no dressing as devils or witches, but apple bobbing was allowed as well as other party games. As the night drew in, Grice lit a bonfire and the boys toasted marshmallows around it and then took turns telling ghost stories. There was a prize for the best.

Most of the stories were predictable and un-scary to anyone older than five. They seemed to be based on whatever cartoon junk their parents allowed them to watch when not in school. Finally the torch was passed to Benjamin. Grice didn't think he would be up to telling a story in front of his classmates, but he was surprised.

The boy concocted a ghastly little tale. The torch's yellow light made his pale little face seem almost translucent. His big, dark eyes looked magnified and gave the illusion of being entirely black. His story was called "The Night The Woods Got In". It was about a frightened old man living alone on the edge of a forest that the boy called 'The Grandfather Woods'. The old man was constantly under siege from the Grandfather Woods. Each night the trees and briars would creep closer to his tumbledown cottage. They would scratch at the walls and doors, and try to pick the glass from the windows. Thorny creepers would try to slip down the chimney so the old man had to keep his fire well stoked, even in the height of summer. He sat alone and frightened each night at the rustling, creaking, hungry sound of the Grandfather Woods.

He nailed the windows shut and blocked the door. The Grandfather Woods only came at night. By day, they were just trees and bushes and he cut them back. But each night they would slither closer. He could not move away, all his relatives were dead and he had nowhere to go. He tried keeping them out with magic charms. Horseshoes nailed to the doors and windows. He sprinkled holy water and salt around his cottage. It seemed to work. The Grandfather Woods retreated and lost their grip on his malodorous shanty.

Then one day he drew some water from his well for a drink. Unbeknown to him some seeds had fallen into the water. The Grandfather Woods had found a new way to get in.

Now the forest was not only in the old man's cottage, but in the old man himself. A great thorny tree grew from the seeds that had germinated deep down in his belly. They sprouted thorns up through his eyes and his mouth. Tendrils gnawed at his brain and split his skull asunder. Leaves vomited up from his mouth. Vines oozed through his veins.

Years later the cottage was gone, but there stood an ugly, thorny, twisted old tree. Deep in its trunk was the face of an old man. An old man screaming.

Benjamin seemed to take a particular delight in telling the story. He seemed to be totally on the side of the Grandfather Woods and sounded as if he thought the old man got what he deserved.

"There are some places people are just not meant to build on or live in. Ancient places, sacred groves, and darksome hilltops. And when the foolish, who don't heed the warnings, tarry in these places there are things that come in the night for them."

The other boys seemed genuinely disturbed and even Grice felt cold. *"Come on boys let's go in now. Well done Ramsey, I think we all agree that was the night's scariest story."*

Benjamin seemed proud. *"Thank you, Sir."*

"And the prize for the best story, as promised, is a book token. There you go lad, you can use that over the Christmas break."

Benjamin grinned as he took the token. *"I know what book I'm going to get,"* he said.

A couple of days later, Grice saw Benjamin standing alone at playtime, as he usually did. He seemed to be holding something and staring out onto the moor as always. A small group of boys approached him. Robert Taylor led them; a boy two years Benjamin's senior, and for whom Grice had a strong dislike.

"Hey look everyone, Benjy's got a doll!" He reached forward and ripped a small figurine out of the younger boy's hands. Benjamin leapt forwards reaching for the doll.

"That's mine Taylor," he shouted.

The bully shoved him violently to the ground.

"Benjy plays with dolls. He must be some kind of a puff!"

The small crowd of Taylor's followers laughed.

Grice strode over. *"Taylor, give that back NOW!"* The bully looked up surprised.

"I was only teasing him, Sir".

"Don't backchat me, boy, or you'll be in the headmaster's office so fast your feet won't touch the ground."

Taylor handed the doll back to Benjamin, and hissed something under his breath before slinking off with his followers.

Grice took a look at the little doll Benjamin was holding. It was a small stick figure made of twigs bound with twine. It was dressed in a blue/grey cloth and about its neck were several turquoise beads in a piece of wire. It bore scant resemblance to the corn dollies Grice had seen at harvest festivals.

"I didn't know you liked crafts, Ramsey. Did you make that yourself?"

"No, Sir."

"Let me guess; Robyn made it for you?"

"Yes, Sir. Robyn made it. It's called a twigling, it's a sort of raggedy man. I gave him some of the apples I won at bobbing over Hallowe'en and he gave me this in return."

With that the boy scampered off laughing and waving the crude doll from side to side. Grice shook his head.

It was quiet for a week or so, and then all hell broke loose. Mrs. Mullany found Father Williamson, the PE teacher, lying in the kitchen unconscious and in a pool of his own blood. A livid bruise tattooed his left temple and a deep knife wound had opened his right thigh. As she looked about, the horrified cook saw that again the kitchens had been robbed of food. Several sets of small footprints outlined in scarlet led to the window that was, this time, wide open.

The police and an ambulance were called and Williamson taken to hospital. The boys were kept in their rooms for several days whilst an investigation was carried out.

In the staff room the tension was high and speculation thick.

"It's those damn new-age travellers," snorted Father Sutton, the geography master. *"That or the bloody gyppos."*

"Same thing as far as I can see, just a new name for old scroungers," Father Wellington, the maths teacher, added looking up from his paper.

Grice remained quiet in a corner and listened.

The headmaster peered down his spectacles at his staff. *"I think it could be worse. Now don't breathe a word of this outside this staff room or all our jobs could be on the line!"*

He now had instant and undiluted attention.

"I think there is more to this than gypsies and filthy travellers. Remember a couple of years back some backpackers disappeared up on the moor? They were never found. Then those hikers down from Liverpool on holiday that vanished. Big police search and nothing was ever turned up. At the time the papers said that they may have fallen down an old tin mine shaft. Well I think there is a gang up on the moor, a dangerous one that has been waylaying folk round here for years."

"Hang on," piped up Father Row the music teacher. *"How do you know all this?"*

"Well for your information, Mr. Row, I have been doing some digging in the library down in Bodmin town. I looked through the papers going back to before the war. People have been vanishing in these parts for years. I think this is a family operation, this gang. Probably goes down from father to son. The devils have been up to it for years."

Grice spoke up. *"Have you told the police this yet, headmaster?"*

"Not yet, Mr. Grice. I'm still piecing it together. I don't want to present it until I feel sure I have a strong enough case. But I have gleaned a few things from them."

"Such as?"

"Well I overheard a few things whilst talking to the police. I was in the kitchens and I saw the gentleman taking fingerprints from the windowpane and the shelves. I heard him say to one of his colleagues that the prints looked wrong."

"How do you mean wrong?"

"I don't know but the fellow had the strangest look on his face. Like he had never seen fingerprints like these ones before. And I'll tell you another thing: the footprints were not made by any pupils here. I got a good look at them and they didn't look like children's feet, they were all odd and wrinkled. I tell you, gentlemen, something very rum is afoot here."

Grice excused himself and walked back to his room. He had hardly believed the farce he had just witnessed; that pompous oaf Dougherty thinking of himself as some kind of Sherlock Holmes. Something else was bugging him, something at the back of his mind that he could not quite remember. Something vaguely un-nerving.

Later that night, as he rifled through his briefcase for some notes, his hand fell upon a slip of paper. Pulling it out he saw the wax crayon rubbing of the marks he had found. He looked again at the curious script. Was it writing or a code? Could there be something to the head's wild theory? He decided to take it to Father Glover, the history teacher.

Glover was one of the few other teachers Grice liked. He was almost as young as Grice and quite passionate about history. He had wanted a teaching position at university but he hated computers. A man born out of his time, Glover was the worst technophobe Grice had ever met. Hence, he ended up in this backwater, a place of chalk dust and blackboards.

Grice had found Glover still up and drinking whisky when he knocked. His friend invited him in for a dram and soon both men were sitting next to the crackling open fire in the history master's room.

"Do you know much about ancient writing, Bill?" Grice asked.

"Well, a little. Why do you ask?"

Grice produced the paper and leaned over. *"What do you make of this?"*

The history teacher took the paper and squinted at it by the firelight. *"Good God man, where did you come by this?"*

"I found it scratched into the wall outside the chapel a few weeks ago, you know when the head had us doing night watch"

Grice saw his friend's expression. *"Look, I can take you there and show you if you like. I assume it's still on the wall."*

The two men were soon outside the chapel, shivering despite their overcoats. Glover played his torch over the sandstone wall.

"There! There it is, see!" The markings were still clearly visible. They were small and so low down a passer-by would hardly notice them.

"Do you recognise them, Bill?"

"They are like nothing I have ever seen in any text book."

"So you don't recognise them?"

"Well, yes and no. Look, back in the 1920s a ploughboy called Emile Fradin unearthed some clay tablets on his farm in Glozel, France. They were covered by some kind of strange writing. A team of archaeologists was brought in to dig on the farm. They found more tablets, urns, lamps, phallic carvings, stone axes, and carved bones all covered with an odd writing. Not one single expert on either side of the English Channel could decipher the writing. Such was the embarrassment that the objects were declared fakes and the dig closed. But in 1974 the objects were dated using thermo luminescence tests. They proved to date from 350 BC. The writing scratched on that wall is almost identical."

"Bill, no kid here could have possibly known about those objects."

"Exactly, the Glozel case is almost totally forgotten even within the archaeological community."

"Then what the hell is it doing here?"

"I'm damned if I know Andrew, damned if I do."

The pair walked back inside and Grice decided to call it a night. He slipped into a fitful sleep. He dreamed it was a summer's twilight. Night-scented stock filled the air and the bats and owls were just beginning to emerge as the sun crept lower on the horizon. He was standing on a hill. The strains of pipe music floated up to his ears and from a copse in a meadow below him, the smoke of a campfire rose.

He set out towards the trees as the sun set. Unhampered by light pollution the stars glittered above in uncanny clarity. As he approached the copse he could hear voices singing, strange and high. An odd, sickly sweet incense was burning. There in a clearing, about a bonfire was a group of children. They were all dressed in hooded robes like tiny monks. Some were playing pipes whilst the others danced in a strange serpentine form about the fire. Hand-in-hand, the children coiled back and forth around the flames and about the bows of the great trees that fringed the clearing.

Suddenly he felt small hands grasp his and before he knew what was happening he had been dragged forwards to join the children in their eerie dance. The serpent of little hooded people coiled faster and faster, in and out of the trees, round, and round the fire. Their voices were high like birdsong. He felt the dance would never end but he was not weary. Indeed he did not want the dance to end, ever. He felt the other things in his head slipping away. The school, his family, his friends, everything was melting away. Now he could not recall who he was or had been. There was just the dance, the pipes, and the song.

He sat bolt upright in bed clammy with sweat. Shakily he got up and staggered to the window. He threw it open and gulped down lungfuls of cold November air. It was then he noticed a sweet, sickly smell in the night air.

Father Williamson made a full recovery and was back in school within a fortnight. Some of the Fathers had visited him in hospital but most, Grice included, were eager to hear him relate his adventure. They gathered around him in the staff room.

"Well I can't tell you chaps much more than I told the police," he began. *"I was walking down the corridor when I saw the kitchen door open and went to have a look."*

His next words hit Grice like a slap in the face.

"As I got closer I thought I heard something like birds singing. I thought some birds might have flown through the window in the daytime and got trapped. I looked inside and saw cans of food rolling on the floor. Then wham! Something hits my head and lights out."

"So you didn't see what hit you?" asked Dougherty.

"Not a sausage, but here's a strange thing. I was talking to the surgeon who stitched me up. He told me what he had found in my leg. Never seen the like of it in thirty years he said. It was a blade."

"What's so odd about a blade, man? The knife just snapped in your leg," said Father Wellington.

"It was a flint blade. Not metal but chipped stone. Like I had been attacked by bloody Barney Rubble."

"There!" snapped Dougherty. *"What did I tell you? Some kind of inbred gypsies. And what do the police do? Take a few prints, ask a few questions then throw up their hands in defeat. They would have been a damn sight more interested if we had been blacks, lesbians, or hippies instead of good God-fearing men. You know we lost eight pupils because of this? Eight families thought that their sons were not safe at Saint Michael's."*

Grice thought of mentioning the marks on the chapel wall but thought better of it.

It was some time after the Christmas break and bitterly cold. The School and the surrounding moor were glazed by ice and wraiths of arctic wind piped strange notes about the building's towers and turrets. The snow was not the crisp, shining stuff of picture postcards, but grey and wet.

During one break Grice found Benjamin reading a book inside whilst the other children mooched miserably about the playground.

"Is this what you brought with the token, lad?"

"Yes, Sir". He looked up and grinned. *"Look,"* he announced proudly holding the book up.

Grice looked at the cover. A bare, ragged, tree scratching at a fat moon.

"The Complete Works of Arthur Machen," he read out loud. *"Isn't that a little deep for you, and a little scary?"*

"No, Sir. Machen was a great man. He knew an awful lot but he used to hide it in stories. That was his way of getting his information out to people, all the stuff he had discovered."

Grice was about to ask just what Benjamin thought Machen had discovered when the bell rang.

Later on, Benjamin built a snowman alone in the corner of a playing field. Somehow he had contrived to make the dirty white slush coalesce into something like a human figure. He had pushed stones into its mushy face, instead of coal, as the eyes.

Grice was about to call the boys in, as the sun was sinking low and the shadows growing.

As he strode out onto the field rubbing his hands against the cold he saw Robert Taylor run over and start savagely kicking Benjamin's snowman to the ground. The younger boy attempted to push Taylor away but the bully grabbed him about the neck and gave him a stinging backhanded slap.

Before Grice could open his mouth to shout, Benjamin's hand flashed down to his pocket and leapt up again into the face of his attacker. Taylor staggered back letting out a girlish scream. Blood gushed from a slash that opened his left cheek. He threw his hands up to his face and squealed again as he saw his own blood on his fingers. Benjamin lunged forward with a quick jabbing motion and the bully staggered away, this time holding his belly. A patch of blood wetly stained his white school shirt.

Grice crossed the field in madly wide bounds and grabbed the younger boy's wrist. As he twisted, a small knife fell down onto the red speckled snow. Grice snatched it up. It was made of flint.

"What the hell are you doing? Where did you get this?"

Benjamin struggled and tried to grab the knife.

"It's mine. Robyn made it for me."

"For Christ's sake, boy, you nearly killed someone."

Losing his temper he shook the boy like a doll.

"Father Williamson was stabbed by a flint knife you bloody little maniac!"

He remembered Taylor and bellowed out for help. After the third shout, a group of teachers emerged from the school and ran over to the prostrate boy.

Ten minutes later an ambulance was on its way. The Fathers had managed to slow Taylor's bleeding and Grice stood before Benjamin in the staff room.

"You know this means expulsion for you, Ramsey?"

"Sir, he attacked me."

"That doesn't give you the right to stab him."

"He deserved what he got. He was always bullying me. All bullies should die."

Grice was momentarily silenced by the formerly timid boy's venom.

"Was it you who attacked Father Williamson?"

"No, no. He never harmed me. I didn't do that!"

"He was stabbed in the leg with a flint knife. How many flint knives do you suppose there are in Saint Michael's School?"

"I let them in but I didn't stab Father Williamson."

"Let who in?"

"They just wanted food so I opened the window for them then closed it after they had gone. It would have all been OK but Father Williamson came down. They weren't expecting him. They panicked."

"Who, for heaven's sake, boy?"

"Robyn and his family. They have flint knifes and flint arrows. They never have metal ones, they don't like iron."

Grice's temper snapped and he slapped the boy hard. *"Look, I've 'phoned your grandparents and the police. They are both on their way and God only knows what Father Dougherty is going to do to you when he gets here as well. So start telling the truth and no more babies' stories."*

The boy looked livid with rage. The pale, angelic face twisted into a daemon by fury.

"I AM TELLING THE TRUTH! They are my friends, they live on the moors, they needed food. I helped them. They took the chickens too. They only attacked because they were frightened by Father Williamson's torch."

"Who are they, gypsies?"

"No, not gypsies. Robyn's family have lived here for centuries. They are people, but not like any people you ever saw."

Exasperated, Grice turned away. *"Save it for the police."* He locked the boy in the staff room and began to walk down the corridor to see how the others were doing with Taylor. He paused to gaze at the four-inch flint blade he had wrapped in his handkerchief. The handle looked like it was made out of bone. Possibly deer.

Back in the staff room Benjamin ran to the window to find it was locked. He pulled a small bone whistle from his pocket and blew hard on it.

In the corridor, Grice heard a shrill note followed by breaking glass. He realised the mistake of leaving the disturbed boy alone in the room and ran back.

He found the window shattered by a chair. He rushed over and saw the boy running across the playing fields towards the moor. Grice pushed aside shards of glass and vaulted out of the window. The drop was no more than four feet and he hit the ground running. He heard the high whistle slice the night air again.

"Ramsey, Ramsey! Don't be a bloody fool. It's freezing, you'll die of cold on the moor."

Even as the words left his mouth he realised how stupid following the boy in the dark would be. Fiddling in his pockets, he found his car keys and rushed the hundred yards or so to his car. He retrieved a torch from the glove compartment and then ran after Benjamin.

Despite the child's head start, the man's longer legs soon gave him the edge. As a lad Grice had been the finest sprinter in his school and still kept fit. Soon he began to gain on the boy. His quarry stopped before a stretch of woodland. A hooded figure no larger than Benjamin stepped from the undergrowth to meet him. Grice skidded to a halt some fifty feet from the pair. A cold sensation, that had nothing to do with the time of year, oozed through him. The hooded child was like the one from his dream.

Shaking himself, he began to run again crashing through the bushes where the children had run. He halted again as he came to a clearing. There were more of the children, all dressed in the same blue/grey hooded robes. There were, perhaps, twenty of them. What the hell were all these children doing out on the moor at this hour?

They had seen him! All of the children, including Benjamin, turned and ran. Again he charged after them, the brambles and branches cutting his hands and face. A hill seemed to rise out of nowhere and the group of fleeing children seemed to run into it. Not up or around it, but into it.

Confused, Grice blundered to a halt. Vines and creepers swathed the hillside. Wrenching them away he found where they had run to: a gaping hole in the side of the hill. Pitch black. He raised his torch, glad that he had stopped to collect it, and switched it on.

The beam illuminated a long, unwholesome passage, leading downwards.

"Ramsey! Ramsey!"

Nothing except an echo. He began to follow the path down. As the yellow beam fell across the passage walls he saw something etched in the stone. The same queer writing he had seen scratched into the chapel wall. The path seemed to go much deeper than the hill. He reasoned it must lead to caves honeycombing the area. He had never read of such caves. It struck him that they must be an undiscovered system, now the passage was branching off both left and right. He swung the beam to the ground to see if he could find the children's footprints. Again the beam picked something out. Some kind of ragged bundle lay on the floor. He bent to look closer. It was a backpack. Dirty, torn, and old. He could just make out a name tag sewn to the rear.

Jill Best
116 Crown Street
Wirral
Liverpool

Grice's mind flashed back several years to the missing hikers. Did they come down here and get lost? He shivered as he imagined them wandering round and round in the caves, getting ever more tired and desperate as their torch batteries failed.

He shouted again. Nothing but an echo. The tracks followed the left hand path and he stumbled after them. Soon the cave widened into a cathedral like cavern. Forests of stalactites and stalagmites sprang from the floor and reached down from the roof. They looked like pallid, diseased teeth as the beam picked them out.

There suddenly came a subdued sound. A little, high, halting sound. Was it crying? A child crying? He followed the sound to the corner of the cave. There, with its back to him, kneeled a hooded child. He could not see if it was a boy or a girl. Its shoulders shook with tiny sobs. Grice was suddenly filled with pity and horror that a child, any child, should be in such a place. He leant forward and placed a gentle hand on the child's shoulder.

The child turned around in the wan torch light. Only it wasn't a child. Huge nocturnal eyes, like a bushbaby, glared from a grey-skinned, wizened face. Silvery white hair dangled over a thick, simian brow ridge as a pug nose snorted. The red tongue darted between sharp little teeth in a thin-lipped mouth as wide as a frog's. The thing had been laughing, not crying. A scrawny arm gripped his. Monkey-like strength ran through its long fingers.

Grice screamed and screamed as he staggered backwards, ripping himself from the thing's clutch. The child-sized creature sprang to its feet slashing with a little flint knife. It made a noise like birdsong through the thin lips.

A soft rustling, a furtive scurrying, more of the things were in here with him! He swung the beam around and saw them shrink from the light, their eyes illuminated an eerie green. They leapt and sprang in the shadows, some in hooded robes some naked despite the cold. Painted in ochre and wode they chittered excitedly to each other. There was a twang and a hiss. Pain exploded in Grice's left leg. An arrow no larger than one in a child's Red Indian costume was buried in his calf.

Using the torch like a club he flailed wildly, running for a passage. He heard the scampering of the tiny, wrinkled men as they loped after him some dropping to run on all fours like little grey apes. He stopped to swing the beam at his pursuers, dazzling them again. A three-foot, flint-tipped spear clattered off the stone wall beside him as he desperately tried to run.
His mind was a maelstrom. Snatches of rhymes from his childhood.

My mother said I never should
Play with fairies in the wood.

They fear iron. Nail a horseshoe above your door.

Up the airy mountain
And down the rushy glen
I dare not go a hunting
For fear of little men.

They will take a human child and leave a changeling in its place.

We must not talk to goblin men
We must not buy their fruits.
We do not know what has fed
Their hungry, thirsty roots.

Grice remembered something in the news. Just last year. Bones of a race of tiny people discovered on the island of Flores in Indonesia. A new species of man.

More spears and arrows flashed by his head. He could hardly feel his leg. Numb below the knee. Was it tipped with some kind of poison?

Could another type of man have evolved here in Britain? Tiny, nocturnal, cave dwelling. This is where the legends of little people came from, real creatures. God, how did they survive undiscovered?

He fell headlong into another chamber and landed on a pile of brittle things that crunched and snapped beneath him. The torch whirled out of his grasp. He clawed himself to his hands and knees. The beam fell across the white brittle things. He gagged as he saw that they were bones, human bones and skulls. They were marked, gnawed by small sharp teeth.

He heard a familiar voice in the darkness.

"You shouldn't have come here, Sir."

"Ramsey? Ben? Is that you? Help me for God's sake!"

A hooded figure pushed its way to the front of the growing crowd of pigmy troglodytes.

"Your God has no power here. We worship our gods, old gods."

"What do you mean, boy? Help me! Stop these things."

"I mean our gods. This is my family. Robyn is my kin, my half brother."
"What are you talking about?"

"We have the same father. My poor dear mother was waylaid one night whilst walking on the moors. I'm the result. Didn't you ever wonder from where the legend of changelings came? Oh yes, I knew a lot more than I let on. Robyn has been coming to me for quite some time now, telling me about my heritage, my birthright. We were here before the Celts, before the Picts."

The boy chattered and whistled to his companions who returned the noise excitedly.

"We have talked long enough. My family are hungry now. I'm sorry, Sir, you where the only one I ever really liked, but you shouldn't have come."

A week after the disappearance of Mr. Grice and Benjamin Ramsey, Saint Michael's Catholic School was closed. The building stood empty for two months before a fire burned it to the ground.

There are some places people are just not meant to build on, or live in.

Lab coats
must be worn
in this area

PAVED WITH GOOD INTENTIONS

From: Dr. James Ash   **Sent:** 4.4.2008
To: Professor Erik Adler
Subject: Project Milk Well

Dear Professor Adler,

Dr. Hammond is still recovering from his unfortunate accident with the saw-scaled viper. It will be some time before he can work again and I gather you have stepped in to fill his boots at short notice. I know it can't be easy taking on someone else's whole project halfway through. However, you need not worry as great strides have been made in the past weeks.

You will be pleased to know that at last we seem to be making progress. A single, female specimen of batch 28B has survived and is taking small prey items. One out of a group of nine may not seem a success but, if you will recall, all hybrids of this nature have died shortly after birth. Our specimen is now four-weeks-old and is growing at an incredible rate.

Early hybrids between snakes of the same family were a success. We raised a number of *Bitis gabonica* X *Bitis nasicornis* as well as *Naja haje* X *Naja mossambica*. But we had trouble hybridising Viperidae with Elapidae. Both were hard to hybridise with the few venomous members, Colubridae.

As you know the Viperids are the most advanced of the snakes and the most recent to evolve. They are genetically incompatible with the more primitive types. Indeed, even species in the same family but separated widely geographically do not take well as hybrids.

Chromosomes that are unmatched in number cannot pair during meiosis. During meiosis, chromosomes duplicate and the cell divides to form daughter cells, which split apart to form gametes, or mature sexual reproductive cells. But with unmatched chromosomes, the split into gametes would be uneven, creating sterility.

Hybrids of Viperids and Elapids will yield venom that can be used in the creation of antivenom for the bites of both parent species and a few closely related species. The aim of Project Milk Well was to hybridise a species whose venom consisted of the elements of a number of different snakes often involved in snakebites. From this a "magic bullet" or universal antivenom could be created. Thus the need for hospitals to stock dozens of formulas would be redundant. Then Lardon Pharmaceuticals could market the super serum around the world.

The breakthrough came when we were attempting DNA transfer into foreign eggs. The technique involves taking genetic matter from the living cells of one species then injecting them into the egg of another species from which the genetic material had been removed.

At first, this only resulted in the host giving birth to or hatching eggs with alien species inside them. As you know Elapids lay eggs but Viperids give birth to live young. The breakthrough came quite by accident from a technician working in another part of the lab on a sister project. We were also studying how venom developed. It is, of course, highly modified saliva and is unknown in more primitive snakes such as the Boidae.

We were studying the ancestral snakes, the basal group known as Scolecophidia. These are sometimes called worm snakes or blind snakes. Palaeontologists think that the first snakes to evolve were akin to these diminutive, burrowing creatures.

We were attempting to see which gene or set of genes needed to be stimulated to encourage venom production. Due to carelessness, some genetic material from a blind snake, species *Rhinotyhphlops gracilus*, contaminated one of our venom hybrid tests.

There was something in the genetic make-up of the ancestral snake that allowed the genetic material from unrelated species of venomous snakes to meld together. We are still unsure as to how this works but it meant that we could now crossbreed any species of snake we chose.

We selected genetic material from differing species on the basis of the following criteria:

1.   Potency of venom
2.   Number of recorded bites on humans each year
3.   Aggressive nature
4.   How close to human habitation the species is found

We then drew up a list of species that would contribute to the creation of our "super snake":

From Viperidae
Vipera russelii (Russell's viper)
Echis carinatus (Saw scaled viper)

Bitis gabonica (Gaboon viper)
Bitis nasicornis (Rhinoceros viper)
Bitis arietans (Puff adder)
Lachesis muta (Bushmaster)
Bothrops asper (Lance head)
Crotalus adamanteus (Eastern diamond backed rattle snake)

From Elapidae
Naja haje (Egyptian cobra)
Naja mossambica (Mozambique spitting cobra)
Ophiophagus hannah (King cobra)
Bungarus caeruleus (Common krait)
Dendroaspis polylepis (Black mamba)
Notechis scutatus (Tiger snake)
Pseudonaja textiles (Eastern brown snake)
Oxyuranus scutellatus (Costal taipan)
Oxyuranus microlepidotus (Fierce snake)
Micrurus fulvius tenere (Coral snake)
Laticauda colubrine (Banded sea snake)

From Colubridae
Dispholidus typus (Boomslang)

The specimen, which we refer to as SS1 was 12 inches long at birth. SS1was carried by a *Bitis nasicornis* X *Naja mossambica* and birthed live as opposed to in an egg. She is an iridescent black except for a red streak on the head. The eyes are large and golden in colour like those of *Bothrops asper*. She seems to bear both Jacobson's organs and heat sensory pits. The birth occurred at 2.35 am on 1.2.2008.

The others in the batch were still born or died within one hour. Within four days of birth SS1 was feeding on mouse pinkies and consumed several per week.

The growth rate is phenomenal. In a little over two months, SS1 has tripled her size and is now over three feet long! We think this is a side effect of her hybrid nature. This fast growth rate has been recorded in other crosses and is known as hybrid vigor. She has progressed onto eating mice and we will shortly be experimenting with the potency of her venom on live prey.

She will soon be large enough for her first milking, whereupon we can examine the chemical make-up of her hybrid venom.

I hope you, Lorraine and the boys are all keeping well.

Your,
Dr. Ash

From: Dr. James Ash   **Sent:** 18.4.2008
To: Professor Erik Adler
Subject: Project Milk Well

Dear Professor Adler,

What amazing discoveries we have made! SS1 is now well over four feet long and still growing. She has the fat body of a Viperid (about as thick as my arm) but displays the threat posture of an Elapid, rearing up like a cobra. The red streak on her head has grown into a crest of scales. She must have inherited this from her *Bitis nasicornis* genes.

However, with the rhinoceros viper, the crest of scales is on the tip of the snout rather than the top of the head as in SS1. Her appearance reminded me of something but I could not recall what it was until I happened across a book on folklore. SS1 looks for all the world like a basilisk, a legendary serpent said to hatch from a rooster's egg incubated by a toad or a snake.

The resulting monster was a snake with a comb like a cockerel and a gaze that could kill any living thing it looked at! The original legend may have begun by mass rye ergot poisoning or plague outbreaks blamed on snakes. Please forgive the frivolity but SS1 is a magnificent specimen and some of the technicians have begun to call her "The Basilisk."

Joking aside, we have found that her venom is remarkable. SS1 seems quite placid and has made no attempt to strike at any of us yet. She does not struggle when we use the snake catching pole on her or when she is milked. Her venom yield is amazing 1000 mg! Its chemical structure is still under analysis but it seems to contain elements of all the snake species used in the experiment. It combines the neurotoxin of the Elapids with the hematoxin of the Viperids.

The venom potency is beyond anything seen in the animal kingdom before. 1.15 mg is sufficient to kill a full-grown Friesian cow weighing over a quarter of a ton. Symptoms include failure of the blood to coagulate, paralysis, muscle spasms, bleeding from eyes, ears and mouth, necrosis, and major organ failure. The tested cows have all died within ten minutes of being injected with SS1's venom. This means a vast amount of antivenom could me made from just one milking of SS1.

The fangs of SS1 are very long and hinged as in *Bitis gabonica* but their structure, hollow with a hole at the front, suggests that SS1 should be able to spit venom in the manner of *Naja mossambica*. All staff wear goggles when dealing with SS1.

We are all genuinely excited at the progress being made here.

Love to the wife and kids.

Yours,
Dr. Ash

From: Dr. James Ash   **Sent:** 6.5.2008
To: Professor Erik Adler
Subject: Project Milk Well

Dear Professor Adler,

Some problems. Had to tighten up security. Animal rights protesters broke into the compound. Thank God they did not get into this lab. The thought of so venomous a snake at liberty in England makes my blood run cold! Thankfully the security guards and police stopped them before they got anywhere near SS1. We have since tripled the guard and installed more CCTV cameras.

Don't these idiots know that we are trying to save lives? 40,000 people worldwide die from snakebite each year. SS1 could put an end to this forever.

The project is progressing better than we could ever have hoped. SS1's venom desiccates very well, making it all the better for packing and shipping. The efforts to perfect a cover - all antivenom look very bright indeed.

The power of SS1's venom is so great that masses of antivenom could be synthesised from it cheaply and shipped all over the world, even to the most remote clinics in the Third World. Lardon Pharmaceuticals is going to be famous.

From a zoological viewpoint, SS1 and her behaviour are truly fascinating. She is now six feet long and we have been feeding her on dead rats. We decided to see how she would deal with live prey.

A large rat was placed in her vivarium. The rat immediately froze upon seeing SS1. SS1 proceeded to slither up to the frozen animal and bite it. Death was instantaneous and she swallowed the rat in less than twenty seconds.

I have always thought that the mesmeric powers attributed to snakes were purely folkloric, the prey animals freezing to avoid detection. Now I am not so sure. SS1 seems to genuinely hypnotise her prey, freezing it to the spot like a statue.

On a personal note, I am suffering from the most horrid headaches of late. I think I'm pushing myself too hard but I cannot afford to take time off at this crucial point in the project.

Hope the family are keeping well.

Yours,
Dr. Ash

From: Dr. James Ash   **Sent:** 22.5.2008
To: Professor Erik Adler
Subject: Project Milk Well

Dear Professor Adler,

We have decided to test out the alleged hypnotic powers of SS1 by offering her more mobile prey, and prey that could put up more of a struggle or is more mobile and adept at escaping.

We placed a domestic cat in with SS1. The cat arched its back and hissed at SS1 but then froze with its back still in threat posture. SS1 was looking at the cat at the time it froze. She then slithered over and bit it in an almost nonchalant manner. SS1 then proceeded to swallow the prey. On a later occasion, we put a rock dove into SS1's vivarium. The bird flew and perched on the highest branch in the enclosure. SS1 merely looked at it and the bird flew down and sat in front of her jaws. It did not so much as flinch when SS1 bit it. We repeated this on a number of occasions and filmed the process. I am more convinced than ever that SS1 has some manner of hypnotic powers.

SS1 has another astounding trick up her sleeve. She is parthenogenic! On the 15th of this month she gave birth to six live young. All were genetically identical to her. All have lived and are taking food with gusto. She must have inherited this from the *Crotalus adamanteus* in her make-up. Rattlesnakes have been known to exhibit parthenogenesis. Females raised in captivity that have never had contact with males are known to have given birth.

Her hybrid nature may give us another clue to this. *Cnemidophorus neomexicanus* the New Mexico whiptailed lizard is a species totally consisting of parthenogenic females. No males exist in this species at all. Herpetologists believe that *Cnemidophorus neomexicanus* arose as a naturally occurring mutant hybrid between *Cnemidophorus inornatus*, the little striped whiptail, and *Cnemidophorus tigris* the western whiptail.

SS1 has a great advantage. Being parthenogenic we need only one of her kind to start a new population. Parthenogenesis is a faster mode of reproduction that standard sexual reproduction as only one individual is needed. Also every member of a population can give birth. It also acts as a buffer for harmful mutations but as beneficial mutations arise they are passed on quickly. SS1 is indeed a remarkable and precious creature. She is worth far more than her weight in gold. She and her young will save hundreds of thousands of lives in the years to come.

Those damn headaches are getting worse!

Did Lorraine and the boys enjoy Malta?

Yours,
Dr. Ash

From: Dr. James Ash   **Sent:**13.7.2008
To: Professor Erik Adler
Subject: Project Milk Well

Dear Professor Adler,

SS1 and her brood must all be killed. They constitute a horrible threat to all mankind! I know that I am not sounding like a level-headed scientist at the moment, but you will understand once I have told you what I have been through.

As SS1 grew bigger and stronger I began to find myself becoming more nervous of working with her, especially when I was in the lab alone at night. At first I put it down to stress and overwork. I constantly felt as if she were watching me. Yes, I know snakes have no eyelids and are - ergo - watching everything all the time but this was a palpable feeling of menace. SS1 had never attempted to bite me, or any of the staff, but when I was alone with her a creeping dread came over me and I began to imagine I knew what those poor prey animals felt when we fed them to her. A morbid imagination? No, far more.

A few nights ago I heard it first. A sibilant, inhuman voice in my head. It addressed me clearly by my name. At first I thought it was one of the younger technicians playing a trick. I became angry, shouted, and searched the lab but there was no one. They had all gone home. I dismissed it as imagination.

The following night I heard it again. It was a hissing voice calling me by name. It seemed to be coming from SS1's vivarium. The next night I asked one of the other scientists, Dr. Leach, to stay behind with me. I used the excuse of wanting help in cataloguing photographs of SS1's venom effects on tissue. I heard nothing. But the next night it was back. SS1 seemed to be speaking to me. She was asking me to open her vivarium and take her out!

I feared for my sanity but then thought it may be some kind of campaign by the animal rights people. Maybe they had rigged up some microphone and were trying to spook me. I searched the lab and found nothing. I had security sweep the whole complex with a fine-toothed comb, nothing! I brought a tape recorder in the next night and switched it on when I heard the SS1 begin to talk.

"Dr. Ash," the voice said, *"Dr. Ash, you must let me out. You must let me out. Me and my daughters, Dr. Ash. You made us, Dr. Ash. You are our father. We will not harm you, Dr. Ash. We will not harm our father."*

It was as if I was talking to the original snake, the primal serpent in the Garden of Eden that tempted Eve.

I tried blocking it out, covering my ears but I could still hear it. When I played the tape recording back there was nothing, it was blank. That was because the voice was inside my head. Not in the sense that I was mad, but in the sense that the voice was beamed directly into my brain.

The SS1 is a telepath. Snakes have no lips, no voice box. Snakes could not form words even if they were intelligent enough to use language. The SS1 is not like other snakes. She is devilishly intelligent but she can no more form words than other snakes due to her physical configuration. But she sends words by thought waves right into my head.

The technicians were right when they called her a basilisk. Remember the legend? The gaze of the basilisk is deadly. SS1 uses her mental powers to mesmerise prey. Lesser animals cannot fight it and become little more than puppets to her will. But humans have reason, they can fight it. Or so I thought.

She reared up, glistening black, her crest the colour of arterial blood. She looked at me with those great amber eyes and willed me to come towards the vivarium. I fought it, I tried so hard but my legs seemed dragged towards the creature. My right hand was fumbling with the catch on her door. I managed to snatch up a polished metal tray from the bench with my free hand and held it up like a shield. The basilisk cannot stand its own reflection. The spell was broken and I fled the laboratory.

Perhaps, in the distant past, some naturally occurring hybrids arose with powers akin to the SS1. They would have been very rare as are most hybrids in nature. Maybe that is from where the basilisk legend arose.

When certain snakes mated, something with abnormal intelligence, cunning, and mental powers was the result. But they would have been so uncommon as never to have meant a real threat for very long. They would probably have not had the advantage of parthenogenesis as well so they could not have spread. Unlike the SS1.

To think I almost released that horror! If just one such creature got free, just imagine it. It could make any human into its mental slave. It would have its slave hide and protect it, bring it food and water as it birthed more and more of its kind. Then they would crawl forth to find slaves of their own.

Perhaps the original slave would plant the young in his friends' houses. Anyone who stood against them would be struck down. Bitten or spat at with venom so deadly the victim would be dead before they hit the ground. God above, what if she and her children were liberated? Within a decade, this world would have a new dominant species.

What have I done? What have I created? Have I condemned all mankind to be the slaves of mythical beasts?

I am returning to the lab with a mirror and a gun.

Yours,
Dr. Ash

From: Dr. James Ash   **Sent:** 14.7.2008
To: Professor Erik Adler
Subject: Project Milk Well

Dear Professor Adler,

What a first rate chump you must have thought me. Psychic snakes indeed! Call the men in white coats! I had indeed been working far too hard. Too many late nights, not enough food, it's bound to catch up with you in the end. I merely fell asleep in the lab and had a very bad dream. Freud would have had a field day with my noggin.

You will be glad to know I am having a week's holiday beginning today. A little R&R will do me the world of good.

The project is a 100% success. The SS1 and her offspring are incredible animals. You will be astounded by them. The lab is ready for your visit on the 30th of this month. I think you will be very pleased with what you find. The project has passed far beyond our wildest expectations. We all eagerly await your visit.

Oh and please feel free to bring your family. I'm sure Lorraine and the boys would find our work most exciting.

Yours,
Dr. Ash

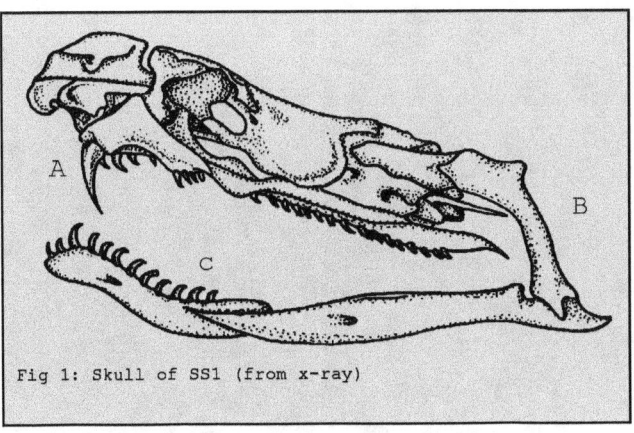

Fig 1: Skull of SS1 (from x-ray)

GOING UNDERGROUND

I'm typing this slowly, with one finger, with my left hand. I am right handed but I can no longer feel my right hand. The whole of my right arm from the shoulder down is numb and there is such an itching in my head, I find it hard to focus.

I suppose the mess I find myself in had its genesis in the 1970s. Curiosity was responsible for the demise of our feline friend. I loved empty houses and building sites. In fact anywhere that I shouldn't be. I would sometimes bunk-off school with a couple of classmates and hang around empty warehouses. In the dark, cold, autumn nights when the acrid smell of bonfires filled the air, and the wind sang odd songs through broken glass and rafters. I found myself entranced by such places, wondering who had lived there and what had transpired between the damp, crumbling walls. Sometimes I would find something; an old book, a broken toy, a discarded shoe, a piece of furniture left behind. These were my treasures. I amassed quite a collection.

My parents thought me strange and hoped I would grow out of my odd obsession, but I did not. As I grew older I grew bolder. The thrill of trespass was almost as attractive as that of decay and emptiness. At *least* I was not in a gang or on drugs; I think my folks were grateful for that and turned a blind eye to my nocturnal ramblings. I embarked on more daring forays, slinking about places that had security guards: factories, offices, the roofs of buildings. I would watch the city sweep away from me in illuminated vistas. It was a little world all of my own. I was lucky to have never been caught, although that now seems infinitely preferable to my current state.

It was on one of my moonlit rooftop constitutionals that I met Julie, a stocky little eighteen-year-old Goth with a mop of unruly black hair. I had never expected to meet anyone on my little adventures far above the city. Julie and I sat talking for hours, perched on a skylight above a disused spiritualist church in Chiswick one night. She introduced me to organised urban exploration.

One of our favourite buildings was Cane Hill Asylum in Coulsdon. A massive place built back in 1883, that tried in vain to contain the madness of Victorian London. It was a collection of spiral staircases and dark corners, a nightmare in brick and mortar. Padded cells were still evident complete with the tiny spy holes in the thick doors. We often wondered who had been locked up in those cells and what kind of madness crept through their brains.

The hobby was in its infancy then. There were only a handful of us. We called ourselves 'Team Fox' after the urban foxes we met most nights. Team Fox consisted of about ten of us from all over London. Not all of us would go on every "mission" but there would usually be at least three. We would meet up in *The Man in the Moon* in Camden and swap stories and ideas for new places to explore. We took cameras on most trips and brought back shots of the places where we had been.

I recall when Kevin first brought up the subject of disused Underground stations. A burly, rugby playing lad from Bromley, he had been with Team Fox from the beginning. He had brought a book to the pub with him one night. He threw it down on the table.

"Look at this," he said.

I picked it up. *London's Lost Tunnels: The Forgotten Underground* by Ted Ganley. Surprisingly it was only a couple of years old.

"The city is swarming with these places," said Kevin. *"I can't believe we never thought of it before. There are miles and miles of abandoned tunnels right beneath our feet and no one has ever been down them. Well not since the war, at least."*

Julie leaned over my shoulder as I leafed through the book. She read off the names of the stations. *"Bull and Bush, Aldwych, Down Street, Brompton Road, Wood Lane. Why did they all close?"*

"How long's a piece of string?" said Kevin. *"Some were never even finished. Economic reasons, mostly. Some of the stations were so underused that it just wasn't worth keeping them open. Others were just built in awkward areas."*

"God," I mused. *"All this time and we didn't know. It's a fucking labyrinth down there. Never mind torches, we'll need a ball of twine and a bloody sword!"*

Sid, another member, looked up from his pint of bitter and mumbled through his long ginger hair. *"How do we get down into them?"*

"Depends which one," Kevin had said. *"Some have had their facades destroyed or totally blocked up. If we do want to explore one of these stations it has to be a branch line. Some were just stops that are not used any more and the tracks are still live as trains still pass them. Some of the old, deep branch lines have had no power for around a hundred years so one of them would be best."*

Julie put down the book. *"Any ideas?"*

"King William Street. It's a very deep, abandoned branch of the Northern line." Kevin warmed to his subject and stood like a lecturer as he enthused over his research.

"It was opened in 1890 and was designed to be cable operated but they switched to electric just before it opened. It's just a single platform because the builders thought it was going to be cable. It lies between Bank and London Bridge but at a much deeper level."

"The station was closed in February 1900. The official story was that it was because of loss of power. The tunnel was on a sharp incline and the station that provided the power was at the other end of the Northern Line. But check this out; I've been looking through old papers from the time in the library. There were several unexplained disappearances before the line was closed. People who had been waiting for late night trains just vanished."

"Ohh, Jack the Ripper then?" butted in Julie.

"There were only two years between the Ripper murders and the station opening. But there is nothing to link the two. There was never any blood or any bodies, the people just vanished. Anyhow it was all forgotten after the station closed down.

It wasn't opened again until World War Two. It was used as an air raid shelter. It was only used for a few months then shut down again."

"What, in the middle of the war? You'd have thought they would have used all the space they could get for shelters," Sid grunted. He was the only one of us seemingly more interested in drinking than pawing over the book.

"I thought that as well," agreed Kevin. *"But I checked in the papers again for that period and there was a load more disappearances. People went down there during air raids and never came back up. The wardens put it about that there had been subsidence and the floors of the tunnel must have caved in. They declared it unsafe and stopped it being used as an air raid shelter. That was the last time anyone was down there, sixty years ago."*

"Hang about," I chipped in, beginning to worry a little. *"If the track has collapsed it would be fucking suicide going down there."*

"Ah, but has it? Has the track fallen in or was it just a cover story? Think about it, guys. If there was subsidence, even at that depth it would be unsafe to build over the tunnel but there are loads of buildings above where it runs. It don't make any sense."

Julie snapped the book shut making us all jump. *"So how do we get down, Kev?"*

"The old facade was totally demolished. None of the above ground station remains. But the stairs down to it and the station itself are intact. A new building was built over the entrance. It's called Regis House. It's a bunch of offices for IT businesses. In the cellar of Regis House is the boarded up entrance to King William Street Station. And Team Fox are gonna bust in."

We had all been enthused, even Sid. The whole idea was so exciting. Kevin had promised to scope out the security in Regis House and the following week he told us how lax it was - just a couple of fixed cameras, primitive alarms that Sid (an electrician) could easily over-ride, and one security guard. He was, by all accounts a lazy youth who spent most of his time drinking coffee and listening to a Walkman. Getting into Regis House should be a doddle. And it was.

I was amazed at how easily we gained entrance. The security guard did a half-hearted sweep of the grounds once every half hour then returned to his cubicle. Kevin, being the biggest of us, gave a leg up to the others across the chain link fence that ran around the building. The thick overalls we wore padded us against the worst of the barbed wire. Kevin himself then scrambled over like a gorilla in a boiler suit.

Hugging the shadows, we followed the building's contours to a fire escape. Half way up, on what we reckoned to be the second floor, was a small window. The framed bulged, perhaps from damp. Julie worked a kitchen knife under the lip and prized it softly open with the skill of a cat burglar. Being the smallest she wriggled through first. I followed, then Sid. It took a little while for us to heave Kevin's six foot five bulk inside but we managed.

We were in a corridor, bare except for a tea machine and several doors leading off into other rooms.

"We need to head down," whispered Kevin. *"The entrance is in the cellar. If we follow the stairs down as far as we can go we should find it."*

Moving slowly in the near dark we found the stairs around a corner in the corridor and began to descend. We were on the second floor of a three-storey building. Two more floors and we should be in the basement.

There were a couple of false starts. A broom closet, and a small windowless office, then we found it. The cellar was obviously being used as a storage room, unwise as it was damp. There were elderly looking filing cabinets, bulging with long forgotten files, anachronisms in this computer-led business, standing against the walls. There were untidy piles of boxes containing God knows what. We were not thieves or vandals; we never even bothered to look into them.

We found the large doors behind some of the rusting cabinets. They were damp and covered with peeling paint. The bolt was rusted into place by sixty years of moisture and non-use. It took Kevin ten minutes of wrenching with a pair of pliers before the corroded metal gave way with a sickening screech of protest and a shower of rust flakes. The four of us heaved the heavy doors apart to be greeted by a foul blast of foetid air. We shrank back momentarily.

"Oh well... Geronimo!" said Sid pulling out his torch. We all followed suit. The beams cut through the darkness illuminating dust motes that danced on the air in the first breeze to disturb them in six decades. The light fell upon the dirt-caked stairs and the verdigris-gnawed copper of the hand rails. We began out descent into the cold, velvety blackness.

We reached the platform. There was an ancient chocolate vending machine, long empty, otherwise the platform seemed bare.

"Well someone has been down here, and fairly recently."

Sid, Kevin, and I all swung round at Julie's comment and our eyes followed the beam of her torch.

"And it looks like they have been riding a bike!" she added.

It was true. Over one area of the platform there were markings about as wide as a bicycle tyre. They criss-crossed many times as if the rider had been going back and forth purposefully. They led from the tunnel to the edge of the stairs. Julie took several snaps with her camera, its flash momentarily blinding us.

"Who the fuck would come down here to ride a bike?" I bent to look closer at the tracks in the dust-caked floor. They seemed to lack any markings. If they were bike tyres, then they had no treads. *"Only one way to find out,"* I said, leaping off the platform and down onto the rail track. We trained our torches into the tunnel and walked blithely in.

The wooden components of the track had mostly rotted but the metal was still there, albeit rusted and distorted. We must have walked for a quarter of a mile in the damp, stinking, man-made cavern when my beam fell across something round and grey on the floor.

"What the hell is that thing?"

As I drew closer I saw that it was about the size of a beach ball. It was grey and rubbery looking. I touched it then withdrew at its clammy feel. There were several more slightly smaller than the first, scattered across the width of this portion of the tunnel. They seemed imbedded in the earth. Julie took some more pictures but said nothing. There was something eerie about the objects. As the camera flashes lit up the tunnel I thought I heard a rustling in the distance. I looked up. We all did.

"Rats," I said, a little too quickly. The others nodded. I don't know if they were any more convinced than I was.

"You reckon we should dig one up and take it back, see what it is?" said Kevin

"Maybe on the way back. We'd better explore the rest of the tunnel first. Don't wanna get bogged down carrying stuff," Sid said.

I was unaccountably relieved.

We wandered on for about another quarter of a mile saying nothing. The place had affected us like no other. We were used to old, uncanny, creepy buildings. Cane Hill had been a madhouse for Christ's sake. But this place had a leaden pall of sheer decay like nowhere else I had ever experienced. The foul air seemed pregnant with a brooding menace. The others felt the same. I could tell from their subdued behaviour.

Sid had wandered on ahead of us. He stopped and we heard him cry out.

"Oi you lot, I've found another of those things."

We all ran forward to where Sid was looking down at another grey, spherical object. He bent to look closer.

"This one's smaller than the others, it looks… OH FUCK!"

As Sid recoiled we saw that the object was a human skull with a shattered cranium. Beside it were the scattered remains of the rest of the skeleton. A few decaying rags hung to the bare bones.

"God, we've got to tell the police," whispered Julie, trying to hold down the panic that was rising in her.

"You what?" bellowed Kevin. *"We have just been breaking and entering in case you hadn't noticed. If we go…"*

He was cut short by Sid turning and running further up the tunnel. Sid was in a blind panic and, forgetting the golden rule of urban exploration, had run off on his own.

"SID, SID! GET BACK HERE YOU DICKHEAD!"

Our shouts echoed up and down the tunnel.

"We've got to go and get him. Christ knows what's down there, he could fall into a sink hole or something." I was edgy and angry now.

"But the body…" started Julie.

"Fuck the bloody body. It's been dead for years. You saw the state of it."

Suddenly a high-pitched, almost feminine scream of terror reverberated through the darkness. We all ran along the track in the direction Sid had stupidly gone, away from the platform and the stairs.

More screams followed and then they abruptly ceased. We swung up our torches and found Sid suspended like some ghastly puppet from the tunnel's ceiling. At first it looked like he had become tangled in the roots of a tree. But what tree had roots this deep? What tree had bone white roots? What tree had roots that squirmed?

Sid was covered in, and suspended by, a mass of writhing, pallid members that resembled titanic worms. By the way his limp body jerked, we could tell he was already dead. The wormy things were burrowing into his flesh, twisting beneath his skin like fingers in a glove.

We ran and screamed. A damp rustling alerted us to the presence of more of the things. They were oozing out of the walls of the tunnel, forcing brickwork and earth before them. They reached blindly for us with their featureless ends. I saw no eyes, no mouths, on the pointed ends of the twisting things, but they followed our movements like predatory hosepipes.

In my mad flight, I tripped across some rusted section of track and fell forward onto one of the rounded, grey objects we came across before. It burst asunder like a huge bladder showering me with a fine white powder. I crawled on all fours gagging. The substance was in my mouth, in my eyes and up my nose.

Kevin and Julie stopped and turned back. Julie wiped the powder from my face. I felt a fumbling about my legs as one of the worm things reached me. It grasped with a strength that made me scream out in pain. If felt its pointed tip questing hungrily for naked skin.

Kevin lifted up a broken section of track and slammed it down onto the thing. It lost its grip on me and I stood. Keith's blow had bisected it. There was no blood, no signs of internal organs, just white flesh. It writhed like an earthworm severed by a spade.

Then a dozen more of them exploded up from the ground at our feet. Before we could react they had whipped about Kevin. Some coiled about his neck like a hangman's noose. Others latched onto his arms and legs. More and more of the vile members coiled out of the darkness behind us like an out-sized mass of twitching vermicelli. Kevin didn't have time to scream before he was pulled back and engulfed.

Julie and I sprinted for the platform and scrambled up of the track. We reached the stairs and began to run up on all fours. Behind me I heard her scream. As I turned she was being dragged back down the stairs by the ropey assailants that had fastened onto her ankles. I grabbed her wrists and pulled with all the strength I could muster. The last I saw of Julie was her screaming face as she was wrenched from my grasp, and drawn back down the stairs by the ghostly tendrils. Back across the filthy platform and into the tunnel where her hysterical screams were cut short.

I smashed aside the doors and ran through the cellar. On fear induced auto-pilot I found the window and heaved myself through. Running down the fire escape, I collided with the security guard and knocked him flying. I didn't stop for breath or heed his profanities. I scrambled over the fence cutting my hands on the wire and fled into the night.

I have no memory of how I got home. I am sitting in front of my computer covered with dirt and blood and white powder. My skin itches. I cannot feel my right arm or the right side of my face. I see only with my left eye now.

What was it? I think I know. The round objects were like huge puffballs. I think the puffballs and the "worms" were part of the same thing. A kind of giant subterranean fungus. The puffballs were its fruiting bodies, the white powder its spores. The wormy things that pulled three of my friends to their deaths were its mycelia, the fungus equivalent of roots. I read once of a honey fungus in the US. It stretched over four square miles and was centuries old. The mycelia formed a network beneath the earth but all people saw of it was its fruiting bodies in the form of tiny toadstools. The whole thing was one macro-organism.

Fungi and their relatives have more in common with animals than plants. Some, like slime moulds are motile and can actively seek prey. This is some vast unknown species. God knows how old it is or how far it stretches beneath London. That must be why the station was closed. They found out about it and tried to cover it up. Tried to stop a panic.

The mycelia feed it. They draw up nutrients from the soil but hunt live prey as well. I also know how it breeds. Something bothered me about the skull we found. The cranium had not been smashed by a blow. It had been ruptured from the inside, blown apart. Christ knows how many of those spores I swallowed. I can feel a rustling inside my head.

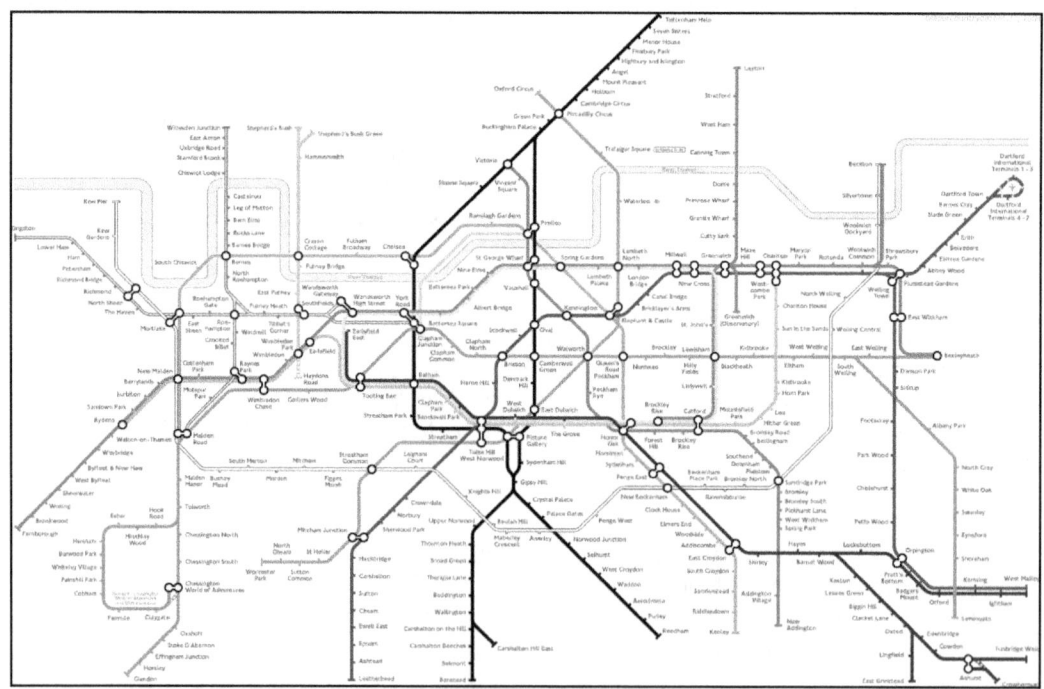

King William Street was the original but short-lived northern terminus of the City & South London Railway (C&SLR), the first deep tube underground railway in London and one of the component parts of the London Underground's Northern Line. It was in the City of London, on King William Street, just south of the present Monument station. When the station was in operation the next station south was Borough and the southern terminus of the line was Stockwell. **(Wikipedia)**

SLEEP OF REASON

As Paul watched, a faceless bleeping monkey with stigmata walked through the liquid wall. As it crossed the room with a sound like a submarine's sonar, the droplets of blood that fell from its wounds blossomed into tiny roses on the Persian carpet. It grasped Paul's hand, the wet, sundered palm feeling like a warm mouth, and shook it vigorously.

"Allow me to introduce myself, Rex," it said in a high voice. *"I'm Frampton."*

To be honest, he thought to himself, this was the last thing I was expecting.

As the blank faced simian led him towards the rippling wall, he recalled what had led him to this irregular situation.

Paul Campbell had a passion for mind-altering substances. For more than two decades he had been a ferocious devourer of psychoactives of all descriptions, starting at the age of fourteen when he had sampled *Psilocybe* mushrooms picked with classmates on a hillside during a school trip to Skye. He moved quickly on to experimenting with fly agaric and henbane. He stole antihistamines from his parents' drug cabinet. At first, like most kids, it was the thrill of actually taking the substances that attracted him. The very illicitness of it was his kick. This swiftly changed.

As a student in Manchester, he was exposed to more mind-altering substances. LSD, brolamfetamine, phencyclidine, dimenhydrinate and dozens of others. He came to know them all like old friends. He savoured their different effects as a wine connoisseur might savour different wines.

He also became adept at procuring these substances. Some were merely over the counter medicines taken in large doses or mixed with another substance. The illegal drugs could always be found if you knew where to look and who to ask. Paul was well off and always had money to spare to feed his habit.

In fact, Paul loathed the terms 'habit' and 'addiction'. He considered himself a psychonaught,

---

an explorer in the realms of perception. Now he ingested, snorted or injected the substances in order to travel to 'other places'. He kept a meticulous journal of what he saw and experienced during his experiments. His writings currently ran to a dozen volumes.

It could be argued that Paul was just as much an addict as any street junkie. But he was addicted to the experience itself and not the drug he took to get himself there. The psychoactives were just a ticket, no different to him in the final analysis than a plane ticket.

After graduation he returned to his native Glasgow and made a reasonably good living as a fantasy writer. He was no Rowling or Pratchett, but his books had a minor cult following. He had used some of his experiences in mental exploration as an inspiration for his books. '*The Amoebic World*' series took place inside a planet-sized protozoan. It was a whole world encased within a vast cell membrane. Its bizarre inhabitants, who lived in the cytoplasm, were all based on things the psychonaught had met on his drug-fuelled journeys.

But Paul's creative well had finally dried-up. His tolerance to drugs was legendary. Now, at the age of 38 he found that even the strongest of substances had very little effect on him. This meant that his inspiration was fast running out. This was not what worried Paul; it was more the fact that he could no longer explore these 'other places'. The books and the money they brought in were of a secondary concern. They were a means to an end. The end itself was the experience.

So when talk of something new, a fresh drug apparently unlike any other, reached him, his ears pricked up. Paul could have called his dealer to deliver the stuff to his upscale apartment in Newlands but he relished venturing into the city's seedier underside and it didn't come any seedier than Castlemilk.

He wandered through the cold night air surrounded by the worst of urban decay. Castlemilk reminded Paul of some post nuclear wasteland in a third rate science fiction film. Filthy, desolate and seemingly abandoned it had a *genius loci* of utter, leaden despair and unyielding hopelessness. At least this was some fodder for his novels.

He pulled his trench coat tighter as his own breath made tiny ghosts in front of his face.

Something moved in the shadows. Like all apocalyptic landscapes, Castlemilk had its mutants. From the darkness of a broken down lift in a half-abandoned block of flats, a trio of youths slouched towards him with a lazy menace.

Pasty-faced, skinny, dressed in dirty tracksuits and Burberry caps, Paul felt the hate rising in him as they slunk closer. He detested chavs. In procuring the fuel for his psychonaught adventures he was brought into close contact with all manner of low-life. But none filled him with such sheer hatred as human sewage like these.

"Oi mate, got any cash?" The vermin seemed to spit out the words rather than speak them.

"No."

"Ye better have, mate, for your sake."

"Or what?"

"We gonna cut you up, mate." One of the youths, they could be no older than seventeen, produced a Stanley knife.

Before he could use it, Paul had grabbed his wrist and yanked him forward. His forehead smashed into the bridge of the boy's nose shattering it in a spray of scarlet.

He dropped the knife and started mewling like a child.

"Ye broke me nose ya bastard, ye broke me fuckin' nose."

His two rat-like comrades advanced. Paul grabbed the first youth by the neck and whipped a gun out of his deep coat pocket. He jammed the cold metal into the boy's bloody face.

"I would love to blow what passes for this little ned's brain all over the fucking pavement. Do you want to give me any more reason to do it?"

A large wet patch had formed around the crotch of the grubby tracksuit bottoms the boy was wearing.

"Fuckin' hell, don't shoot, mate, don't shoot," he whimpered like a little girl, and went as loose as a rag doll.

His two friends took one look at the gun and ran into the night. Paul hoisted the youth up and glared into his dull eyes nose to shattered nose.

"If I ever see your ugly little face again I'm going to ventilate you. Do you understand, you cockweasel?"

He nodded frantically.

"Now get the fucking fuck out of here before I get too tempted to put a hole in your slimy hide here and now."

He dropped the soiled chav who crawled away still sobbing.

Paul relished such encounters. He replaced the gun with a gentle pat and carried on walking to his rendezvous.

'The Boy Wonder' was a name the locals gave to a statue in Castlemilk. The title its sculptor Kenny Hunter had given it was 'King of the Castle'. Castlemilk residents thought it bore more than a passing resemblance to Batman's youthful sidekick, so the name stuck. The Boy Wonder was rendered in white plaster and stood, holding a pair of binoculars on a graffiti defaced hemisphere. Leaning against the dome in a long, shabby leather overcoat was Hugh McPherson.

"The psychonaught returns," he grinned through rotting teeth. *"Any trouble, Paulie?"*

"It's Castlemilk, there's always trouble. Nothing I couldn't handle though." Paul playfully patted the gun in his pocket as if it were a small animal.

Hugh had an untidy mop of grey/brown hair and habitually wore small round sunglasses even in the middle of the night. Paul had never seen his eyes.

"So what's the new stuff, Hugh? It better be good, you know that lately I have being getting, shall we say... accustomed to the regular items on your menu."

"This is different from any other drug I have ever seen and I have been dealing for years. I have other customers who thought they had tried it all. This stuff blew their minds."

"Nice to know I'm not a guinea pig."

"No worries, you know I would never sell anything I ain't tried myself."

What Hugh said was true. He never sold poor grade drugs or drugs cut with unknown substances. His appetite was almost as legendary as Paul's and he was often the first to sample anything new that arrived in the city.

Hugh reached into his pocket and retrieved a glass vial. He held it up in the moonlight and Paul looked closer. It was filled with a thick liquid. As Hugh gently tilted the vial the liquid seemed to change colour. One moment it seemed purple, another green. The effect reminded him of when he had seen the Northern Lights as a boy up in the Highlands. It was quite beautiful and he gazed at it for a while.

"What's it called?"

"The manufacturer refers to it as 'Writhe'".

"Why?"

"I have no idea; maybe it makes some folks Writhe in pleasure."

"Do you know what's in it?"

"Of course I do. You know I never put anything into my system without knowing what it is and where it came from."

"Well?"

"The gentleman who is currently supplying me wants to keep his production methods secret for the time being but rest assured Writhe is 100% organic and totally natural. In fact you could call it green."

"So what are the effects?"

"Paul, Writhe will take you to places even you have never been to. Forget about machine elves, you'll see some really weird stuff on this. Trust me, this shit will fuck with your mind big time. It's like no other psychoactive I have ever known of. And, as agreed, the first trip is on the house."

He passed the vial to Paul who looked at it more closely. The liquid almost seemed to be alive in the way it swirled. He put it into his breast pocket carefully.

"So what do I do, inject or drink?"

"Drink, the taste is not unpleasant."

"I'll look forward to it."

"Oh and Paulie, be careful where you take this. Ingest it at home and alone. Lock all the doors and windows. The drug itself won't do you no harm, but like I said the trip is a mind fuck. One guy I know of stepped out in front of a train when he was high on Writhe."

"I'll wait till I get home."

Back in his apartment Paul lay on his couch. The doors and windows were locked and the 'phone off the hook. He pulled the cap of the vial and sniffed the liquid. It smelled like a mixture of lime and violets.

He took the vial to his lips and sipped. It had a sweet sticky taste. The nearest analogue he could think of was some boiled sweets he had left beside a window one hot summer's day. Melted boiled sweets, yes that was what it tasted of. He swallowed the rest of the liquid and lay back on the couch.

He felt no difference. There was no mental shift. Another disappointment. At least he hadn't paid for this one. It was then he had heard the rustling sound and looked up to see that the wall of his apartment was rippling like water that had a stone cast into it. And then the faceless, stigmatic, bleeping, chimp-sized monkey had walked through the wall.

Frampton led him through the wall. It had a sensation on his skin that felt like passing through a bead curtain. He found himself on a set of shining steps suspended sixty feet above the ground. The steps led to a narwhal made of solid light. The tusked light-whale was as long as a train carriage and had rows of portholes set in its sides. A door opened in its glowing flank and man and monkey entered.

Inside were rows of high leather back seats. In the Victorian-style cockpit a being identical to Frampton sat at a brass and mahogany control panel.

"Rex, this is my brother Marzipan. Marzipan this is Rex. We are known as Ouch Monkeys."

The second faceless monkey turned and waved whilst bleeping like his brother.

"Hello there, Rex," it squeaked in a voice as camp as its brother's.

Paul didn't think to ask why they were calling him Rex or even how they managed to speak without mouths.

"Ouch Monkeys like us are employed to show freshers like you around," said Marzipan.

"Strap yourself in, Rex," squeaked Frampton. *"A ride in Roscoe can be quite bumpy."*

Paul sat in a chair by a porthole and strapped himself in with a brass and leather belt. Frampton scurried over and sat beside his brother in the narwhal's cockpit. They fiddled with some wheels and levers and the machine beast rose, the stairs retracting and folding like a concertina.

For the first time he looked out on the city. The city he knew was gone. Where the Clyde once flowed there was a river of purple smoke that rose in great plumes high above the city. Most of the buildings looked like architectural impossibilities. Towering, branching structures, hundreds of feet tall that looked as if they were made from glass. Spherical blue and gold objects Paul took to be dwellings hung from them like fruit. Other buildings seemed to be suspended from vast zeppelin type balloons that were anchored via great chains. The dwellings hung like gondolas beneath them.

The sky was a dark, moody green with titan clouds obscuring the sun. Occasionally the clouds would be lit up by blue flashes like sheet lightning that outlined them or threw them into relief.

Paul noticed dark shapes against the clouds that seemed to be drawing closer. As they swooped towards Roscoe, he saw that they seemed to be hybrids of angels and scarecrows. Ragged, spindly things, the scarecrow angels looked to be composed of twigs and burlap with tattered wings of woven corn stalks over a wicker framework. One swung in close and seemed to be saying something through its lips of straw and gesticulating with crooked twig fingers. From inside the whale he could hear nothing.

"Look! What are those things?"

The monkey glanced over.

"No need to worry, Rex," chirped Marzipan. *"Those are just scrapfaggots."*

"Scrapfaggots?"

"Etheric scavengers," continued Marzipan. *"They feed on decaying etheric matter like flies feed on rotting meat. They are of no danger to us, Rex."*

Frampton seemed a little more concerned.

"They generally hang around the large predators of the ether. Ready to gobble up the scraps

they leave. Rex, look out of the porthole and please tell me how many you count?"

Paul looked at the scrapfaggots as they beat their wings like tatty dishrags flapping in the wind.

"Nine as far as I can see."

"Nine, nine, nine," squeaked Frampton. *"Nine of them. That might mean there is large predator at large."*

Behind them, in the clouds Paul saw something coiling in the verdant clouds. Whatever it was seemed to be stalking them. It was using cloud cover much like a stalking leopard might use bushes on the African savannah. From the glimpses he got, Paul thought it was an elongate creature about as long as Roscoe.

Suddenly it came whipping out of the clouds in a frantic zigzag flight pattern. The scrapfaggots scattered in alarm, screaming like children. Within seconds the creature was alongside the narwhal.

It was over thirty feet long and shaped like a huge eel. Paul could see what looked like gill slits on its side. Its colour was a light violet but the skin was translucent revealing the stomach and organs inside like an out of focus picture on a monitor. A little, piggy eye glared in at him. Where the mouth should have been was a huge sucker surrounded by rings of fangs. It drooled yellow saliva in great loops and strands.

"Etheric hagfish," the monkeys screamed in unison and began fiddling madly at the controls with their hands and prehensile tails. Their bleeping increased in frequency and volume.

The narwhal banked away sharply trying to evade the airborne hunter. With a flick of its slimy tail the ghostly predator was beside them again and maneuvering for an attack. As it turned its pallid underside towards them, Paul saw that the rings of teeth were all moving independently of each other like a cross between a chainsaw and a drill. The etheric hagfish made a noise like an outsized tuba and lunged at Roscoe's side, its teeth whirring.

Again the whale of light dived. This time the monster only just missed.

"The tusk, use the tusk!" squealed Marzipan.

Frampton grasped a brazen steering wheel and whirled the machine beast around to face the slavering monster. The etheric hagfish looked insubstantial, almost like a phantom but Paul had no doubt it could do untold damage. It clamped its horrid sucker onto Roscoe.

The narwhal thundered forward powered by its muscular tail. The lamppost-sized, spiralling horn of hard light aimed at the coiling hagfish. With an almost idle flick of the tail the monster sailed clear of the spearing horn and span round to attack. Like a striking cobra its head rose and fell in a heart beat. The sucker clamped onto the whale's side and the tooth circles began to spin and bore. Shards of light fell from Roscoe's side like gold fish. The scrapfaggots swooped in to snatch them up and devour them greedily. Roscoe bellowed like a church organ.

"It's got us, it's got us!" yelped Marzipan.

"Look," Frampton shrieked. *"Up ahead. Cloud urchin!"*

Looming out of the green clouds was a spiky, floating mass the size of small block of flats. It was roughly spherical and seemed to be composed of long shards of silvery crystal. Frampton steered the narwhal straight towards the cloud urchin's razor spines.

"We'll crash," shouted Paul

"No, Rex, trust me the urchin is our salvation."

At the last moment, the faceless monkey twisted the brass wheel sharply to the right avoiding the cloud urchin's crystal spines but whipping the etheric hagfish straight into them. The impaled monster disengaged its sucker in a spray of gold strips. Skewered on the spines it thrashed in a frantic but futile frenzy. Blue blood poured from its rent innards and turned solid on contact with the air, falling down like a rain of opals. The cloud urchin shook and made a piping, tinkling noise reminiscent of a fairground organ.

There was a ragged hole as big as a dustbin lid in Roscoe's side.

"He needs repairs," said Marzipan.

"I'll take him down into the city," replied Frampton. He steered the wounded narwhal down from the green skies and over the busy streets of the city. Finally they came to some form of landing strip. Other crazily-shaped aircraft were parked there. Roscoe landed between a giant yellow dodecahedron, and what looked like an 80-foot caterpillar made of chrome.

Frampton led him down the unfurling stairs. *"You show Rex the city and I'll patch up Roscoe,"* said Marzipan as he waved them off.

"Come on, Rex, I need a drink after that." Frampton's wet palm gripped Paul's again and he led him off into the streets.

There seemed to be multiple races in the city, some humanoid, others not. Even the ones that superficially resembled humans had differences. There were people with skin colours never heard of, green, blue, and magenta. The clothes were equally as weird. Some seemed to be made of tiny living birds that roosted communally on their host like hundreds of miniature oxpeckers. Others wore clothes that seemed to change colour with the wearer's mood. Some seemed to be impossibly intricate patchworks of thousands of tiny rags from wildly clashing fashion styles. Some wore nothing. One green-skinned priapic man carried several stingray-like creatures that coiled about his phallus with long tails.

Here and there heavily armoured men mounted on vast, tank-like rhinos with massive horns, sat brooding. They looked like some sort of police force. No wonder there seemed to be little trouble on the streets.

Of the other races he could have written volumes, huge upright insects and reptiles, fish-headed men (or man-bodied fish), beings that hid under black, spiked, rounded shells and scurried like living sea mines. They met another pair of Ouch Monkeys that were introduced as 'Bromley and Sherbet'. One creature lumbered past on two horse-like hind legs. It was seemingly encased in black rubber. Spindly arms hung at its sides and its face was hidden by a massive gas mask. Organic looking pipes led from the mask and seemed to terminate in the thing's rear end.

"What the hell is that?" Paul whispered.

"It's a podlasp, a creature that breathes only its own internal gasses."

They paused at a road to let an elephant-sized beast resembling an armadillo thunder past. People were sitting in chairs bolted onto its shell. The driver had a pink, pumpkin-sized head that was attached the creatures own head by a series of vein like cables.

Frampton seemed to know where he was going so Paul followed in a constant state of awe. Every turn brought some new wonder. Dog-faced nuns in habits of uncured skin with halos of flies, a skyscraper constructed of human femurs, a ten-foot chalk white hive that walked on four nubbin legs, dripping pink honey. It was home to black, fist-sized bees whose humming approximated human speech, but the speech of a raving imbecile.

Paul realised that he did not even know the name of the city or indeed the world.

"What's this place called?"

"*Haythornthwaite*," replied Frampton.

Haythornthwaite, it sounded totally inappropriate, more like some little Dorset village than this crescendo of madness.

"And the wider world, does that have a name?"

"We call this world 'Goitre'."

Goitre, it made about as much sense as anything else.

Finally, down a winding back street paved in rook skulls and mummified wasps they reached their destination, *The Anal Star*. A lurid painting of a puckered sphincter hung over the inn's gaily painted door. Frampton pushed it open and entered. *"Drinks are on me, Rex"* he piped.

The pub was dimly lit by candles whose tallow had grown into fantastical shapes like wax stalactites. Where the bar should have been was a pallid, recumbrant beast. It reminded Paul of some ungodly cross between an insanely bloated termite queen and a human woman. A vaguely human looking head was at one end of the creature, almost buried in rolls of white fat. In comparison to the obese salami that was its body, the head seemed almost vestigial. The thing had multiple, tenticular breasts. About half a dozen patrons were sitting on stools and suckling from the snake-like paps. The thing must be internally producing some form of liquor like other mammals produce milk. It looked as if it had been bred for that very reason.

A young girl was constantly feeding the head of the creature with what appeared to be kitchen waste. A burly, bald man with what seemed to be ritual scars on his head and an apron of pigskin, smiled at them.

"What's it to be, gents?"

"What would you recommend?" asked Frampton

"Well we have some new drinks available, Graveworm Anaesthesia, Stranger in the Pigsty, Leper Fat *and* Tethered Crone. *Then there's the old favourites like* Blasphemous Litany *or* Cannibal Satin. *"*

"Oh, I just love Stranger in the Pigsty, *"* squeaked Frampton. He reached into his left stigmatic wound as if it were a bloody purse of meat and produced two hexagonal gold coins with holes in them. He handed them to the landlord.

"Two suckles of Stranger in the Pigsty *coming up gents. Hear that Tallulah? Two Pigsties?"*

He reached down and took up two lengths of teat as if they were hoses.

"Here you go. Enjoy."

Paul thought he should have been revolted at suckling from such a horror and ingesting something fermented inside the body of such an abomination but he did not. Here it seemed totally natural. He took the chapped, thumb-sized nipple to his mouth and suckled like a newborn. A warm, bubbly liquid fizzed into his mouth. It tasted like pork and apple sauce liquidised in a blender with yogurt and heated up ginger beer.

He glanced over at Frampton. He was audibly sucking without dint of a mouth. Tallulah's nipple just vanishing into the suggestive blank where the big monkey's face should have been.

As it turned out *Stranger in the Pigsty* was a powerful brew and Paul found himself getting intoxicated vey quickly.

An hour or so later Marzipan joined them. He said that Roscoe had been repaired and refuelled. He joined Paul and his brother at the teat. As the night drew on the patrons of *The Anal Star* began singing drinking songs. Though Paul had never heard them before he joined in and sung like a local. All the bawdy lyrics to ditties such as *Maidenhead in Tatters* and *Hormone Shoals* just popped right into his head and onto his lips. He had no idea how much *Stranger in the Pigsty* he had drunk but his head was swimming. The last thing he remembered was dancing on a table with two sapphic, ruby-skinned midgets as he sung *The Jolly Cadaver in Farrow,* which was - apparently - part of the *Sepulchre Tykes* opera.

He awoke on the couch back in his apartment. His mouth was dry and he needed the bathroom. He staggered to his feet. As he relieved himself he looked in the mirror. His reflection looked as if it had been on a memorable night out.

He drank strong coffee and ate scrambled eggs then reached for his notepad and pen. Last night had been, without a doubt, the most amazing journey in his psychonaught career. He had to get it down whilst it was still fresh in his head.

When he had scribbled it all down in excited, untidy writing he telephoned Hugh.

"Well, psychonaught how was your expedition?"

"Hugh, I can't even begin to describe what I saw. It was so real, the sounds, the smells, everything. I can't believe it; it's like nothing else, a total mind fuck. I have to get back to that world."

Hugh laughed, *"I told you so. Writhe is something else, isn't it?"*

"I need more, quickly. Money is no object. When can I have more?"

"There will be another batch ready on Thursday."

Paul gagged: *"Thursday? I can't wait that long!"*

"Hold on there, have a bit of patience. It takes time to produce. We are talking about a quality product here. Good things are worth waiting for. You get on with some writing and ring me on Thursday. The next trip will cost you £500."

Paul didn't flinch at the price. It was the idea of waiting three days before he could return to Haythornthwaite that was galling.

He spent the intervening days typing up an intricately detailed account of what he had seen. It reached over 100,000 words. After what seemed like forever, Thursday rolled around and he rang Hugh. This time he didn't waste valuable time picking the drug up but had him deliver it direct to him. He handed over the money and ushered his dealer out as quickly as he could. Swallowing the liquid in one gulp he lay back on the couch and waited.

Frampton entered the room through the shimmering liquid wall in a state of excitement. He capered round the room in a repetitive, circular dance, stamping his feet.

"We're going to the circus, Rex. I have tickets to the circus!" He produced three damp tickets from his bloody palm and flourished them on high. He grabbed Paul's hand and practically dragged him through the wall onto the waiting, luminous stairs. Roscoe seemed to have been well repaired since their last adventure. The giant, flying, solid light, machine narwhal showed no signs of the etheric hagfish attack.

Inside, Marzipan was as excited as his brother . *"Circus, circus, circus!"* he trilled.

This time they flew Roscoe low, avoiding the deep green clouds and soon arrived at the airport Paul recalled from his last trip. They strode quickly through the twisting streets with their insane crowds until they came to what Paul took to be the circus tent.

The tent looked more like a quivering lime coloured jellyfish, if jellyfishes were the size of the dome of Saint Paul's Cathedral. Frampton handed over the three tickets to a woman with a four-foot long, forked beard that had cat skulls woven into it, and they entered through a trembling hole in the green slime.

Inside where circular rows of PVC seats that squeaked when sat on and were incredibly sweaty. Paul and the Ouch Monkeys had front row seats.

A darkness and hush fell over the crowd. A red spotlight fell on a tall man in the ring. He had silver hair woven into dreadlocks. He wore jackboots and jodhpurs with a frilly white shirt and scarlet-tailed coat. His stovepipe hat seemed to be constructed out of some kind of preserved meat like jerky. Stranger still, the ringmaster seemed to have no skin, his tendons and muscles of his hands and face on display as if he had been flayed alive.

"Ladies and gentlemen, boys and girls, things and creatures, I am Dr. Feverclaw ringmaster of the Fibrillating Circus. Tonight you will witness things that will amaze and appall you, things that will excite and repel you. Will you put out your own eyes with teaspoons or become moist and aroused? It's all down to you my little corpuscles. But now without further ado let me introduce the first act the comical, hilarious Distemper Clowns*!"*

Four creatures came jogging into the ring. They seemed bereft of arms and heads and their flat, toad-like faces were situated in their chests. They had massive buttocks and thin, knock-kneed legs with long, gaudy boots on their feet. It was hard to tell if they were wearing make-up or if the red lips, racoonish eye patches and circular ruby noses were part of their natural physiognomy. They sported three orange pom-poms on their distended bellies. Each bore a shock of green or red hair just above the face on what would have been the shoulders if they had any arms. Their wide mouths were turned down in permanent frowns and their deep set, black ringed eyes seemed screwed up in misery.

The *Distemper Clowns'* act seemed to consist of clumsily running around the ring whilst catching fly-headed, winged cats, with their extraordinarily long and flexible tongues, then devouring them noisily in their sharp-toothed mouths. Every so often one of them would stop and relate some *non sequitur* to the crowd such as, *"An egg preacher is amongst us!", "Beneath macabre awnings I smell carrion!"* or *"A chain of embolism has extinguished reason!"* These statements brought roars of laughter from the audience as if they had been listening to the sharpest stand up on Earth. Paul found himself laughing too. Laughing uncontrollably, laughing until he wept.

After the waddling clowns had left the stage, the ringmaster re-appeared.

"And now for that master of the whip, that tamer of feral beasts, the man who knows no fear, a big round of applause for The Jack of Satyrs and his Plague Swarm.*"*

A goat-horned and cloven-hoofed figure that was formidably male trotted into the ring holding a tall wicker basket and razor barbed leather whip. He sat the basket down and bowed to the audience. Taking the lid off the basket, he cracked the whip causing a blue flash at its end.

There was a brief rustling then a swarm of nightmare creatures flapped up out of the basket. They looked like fanged human skulls that burned with a cold green fire. Each had a pair of bat-like wings sprouting from its sides and a point of red light in each eye socket. The creatures stank like rotting horsemeat. They clattered their jaws and fluttered about wildly until Jack cracked the whip again and they fell into a tight formation.

For a quarter of an hour Jack had the Plague Swarm performing mind boggling aerial stunts like some hell spawn version of *The Red Arrows*. Sometimes they flew close to the folk in the front row and seemed to eye them with a disturbing longing.

Many other acts followed: a beast with the face of a scholar and the body of a wild ass recited epic poetry written by a ditch-dwelling hermit four thousand years in the future; a gibbering priest with an entrail noose about his neck and a pig's head grafted between his thighs, excommunicated some flies drawing "oohs" and "aahs" from the watchers; a scab covered bag lady summoned misty orange poltergeists from her own ulcers by scratching at them and speaking in tongues; what looked like a dozen four-foot tall tar babies, each with a single, compound red eye, performed impossible acrobatics, often melting into one another.

But it seemed that all these acts were just a prelude to the main event. Something big was happening and the excitement from the audience was rising to fever pitch.

The skinless ringmaster re-entered.

"And now, my dearest little pox vectors, the main attraction, the thing you have all been waiting for, the grand death struggle. Here you will witness unbound barbarism in the combat of primordial gladiators in a gore-lust fuelled killing frenzy that brands them with an intolerable degradation. Ladies and gentlemen I give you The Evangelists of Butchery!*"*

The lights fell as he scooted off stage and a discordant herald of trumpets rent the air. His voice rang out from the wings.

"Our reigning champion, a frenzied killer, more rabid beast than woman, red in tooth and claw, the beautiful Lucretia Fleshrender."

A spotlight fell on a woman who slinked from the shadows with animalistic grace. She was totally naked and her skin was a powder blue in colour. Swirling tattoos like those of Maori warriors covered her body from head to foot. She was immensely tall; around seven feet. Her height was extenuated by a two-foot, electric blue Mohican. Her body had an appearance of sinuous strength, the muscles rippling just beneath her skin. Her golden eyes were catlike with vertical pupils. She grinned in a predatory manner revealing sharp metal fangs. Her fingers and long elegant toes ended in cruel metal claws.

The crowd went wild at her appearance and she circled the ring pumping her fist in the air and occasionally stopping to strike a pose with her blue muscles glistening. Paul's eyes never left her form. Finally, she bowed and moved to the side of the ring.

Dr. Feverclaw called out again. *"And now the brave challenger who would dare to claim this butcher queen's crown. Fresh from the streets of Haythornthwaite, Mottleclutch."*

From the opposite side of the ring a large podlasp trotted on his horsey hind legs. The rubber of his suit shone wetly in the hot atmosphere. It held its spindly forearms up in front of it like a kangaroo. Each hand held a bladed knuckle-duster. Behind his gas mask only the eyes could be discerned. They were large, white and unblinking with tiny black pupils. Pipes and tubes ran from the mask, down his long neck, over his rotund body, between the hoofed legs and entered his own bowels.

Both combatants moved towards the centre of the ring and eyed one another. The podlasp was far more massive than the woman.

"Remember," said Dr. Feverclaw. *"There is to be no quarter given. This is a fight to the death. Only one will leave the ring alive. Now when I blow this whistle you will fight. There are no rounds, just fight."*

He blew on a rusty penny whistle. The podlasp trotted forward and kicked out with a hoof. Lucretia dodged it with ease, but he kicked again and again. The blue skinned, naked Amazon leapt and somersaulted out of the slashing hooves' way every time. The podlasp looked as if he were doing some kind of clumsy dance. Mottleclutch seemed to tire of kicking and tried to punch with his guillotine like knuckle-dusters. Again the powder blue girl danced out of range or ducked under the swiping fists.

Finally she caught one of the thin arms and snapped it like a dry twig with her muscular one. There was a sharp retort like the shot of a gun. The podlasp bleated and capered from side to side his broken arm hanging at a weird angle. Lucretia giggled like an excited schoolgirl and flung herself into a cartwheel. As she careered between the ungainly creatures legs her clawed hand slashed, severing the podlasp's gas tubes.

The rubber-clad beast bleated and screamed as the sundered pipes spewed a beige gas with a stomach-churning stench. Mottleclutch was staggering about like a punch-drunk puppet with a head full of mud. An openhanded chop from Lucretia shattered his other arm leaving it as limp and useless as the other. Unable to breathe in his own vital bowel gasses the podlasp was suffocating.

Lucretia bounded onto its back and whipped her long muscular legs about the base of the neck with vertebra crushing strength. The claws on her toes ripped through the rubber and buried themselves deep within the flesh beneath causing rills of white blood to cascade down the fat, black rubber encased body. At the same time she wrapped her powerful arms around her victim's neck but further up. She drilled her claws into the throat. Finally, she bit into the podlasp's neck like a rabid dog worrying a sheep, ripping out chunks of flesh and rubber and spitting it towards the crowd between whoops of feral glee. At this point Mottleclutch lost control of his bowels in a spectacular fashion.

Finally Mottleclutch collapsed in a tattered heap. Lucretia continued to tear at his corpse with her fangs, claws and toenails for fully eight minutes after he was dead. She seemed to be in orgasmic euphoria at the act of killing, lost in her own private ecstasy.

Paul, whose reasoning mind told him he should have found the spectacle appalling, in fact found himself becoming highly aroused at the sight of the gladiatrix at kill.

Finally, she disentangled herself from the ragged cadaver that was now little more than a mass of shredded flesh and shattered bone. A team of mutant carnies dragged the podlasp's remains off to be rendered down into machine lubricant.

Lucretia clapped her hands and two girls in sailor suits came running from the wings to sponge off the blood and organic splatter from her exquisite body.

Dr. Feverclaw walked over to congratulate her.

"Lucretia, another wonderful kill. I do believe it was your best yet."

"Why, thank you Doctor," she purred. *"You know I live to kill and kill to live. It is my sacred duty and my deepest pleasure. Do I have a second challenger tonight?"* She asked hopefully.

"Indeed you do. Once this mess has been cleared away we will bring the new challenger in."

"Ohhhhhh, how perfectly wonderful, I get seconds!" She sounded like an excited child at Christmas. Paul found her voice like a thick, entrapping honey. His loins were achingly taut.

"And our new challenger from the gorgon latitudes of the undercity, the living nest who calls herself the Broodmother."

A flabby woman whose obesity seemed to be constructed of rolls of tallow lumbered into the ring. She stroked her hugely distended stomach and crooned. *"There, there my little ones, Mummy will feed you soon."* Her bloated gut seemed to shift and heave.

Again the rules were read and the whistle blown.

She stood with her thick legs wide apart, squatting like a sumo wrestler. Her face twisted into a mask of strain. With a pop like a cork fired from a champagne bottle an albino crab spider the size of a baby's head shot from her womb trailing an umbilical cord of mucus. There was another grunt and another outsized arachnid plopped to the floor. It was followed by several more.

Mandibles clicking, the creatures scuttled towards the blue Amazon. The first of them sprang like a demented jack-in-the-box at her face with venom dripping fangs.

Her razor claws bisected it before it could bite her.

"You murdering bitch," squealed the Broodmother. *"Avenge your sister, little ones."*

More of the spiders sprang at Lucretia but the Amazon was faster and shredded chitin spattered into the dust. More spiders were brought forth and as they fell the Broodmother's obese gut deflated like an old balloon.

The pale arthropods now changed their tactics. They raised their rear ends and pointed their spinnerettes at Lucretia. They spat strands of silk that fell about her and hardened like steel cords. They seemed to be trying to pin her to the floor. The webs fell across her left arm and her left leg.

Again her claws flashed and were joined by her savage teeth. They sundered the bonds as if they had been cotton. Then the sapphire hellcat was upon the spiders, leaping and stamping as they scurried for cover. Soon all were dead and the Broodmother's womb as empty as a deconsecrated church.

The Broodmother realised she was undone and let out a scream of terror. She tried to run but the blue gladiatrix's powerful legs meant that she didn't get far. Lucretia gutted the Broodmother at her leisure, brutally taking her time and delighting in the heart-rending shrieks of anguish her foe let out. She crunched on nasal cartilage and played gaily with her victim's viscera.

Soon the carnies dragged away the shreds and the teenagers in sailor suits were washing their mistress once more whilst gazing adoringly at her.

Dr. Feverclaw returned holding a large sack of coins.

"Your winnings, Madame."

"Why thank you, Doctor," she took a bow to thunderous applause. Paul felt giddy with lust.

"And now as is tradition, shouted the ringmaster, the winner will select a lover from the audience. Any gender, any species, whatever takes her fancy."

The incredible warrior stalked around the front row, those seated by turn were looking excited and scared. Paul himself was sweating and trembling. She stopped in front of him, her slanted, cat-like gold eyes looking him up and down as a sailor on shore leave might ogle a schoolgirl. She lifted her hand and pointed a clawed finger at Paul. A long red tongue flashed across her full blue lips.

"You, little man, I would rut with you."

She reached down and lifted him up with a hand under each arm like a mother might lift up an infant. In a trice her mouth covered his and her long prehensile tongue whipped about his. Marzipan and Frampton seemed a little nervous in her presence. He couldn't blame them. *"She chose Rex, she chose Rex,"* they squeaked and bleeped.

Lucretia, her sailor girls (whom she referred to as Tog and Pippin) and the Ouch Monkeys, all left the organic slime curtains of the circus tent and headed for a restaurant that the warrior woman often frequented. At the *Cobalt Pomegranate* Lucretia bought the feast with a handful of coins from her winnings. Fawning hierophants brought platters groaning with food and drink. They dined on cat flesh in exotic spices, the fruits of trees thought extinct before the first ape screeched, the livers of deep-sea fish no man had ever set eyes on in their living form, and honeydew dripped from the teats of dryads. The heady wine was of a fine Hyperborean vintage.

Afterwards the Ouch Monkeys left and Paul was practically dragged into one of the buildings that looked like titan blue glass trees. A lift transported them hundreds of feet up the 'trunk'. Then they walked along crazily twisting stairs to Lucretia's luxury apartment. A gold building that hung like an over ripe fruit from the blue 'branch'. Inside it was furnished with red furred beds, couches and walls.

The sailor girls left hand in hand for their own room.

Paul spent the night making love to the seven-foot blue-skinned goddess. His nose, lips and tongue explored every inch of her body from the soles of her feet to her shaved temples. She was a rough and demanding lover and he felt like a teddy bear entwined in her long steely limbs. He made a conservative estimate that she was ten times stronger than him. Though exhausting it was the most satisfying lovemaking he had ever known. She, herself referred to it as 'mating' or 'rutting'. Lucretia surprisingly managed to keep in near perfect control of her teeth and claws. The savage talons and fangs that could have disembowelled him in an eye blink only nicked him a couple of times - once on the tongue and once across the shoulder.

Finally, coated in mingled sweat the lovers fell asleep, the warrior woman cradling her mate to her neck.

Paul awoke on his couch. His clothes were strewn about the room. His body felt stiff and drained. He staggered through to the bathroom and eyed himself in the mirror. His tongue felt dry again. Poking it out, he found that it had dried blood on it. Had he bitten himself during his trip? He touched his left shoulder and found dried blood there too. In both of the places his dream lover's teeth and claws had rent his flesh, he bore a wound.

He frantically dialled Hugh.

"It left physical marks this time. I was cut in the other world, Haythornthwaite the city was called, on my tongue and shoulder and the marks are here in the real world. There was this woman, this amazing..."

"Slow down, psychonaut Joe, what are you on about?"

"The place the drug sent me to, Haythornthwaite..."

Hugh snorted in amusement.

"Haythornthwaite, what kind of name is that?"

"Look, I know it sounds silly, the world itself is called Goitre."

"Isn't that a disease of the throat?"

"The name doesn't matter. The point is I got cut in two places in that world. When I woke up here, I had the wounds I received over there in exactly the same places. What are the chances of that? This means that the other world has some kind of reality. It is in some way empirical!"

"You probably injured yourself thrashing round when you were high and the injuries influenced the hallucinations not vice versa."

"I don't care what you think but I need more fast."

"There will be another batch ready by Monday."

Paul gagged. "Monday... shit... I'll pay double if I can have some more tonight."

"There isn't any Paul. I told you it takes along time to produce. I can't give you what I haven't got. I'll bring you another tube on Monday, OK?"

Again Paul threw himself into writing despite being haunted by thoughts of the pale blue gladiator. He 'phoned his agent and told him of a whole new direction he wanted to take his writing. His agent seemed to be enthusiastic. It was nearly six months since Paul's last novel and he had been beginning to worry that he had writer's block.

To Paul, Glasgow seemed drab, colourless, unreal, like some cardboard set in a primary school nativity play. The hours seemed to drag and at night he lay awake thinking of coiling tattoos down long legs.

Finally Monday came. Hugh was paid and the *Writhe* swallowed greedily. He lay back and waited with his heart pounding in excitement.

He smelled her before he saw her, that sensual musk that he had inhaled so deeply in their night together. She strode through the wall with the Ouch Monkeys and sailor girls in tow. She snatched him up and kissed him whilst her hands roamed freely and wantonly about his person.

*"Come, she said, I have **such sights** to show you."*

Once inside Roscoe, Paul had little chance to look at the view of the city as he was entangled in Lucretia's long limbs. She kissed him franticly and hungrily. He offered no resistance. Once Roscoe had landed and they disembarked, he finally enquired as to where they were headed.

The bleeping simians squeaked in unison, *"Beneath the Smoking River, we are taking you to see the things that swarm and multiply in the purple mists."*

On his previous visits to Haythornthwaite, Paul had noticed that the purple smoke that rose from the river seemed to rise directly up and defuse. People seemed to keep well back from the edges of the river. He thought the smoke might be poisonous.

They walked down towards the river where a crowd of people were queuing a respectful distance away from the smoke, beside a globe-shaped craft. It was a massive, hollow glass ball in a brass cage frame balanced on caterpillar tracks. People were giving coins to a wildly eccentric looking man and taking seats inside the craft.

"Does this thing go into the smoke?"

"He catches on fast," said Tog.

"Clever boy," said Pippin.

Lucretia paid the man and they all took their seats. At the front of the weird vehicle a man in goggles sat in what looked like a cross between a dentist's chair and a tricycle. He began to tug at levers as they strapped themselves into the leather seats.

The eccentric man who took their money stood up. He was dressed in a burgundy swallow-tailed coat with knee-high boots and pantaloons. He had an impressively frilled and cuffed shirt and a paisley waistcoat. His white sideburns were the most absurdly largest that Paul had ever seen.

The man took a hearty swig from a bottle of port and regarded the visitors over his little glasses.

"Dutch courage," he waved the bottle. *"The things we will see on this journey would make the stoutest heart fail. Allow me to introduce myself. I am Professor Thaddeus Clasp inventor of the* mistrig.*"* He raised his hands to indicate the fantastical machine around him.

"This bubble of re-enforced glass is pumped full of air and allows us to enter the Smoking River without any ill effects. Were you to breathe in a decent amount of the vapours, you could be be-jinxed by any one of a dozen agues such as ditch cancer *or* dogstar pox. *The tracks of the* mistrig *give the craft motility so that we can explore what lies behind the violet curtain. We can study the creatures that call this hostile environment home and my specially strengthened glass ensures that they cannot study us as closely as they would like to! I shall be your guide on this amazing journey of terror and discovery. You will find that the two often go hand in hand."*

He turned to the driver. *"Meredith start her up if you please."*

The man in the goggles pulled more levers and pressed more buttons. There was a hissing, grinding, clanking sound as the caterpillar tracks began to move. The mistrig jerked into life and turned towards the wall of purple smoke. The tracks dragged the cumbersome machine into the miasma and the glass globe was entirely shrouded in the violet mists.

Professor Clasp began to explain about the surreal environment.

"The purple smoke has its genesis deep beneath the Earth. The gasses that compose the smoke are forced through fissures in the Earth's crust. These run like fault lines for miles creating 'rivers' of smoke just as there are rivers of water. And as we know water is the most fecund of elements. Likewise, the purple smoke has many life forms endemic only to it. Hopefully we will see some of them."

Distorted shapes loomed up from the vapour. They looked like massive coral outcroppings.

"Ahead we can see some of the outcroppings. These are actually solidified smoke. Under certain conditions that are poorly understood the smoke can take on solid form rather like cement drying. I think it has something to do with the chemical composition of the smoke. We know that it can change at certain times and in certain places."

Clinging to the solid smoke were snail-like creatures the size of barrels. Each had a coiling shell and a neck ending in feathery tentacles that they were waving about around them.

"Here we see a colony of gastroplumes. They feed by filtering micro-organisms from the smoke."

As the mistrig lumbered onwards, they came to a forest of gaily-coloured streamer-like plants hundreds of feet long. They swayed in motion with the smoke.

"These vapourweeds are the equivalent of kelp in the ocean. They extract nutrients and moisture directly from the smoke itself. They are anchored to the ground by clawed roots. Unlike most other plants they can pull these roots up and crawl about. They provide a home for many smaller creatures."

A shoal of ghostly creatures were flitting in and out of the vapourweeds. They looked absurdly like childhood 'bed sheet' ghosts. Pale, insubstantial and vaguely pepper pot shaped they bobbed around regarding the watchers with mournful looking jet black eyes above mouths like inverted ebony crescents.

"Smogwraiths," said the Professor, warming to his subject. *"They consist of little more than stomachs and envelop smaller creatures, slowly digesting them alive. They use psychic waves much as a bat employs sonar."*

A few of the smogwraiths drifted closer and looked in through the glass. Paul could detect nothing but darkness in the eyes. Finally, they oozed back into the safety of the weeds.

As the tour continued a waddling, upright creature as tall as a giraffe emerged from the smoke. It walked on two flabby legs and had what looked like a hollow tube as a beak. Its eyes swivelled independently like a chameleon. Four dexterous arms hung down from its turquoise body.

"A spitebile," said the professor clapping his hands in child-like joy. *"The spitebile has a gut that contains volatile chemicals. When mixed from its multiple stomachs this can act as an*

explosive. The creature places rocks in it beak and fires them at anything it perceives as a threat using the chemical propellants from its own innards. It is, in essence, a living cannon."

The creature scooped up a football-sized rock up and inserted it into its hollow beak. The swivelling eyes came to rest on the mistrig. The spitebile's gut seemed to expand and then with a bang the gut deflated the gasses forcing the rock out of its beak like a cannon. The passengers cringed but the rock merely glanced off the hardened glass.

"No need to fear, my friends. I personally developed this glass. It is as tough as three foot thick steel."

On seeing that its defence had little effect on the intruder, the spitebile waddled back into the swirling curtains of purple smog.

As the purple smoke thickened, Meredith switched on two powerful headlights that illuminated the area and sent tiny, bio-luminescent creatures flying for cover. But something larger was stirring in the shadows.

Of all the cavalcade of renegade zoology Paul had witnessed in this world, the thing that flopped, heaved and dragged itself out of the deep purple recesses was by far the chief abomination. Its snaky, grey/green body must have been close to a hundred feet long. Where its head should have been was an appendage shaped somewhat like a human hand. It was four feet across with long, bony fingers ending in sharp claws and what looked like a similarly armed, opposable thumb. The fingers clawed about blindly on the ground as if searching for something.

Though the thing had no visible eyes or ears it must have possessed other senses that served it just as well for at the mistrig's approach, it rose up and swayed back and forth like a cobra before a snake charmer.

The professor jumped for joy.

"Oh, my friends, we are indeed lucky! This is meatsnatcher, one of the purple smoke's most magnificent predators. And ooh look, it's a female, she has fingerlings."

Indeed, as the meatsnatcher drew closer they could see hundreds of young, tiny replicas of the adult, hanging to the creatures back. Each was about four feet long.

The beast hurled herself at the mistrig, clawing the glass and causing even Lucretia to jump in fear. The meatsnatcher's nails made an intolerable screeching on the glass bubble. Failing to claw its way through, the horror flipped several coils around the machine like a giant anaconda and began to squeeze. The palm of its 'hand' has pressed up against the glass.

"If you look closely at the palm," said Professor Clasp, *"you will see special pores. The meatsnatcher crushes its victims and ingests their vital juices via these pores."*

The mistrig was making a strained creaking sound and could not move whilst in its vast attacker's thrall.

The Professor took a generous swig of port.

"Meredith, one thousand amps to the outer casing, if you please."

The driver pushed a large red button and the outside of the machine was bathed in a white light and an intense crackling sound. Arcs of electricity danced over the mistrig and the meatsnatcher. The latter loosened its coils and slithered back into the indigo haze.

"She will be none the worse for wear," chortled the professor. *"And hopefully she'll think twice about attacking my beloved machine again".*

The mistrig trundled back again passing pulpy, soft-bodied octopi that hid inside human skulls and protruded their tentacles out from the eye sockets, and creatures that seemed to have pink glass exoskeletons.

After the tour, they all thanked the professor and showered him with questions about his lifelong study of the purple smoke and its weird inhabitants. They had taken a shine to the jolly little scientist.

Back at Lucretia's apartment, Tog and Pippin joined the fun. The blue Amazon insisted that Paul wrestled Tog, then Pippin, both naked. Though much smaller than their mistress both were more than a match for Paul and tied him up in painful holds that had him begging shamelessly for mercy.

Afterwards a new game began with Lucretia tossing Paul into the air like an infant and catching him. She then lay on her back, balanced him on her feet, and tossed him into the air again and again.

Tog went out the kitchen and returned with a glass of pink liquid.

"Here love muffin, drink this. Its honey from the glossinalia hives. It will help you 'perform'," she purred.

He gulped it down. It tasted like warm fizzy syrup.

That night Paul had to satisfy not only a seven-foot Amazon, but her two insatiable, girlish lovers. The honey made by the giant, nonsense-ranting bees in their mobile hives worked wonders. He appeased all three several times before falling to sleep.

He woke up sore and bruised on his couch.

He phoned Hugh again.

"I suppose you will be asking me for more of what I haven't got again."

He had anticipated well.

"Hugh, I have to get Writhe *on a daily basis."*

"Well that's tough shit because I can't get it on a daily basis"

"It seems like my trips aren't lasting as long."

"Jesus, what is it with you? A couple of hits and you're getting immune to it already."

"That's why I need more. Look, if you know who is making this take me to them so I can talk to them face to face. Tell them I'm prepared to pay a lot of money for a daily supply."

"You will end up living your life on the trip rather than in the real world."

"Who is to say which is the real world? Haythornthwaite seems a lot more real than Glasgow at the moment."

There was a pause.

"Look, I might be able to take you to the guy that makes Writhe but I can't promise. There is no guarantee that he will be able to give you more than you're already getting though. I'll ring you later if I have any news."

"Thanks Hugh, I appreciate it."

"Well you owe me one if this comes off, you awkward bastard."

Paul returned to writing down his adventures. The things he had seen in the purple smoke were mind-warping even by the standards of Goitre.

Later than night his 'phone rang. He leapt on it in excitement.

"Paul, I've been talking with Mr. McEwen, and I have persuaded him to have a meeting with you. He says he is willing to give you a lifetime's supply of Writhe *but it will cost you."*

"How much?" His voice was trembling.

"Fifty grand and you're sorted for life."

"For life?"

"As much as you want, every day. You can live in that world of yours 24/7 if you have a mind to."

"When? Where?"

"Don't go dragging £50,000 round Castlemilk. Myself and couple of Mr. McEwen's employees

will pick you up at eight on Friday night. Be outside the flats, we won't wait around."

For the next three days he lived like an automaton. Eating, drinking, sleeping but taking little of his surroundings in. He moved as a puppet through the ghost grey world he called Glasgow.

He was waiting impatiently, the cash counted and neatly placed in a leather hold all. A sleek black jaguar pulled over. One of the tinted windows rolled down and Hugh's head with its unruly mop of hair popped innocuously out.

"Don't dilly-dally, Paulie, get in."

Inside he found himself next to a tall man in an immaculate suit. He gave the briefest of nods in acknowledgement. A man who could have been his twin was driving whilst Hugh sat in the front passenger seat.

"Mr. McEwen lives a little out of town. He wouldn't want his operation being carried out with too many eyes and ears about," said Hugh.

"What convinced him to cut this deal then?"

"Fifty thousand pounds and my charm, of course. I explained how much you enjoyed Writhe *and he asked me if you would like to see how it's made."*

The car ate up the miles of road that led from the city out into the countryside of Lanarkshire. About twenty miles out of the city, the car pulled down a narrow country lane. A large country house, early late Georgian, loomed into view. Its windows looked dark.

The car pulled up outside of wrought iron gates. The man sitting next to Paul got out and spoke into a little intercom beside the gates. They grinded open and the car trundled up the drive.

By the time they got to the house the door was already open and light was streaming out. A small man was waiting for them. He could have been no more than five-feet-tall and was quite bald. He wore thick glasses and an immaculate white suit with a matching tie, waistcoat and shirt. His pale white head looked like an extension of his suit.

He grinned widely and extended a hand.

"You must be Mr. Campbell, the man who is so interested in my product."

Paul shook his clammy little hand.

"Yes, Mr. McEwen, Writhe *is quite unlike any other drug I have ever experienced."*

"Indeed it is, my boy. It's all down to the way we make it. It's all done here in the country, nice and healthy, none of your city rubbish full of nasty chemicals and God alone knows what else. Writhe *is 100% organic and aside from a little headache there are no nasty side effects.*

But I'm getting ahead of myself, where are my manners? Come on in."

Paul was led through the large hall to a plush room with high backed leather chairs and a roaring log fire. Around him were cases of mounted butterflies and beetles. A massive, preserved tarantula as wide as a dinner plate hung above the fireplace. Paul declined a Cuban cigar but accepted a large brandy.

"I'm sure I'm preaching to the converted here," McEwen continued, *"but most drugs per se are not dangerous. It's the shit they're mixed with."*

Paul nodded in agreement.

"Now if alcohol were mixed with, say, weed killer, there would be an uproar. So why are drugs so different? I have found a way to produce a powerful psychoactive drug that is completely safe in itself. To be sure, you don't want to go taking it in the middle of a busy road, or on the roof of a tall building, but that's just common sense."

"I hear you are willing to buy a lifetimes supply of this drug, Mr. Campbell."

Again Paul nodded and raised the hold all.

"We'll talk money later; for now let me show you how it's done."

McEwen led the way down a flight of stairs to a basement. Using a small stool, he reached up to a shelf of jars and brought one down. He held it up to the light and Paul saw it had some kind of small creature inside it. The thing was about the size and shape of an average sausage. It was bright red in colour and was formed of chubby segments. It raised what Paul took to be its head towards the light. It looked like a bloated, scarlet earthworm except that along its sides it had hundreds of stubby legs.

"This, my boy, is a fillan.*"*

"A what?" Paul bent to look closer at the writhing invertebrate. A long thin organ began to protrude from the *fillan's* anterior.

"A fillan, *it is a worm-like creature found only on the Hebridean Islands. It was written of widely in medieval times but was assumed to have become extinct. I rediscovered a colony on the Monarch Islands off the north Uist five years ago. I have been breeding and studying them ever since.*

You see, drugs are not actually my business, I'm an entomologist. I study invertebrates, the silent majority of the animal world. Invertebrates are endlessly fascinating; we derive many medical drugs from chemicals produced by invertebrates. Science has already proven the existence of immunological, analgesic, antibacterial, diuretic, anesthetic, and antirheumatic properties in the bodies of insects. Several authors have surveyed the therapeutic potential of insects, either recording traditional medical practices or employing insects and their products at the laboratory and/or clinical level.

Treatment by invertebrate related drugs even has a name: entomatherapy!

Now when I discovered the fillan *I was all ready to share my findings with the scientific community, but quite by accident I discovered the powerful but harmless hallucinogens in their secretions. I thought to myself that I could make millions by being the only producer of this substance and I was correct. Now I breed the* fillan en masse *here."*

"So that's why they call the drug Writhe," observed Paul as the fillan continued to squirm. "How do you extract the chemicals from them?"

"It's quite simple. We milk them much in the same way as ants milk aphids for honeydew. We provide them with food and once per week we apply a gentle electrical stimulation that causes them to secrete the substance we collect and use raw as the drug. Come on I'll show you the milking room."

They entered another room. In fact it was more like hospital ward, long white, and clinical. Beds lined the walls of the room and on each lay a man or woman. All were writhing slowly, almost rhythmically. Some seemed to let out little moans. *"Are they drugged?"* asked Paul.

"Each are in their own private wonderland."

Paul approached a red haired woman on the nearest bed. She wore a simple white smock like all the others. He waved a hand in front of her but her eyes were focused on something distant, something he couldn't see. Her lips were upturned in a sensual smile.

McEwen gently rolled her on to her back and parted her long red hair. There, at the base of her skull was a *fillan*. It was attached like a leech to her.

"The fillan *has its proboscis deep within her parietal lobe. It is secreting the psychoactive chemicals directly into her brain and in return feeding off the endorphins she is releasing. Electrical stimuli applied to the* fillan *will cause it to excrete its chemicals from the other end of its body so we can collect them."*

"How about the girl?" asked Paul as McEwen gently turned her back again.

"She came here of her own free will, as did every one you see." He gestured around him. There were fifty or so people on the 'ward'.

"We feed them via drips. They have everything they need including a lifetime ticket to wonderland."

Paul noticed an empty bed at the far side of the room. *"I suppose that has been made ready for me?"*

"If you have the money. Think about it. A life free of worries, of bills, of hardship. A life lived in your wonderland, your own private world wherein you will never grow old, never know boredom and the only pain you will experience will be of the pleasurable kind. What do you

say, Mr. Campbell?"

A thousand foot serpent that seemed to be made of burning stone was coiling above the city in a mating dance that lit up the sky in flashes. Beneath it a middle aged Scot and a seven-foot blue Amazon watched its awesome display, hand in hand.

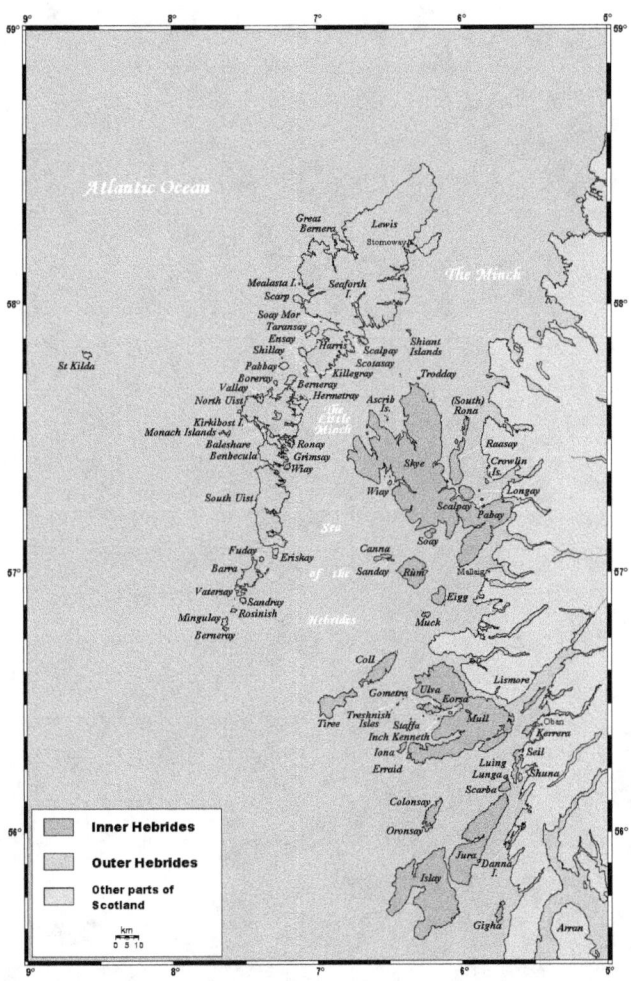

The Monach Islands, also known as Heisker (Scottish Gaelic: Eilean Heisgeir / Heisgeir) are an island group west of North Uist in the Outer Hebrides of Scotland. The islands are not to be confused with Hyskeir in the Inner Hebrides, or Haskeir which is also off North Uist and visible from the group. **(Wikipedia)**

ARABELLA'S BIRTHDAY

T he piles of wrapping paper were scattered about the floor like gaily coloured leaves. Boxes hastily ripped open had been tossed aside and their contents examined before a new parcel was demanded. There were dolls, games, a bright pink bicycle, new shoes, clothes, chocolates and sweets. They all added to the pile of presents that, if they were lucky, had held the recipient's attention for 30 seconds or so. Finally, the conveyer belt of presents drew to an end.

"Mummy, how much longer 'til my party?" Arabella pouted at her mother, gifts forgotten.

"Your friends will be arriving at four o'clock, darling."

"Well you'd better start clearing up all this paper, Mummy. I don't want my friends seeing all this mess."

Arabella snatched up a box of continental chocolates and a doll then flounced off to her bedroom. Leaving her mother and father to clean up the wrapping paper and tidy away the army of gifts, she spent the intervening hours playing 'Animal Crossing' on her computer.

Arabella's 9th birthday party was a grand affair. It was just as well her parents were rich as she had demanded so much. Fifty 'friends' arrived that afternoon with their parents in tow. Most of them were just vague acquaintances from Arabella's school or the children of her parents' friends. Arabella didn't have many true friends; most of the other children disliked her acerbic nature. Some pretended to be her friend because she had so many toys. Often she would take several of her 'friends' on trips with her mother and father. A week or so of listening to Arabella's narcissistic whining was a fair exchange for a trip to Disneyland.

Caterers had laid on cakes, sweets, ice cream and other treats, all handmade of course. Arabella would not countenance anything bought from a supermarket. The central birthday cake was four feet high and consisted of several layers of chocolate cake studded with black cherries and covered in a white chocolate coating, separated from one another by edible columns made from icing sugar. Each guest had a name at their place and a gift bag of expensive sweets.

Then there were the entertainers, *Fumbles the Clown*, *The Amazing Brondo* and *Madame Fi-Fi's Performing Poodles*. To top it all, Arabella's parents had managed to book her favourite boy band *Everest Allotment* to sing at the party. Thankfully the father of one of the band members was in the same lodge as Arabella's father; still the whole enterprise cost the better part of £20,000.

Of course at the height of the party Arabella had to make a speech. She screeched for attention and banged her glass petulantly until there was silence. For the next ten minutes she held forth, boasting about her presents and how important she was. There were audible sighs from the audience, but she didn't seem to notice. She rounded off her address by promising an even bigger and better party the following year.

"And Daddy says I can have whatever I like for my birthday next year, isn't that right, Daddy?"

"Of course you can, my darling, anything you like."

"Anything at all, Daddy?"

"Anything at all, sweetheart."

"In that case I want a unicorn!"

"What? A cuddly one, darling? You already have half a dozen."

"No, Daddy, not a toy. I want a real unicorn, a live one. I want it as a pet."

The room fell silent until broken by her mother's laughter.

"Seriously, cherub, what do you really want for next year?"

"I already told you. I want a real unicorn. Daddy told me I could have anything I like for my birthday next year, anything, and I want a unicorn."

"Unicorns aren't real darling, you're old enough to know that. They only live in storybooks," her father chipped in again as mumblings from the crowd began to grow. *"How do you expect me to get you something that doesn't exist?"*

"Then you make it exist," she snapped. *"You're rich enough. Everybody heard you promise to me. I want a unicorn next year."*

The evening went downhill from then on. Arabella sat in a corner sucking her thumb like a toddler and not speaking. The guests gradually dissipated. Things did not improve in the days that followed. Arabella reminded her farther of his promise at every opportunity. She would not accept that unicorns were mythical animals as a valid excuse for her not having one.

It was a couple of weeks later when Arabella's father was at the lodge bar when he was approached by another member, a tall man with thinning black hair and a checked waistcoat. He only vaguely knew the man but he had been a member at least as long as he had.

"Doug?" The man held out his hand and he shook it.

"Yes, sorry, but I've forgotten your name." He felt a tad embarrassed.

"Oh don't worry, I'm bloody useless at remembering names. My daughter was at your daughter's birthday party a couple of weeks ago. I'm Ken Barber."

"Ah, Louise's father. I hope she enjoyed herself."

Ken took a seat, deposited his briefcase and ordered a drink. *"She had a lovely time, thanks. She told me about what your daughter wants for next year as well."*

Doug took a swig of beer and rolled his eyes. *"Bloody kids, a pain in the arse. I suppose Rachel and I made a rod for our own backs by spoiling her. God knows how she expects me to produce a unicorn. She'll be asking me to walk on water next!"*

"Yes, a trifle demanding aren't they?"

"That's the understatement of the year. All I've heard for the last few weeks is 'Daddy get me a unicorn, Daddy get me a unicorn'."

Ken took a nip of whisky. *"Well, that's what I wanted to talk to you about. I could help you out there."*

Doug looked confused. *"How?"*

"Well if your little girl really wants a unicorn, I could get her one." He ran his fingers through his sparse hair and smiled. *"I can tell by your expression that you are thinking that I should take it with water next time."* He reached inside his tweed jacked and took something out. *"My card."* Doug took it.

> Dr. K. Barber
> Absolute Yield & Co
> www.absoluteyield.com
> Livestock Husbandry and Animal Breeding Research

"You breed livestock?"

"Indeed my company does research into the husbandry of domestic animals, sheep, cattle, pigs and so on. We have found that a stronger bloodline can be established by incorporating the genes of rare breeds, old strains of domestic animals that have almost died out. The mixing of genes makes for healthier animals and greater yields of milk, meat and so on."

"That's interesting, Ken, but what has it got to do with unicorns? You're not going to tell me

your breeding unicorns down on your farm?"

Ken chuckled. *"Yes, Doug, that's exactly what I'm going to tell you."* Then reached down to his briefcase and fumbled about. He produced a large glossy photograph. It showed a beautiful, white furred animal with cloven hooves and a silvery beard. From its forehead a single horn sprouted. Even in a photograph the animal seemed to exude a regal air.

Doug put down his beer and examined it closer. *"This can't be what it looks like!"*

"It's exactly what it looks like. Don't you think this animal is a dead ringer for the one on the British coat of arms?"

"Yes it is, but how do you do it? Do you graft the horn on or is it prosthetic?"

It's neither. It's a real horn on a real unicorn. The unicorn is a real animal but it's not an individual species. The unicorn is a man-made beast and it had its genesis with African tribes back in the mists of time. It was developed to defend herds of livestock against predators."

"The lion and the unicorn?"

"Exactly, any animal that grows horns, true horns not antlers like a deer, can become a unicorn. When the stories of these one-horned beasts reached Europe they had become so garbled that the unicorn was portrayed as a horse with a horn. Of course it is nothing of the sort."

Doug could hardly believe what he was hearing and took another long swig of his beer.

"How are they created?"

"Like I said, some African tribes have been creating them for centuries, but their secret was uncovered by a man named Dr. Franklin Dove. Dr. Dove was an expert in animal horn growth. He worked at the University of Maine. He uncovered the secrets of the tribesmen on his travels in Africa and wrote about them in a book, The Physiology of Horn Growth. *The work was all but forgotten when I stumbled upon it. Dr. Dove discovered that horned mammals have horn buds embedded in the skin of their heads. A few hours after birth the buds begin to secrete an enzyme that causes the bone beneath them to grow up into the bud becoming the core of the horn. Now these buds are soft and can be painlessly manipulated. If they are pushed together, into the centre of the animal's head then they will cause the bone below to develop into one large horn instead of two. The horn will point forward from the animals head rather than backwards or sideways. Dove did this with a bull calf who developed one large horn like a unicorn. The technique was also used on goats. And it is the goat that is the origin of the unicorn legend."*

"And you breed these?" asked Doug incredulously.

"'Create' would be a better term. We use male angora goat kids. Soon after birth, we push the horn buds together and tie them in place. Then the kid is returned to its mother and develops naturally, save for its one forward pointing horn. The photograph you saw was of a unicorn

we created for a girl in Scotland last year. He is called Moonlight. I'm sure you will agree he is quite splendid."

"Yes, he was beautiful. Could you create a unicorn for me? How much would it cost and how long would it take?"

Ken paused, seemingly to do some arithmetic in his head. *"Well a Billy angora changes hands for about £700, then we have the process of manipulating his horn buds and raising him and his mother until he's weaned. Shall we say £3000?"*

"Hell, £3000 for a living unicorn, that's nothing!

"Now there's a line I bet you never thought you'd say."

"How long will this process take?"

"Well the gestation for an angora is about 148 days then the weaning about 140 days. That means if we start the project quickly your little girl will be getting her unicorn next birthday. There are certain drugs I can feed the nanny shortly after conception that will ensure her kid is male."

"How about maintenance, the nearest thing to this I've kept is Arabella's ponies."

"There's no real difference to keeping a normal angora goat. You'll need a pen with a large outdoor run; they love to roam and forage. He'll need to be sheared twice a year and have his hooves trimmed. Then there are inoculations and such. At our facility, we feed angoras on a diet of 75 percent alfalfa and 25 percent corn mix. We also feed them lucern for roughage and sea kelp. Of course your animal will graze on the grass in his paddock as well so make sure there is no ragwort or anything poisonous growing there. As a treat they love rolled oats. It will need access to clean drinking water at all times. I'll give you book on goat maintenance. It will tell you everything you need to know."

"Ken I believe you have just sold me a unicorn."

"Just call me the man who makes dreams come true."

In the months that followed, Doug visited the research the Absolute Yield facility. Ken had selected a fine angora Billy and nanny to breed. The nanny was monitored through pregnancy and suffered no complications. She delivered a male kid in good health. The newborn was allowed to suckle and bond with the mother before having its horn buds realigned and bound in place. It was then returned and to the nanny and grew as any other goat would, save for the little horn that began to sprout from its forehead.

In the meantime, Doug and his wife Harriet had builders construct a 'unicorn' house. It was a basic goat pen but decorated to look like a fairy castle with turrets and towers, for the benefit of Arabella rather than the animal of course. It had a large paddock that would allow the beast to roam around and forage.

Arabella had been beside herself with excitement at the news she was indeed getting a unicorn for her birthday. "Oh, Daddy, thank you, thank you! I'll call him Magick and he'll be my best friend ever and live in his fairy castle."

The creature grew fast and began to take solid food. Its horn, once a pulpy stump had grown long and strong. When Doug visited him shortly before his daughter's birthday he was the mirror image of the best he had seen in the photograph. He had been shorn leaving a mane of white curls along his neck. His coat and beard were silvery white and a sturdy 18-inch horn sprouted from his forehead. His eyes were a striking bright blue and he frolicked about his run like a lamb, occasionally stopping snatch a mouthful of grass. When Doug approached him he trotted over to be scratched behind his ear like a dog. Ken entered his paddock with a bucket of rolled oats and he galloped over excitedly.

"Frisky little fellow isn't he?" said Doug.

"I think he'll make an excellent pet for Arabella." grinned Ken.

It was a beautiful day and Arabella had decided to hold her party in her parents' extensive garden. There was a marquee, a bouncy castle and a little stage for the band to play on. Arabella's fickle interest had now switched from *Everest Allotment* to another boy band *Confectionary Factory*. At the height of the party, Doug arrived in his Landover pulling a horsebox behind him. Harriet handed her daughter a bucket of rolled oats.

"It looks like your very own unicorn has arrived. These are his favourite treat darling."

Arabella left the table and rushed over the lawn. Her father had parked and was opening the horse box. Magick the unicorn pranced down the ramp to gasps from the assembled guests. His mane and beard shone, his coat was a dazzling white and he tossed his head, waving his magnificent horn from side to side. Doug had brought a gold chain that he had strung about the creature's neck. He was truly a thing of wonder.

"Magick, Magick," squealed Arabella, *"look what Mummy's got for you, your favourite."* She shook the bucket of rolled oats.

The unicorn stopped his frisking and sniffed the air. His ears lifted up and he gave an excited bleat at the smell of his most esteemed snack. Eagerly he began to run across the lawn with the bucket in sight. Arabella shrieked in delight as her imposable pet galloped towards her. Head bent towards the bucket of oats the unicorn slammed into the girl at fifteen miles per hour. His strong, sharp, 18-inch horn punched its way through her ribcage and pierced the right pulmonary artery in her heart.

BULL WITH SINGLE HORN
IS MODERN UNICORN

WHAT might be called a modern unicorn has been produced by Dr. W. F. Dove, University of Maine biologist. From a day-old bull calf, Dr. Dove removed the two small knots of tissue which normally develop into horns. These horn buds he transplanted in the center of the bull's forehead, thereby inducing the growth of a single massive horn. The bull, now nearly three years old, has developed much of the proud bearing ascribed to the mythical unicorn.

SEE HOW THEY RUN

I've been working in pest control for twenty years now and I've never heard of moles causing subsidence on the levels you're telling me about, Reverend. Are you sure it's not badgers?"

"Well, there are things that look like great big mole hills all over the churchyard and a number of the graves have fallen in. To be frank I'm worried about the structural integrity of the church if this carries on. It's 16th Century, you know."

"It sounds more like badgers to me. I have had a number of cases where big badger setts have caused damage in graveyards"

"Will you be able to move them to another area?"

"Well, Reverend, badgers are protected by law; you need a special license from the Department of the Environment if you want to interfere with them. But if it is moles, that's no problem. Moles are classed as vermin and I could just trap them."

"Well could you come and have a look sometime?"

"Well I've got a wasps' nest to get out of an attic in Peterhead but I could drop by this afternoon. I'll bring some mole traps just in case. Now how do you get to Radan Cladhiac?"

"It's the first turning on the road between Huntley and Keith, you follow the road for about five miles and you'll find the village, if that's what you want to call it. It's just a handful of houses these days."

"All things being equal I should be there for about two in the afternoon."

It didn't take long to deal with the wasps' nest in Peterhead. It had been long abandoned and was little more than a fragile paper sculpture. The old lady whose attic it had been in seemed glad of the company and had been generous with tea and chocolate hobnobs.

The council van bumped and trundled along the pitted roads of Banffshire in the afternoon sun.

"I wish all jobs were that easy," Dave took a drag on his cigarette as he steered one handed.

"God yes, remember when we had to fumigate that cafe in Aberdeen?" Colin, the trainee wrinkled up his nose in disgust.

"I don't think I'll ever forget the smell in those kitchens. And to think people bloody well ate in there!"

Dave laughed, *"Some of them cockroaches were as big as mice. Dirty bastards couldn't have cleaned the place in donkey's years."*

"So, where are we going again?" said Colin looking at an old AA map he had unfurled in his lap.

"Radan Cladhiac, apparently."

"Weird name".

"It's Gaelic I think, tiny place by all accounts. Don't even have a pub."

Colin sighed audibly. *"I'm sick of packed lunches."*

"Well, we've only got to drop down a couple of mole traps for a vicar then we can knock off." He took another deep drag on his fag and blew the smoke out of the window."

"That'll kill you, you know."

"Yes I'm sure it will."

They found Radan Cladhiac and drove through it in an eye blink. It was, as the vicar had said, no more than a handful of houses. The church loomed a few hundred yards from the village. The vicar was waiting by the gate.

The Reverend Landsdale was younger than they had expected, perhaps thirty. He had blond hair and an untidy beard.

"Ah, you must me the gentlemen from the council?"

"Reverend Landsdale?"

"Call me Trevor." The vicar shook both men's hands.

"Let me show you the mess these little blighters have left."

He led them into the churchyard. It was badly overgrown. The grass was waist high with stunted trees and brambles rampant.

"Sorry about the state it's in. I'd like to spend some time tending to the grounds but I'm too busy. You see I have three churches in my parish and I have to split my time between them. No one has attended this church in years. Only the fact that it's a listed building is stopping it being deconsecrated and left to rot. Radan Cladhiac was a lot bigger before World War One. All the younger generation were killed in the trenches; the village never recovered. Most of the place was demolished in the 1930s. The few houses you see now are owned by city folks who use them for weekend getaways.

Anyhow, I'm rambling. Let me show you what these moles - or whatever - have done."

At the back of the church, the old lichen encrusted headstones were leaning at crazy angles. Several had fallen over. Amidst the graves what looked like huge molehills rose up to three feet or more.

"Blimey, in all my years on the council I have never seen molehills that size," gasped Dave.

"So they are moles then?" The vicar enquired.

"Well, that's certainly not a badger's sett, I can tell you that for sure. I'll have a closer look."

"Be careful, a couple of weeks ago I slipped into one of the graves that had been hollowed out and twisted my ankle."

Several of the graves had indeed fallen in. On closer inspection the mounds looked exactly like molehills, but much larger.

Dave scratched his head.

"Well, nothing else makes mounds like these. You must have some king-sized moles round here. Colin, fetch me the gear will you?"

The youth disappeared and returned with his arms full of tools.

"Now, we need to see where their tunnels are leading," said Dave taking up a metal rod.

He walked around pushing it into the ground every few steps and being careful to avoid the graves. Finally, the pole slipped deeper into the earth.

"A-ha, I've found a tunnel. Pass me a spade Colin."

Dave took the short, narrow spade and cut a hole in the roof of the tunnel. He heaved the sod away and peered in. Taking a torch from his pocket, he crouched down.

"It goes on a long way. I've never seen a mole tunnel this wide either. Amazing!"

He took a trap from Colin, a long-handled, spring-loaded affair with nasty looking jaws. He heaved the handles apart and set the trigger. The trap was positioned and the sod placed over it.

"Now when the little devil crawls over that... BAM! We've got him."

He placed several more traps around the graveyard where his probing found tunnels.

"I'll be back tomorrow and check these. Is the same time OK for you?"

"Yes fine, thanks for coming."

"Money for old rope," said Dave as they wandered back to the van.

After a morning of laying rat poison in drains around Stonehaven, Dave and Colin drove back up to Radan Cladhiac to inspect the traps. It seemed like all three had been set off.

Colin reached in, and retrieved the nearest one and pulled it from the earth. The trap was empty except for half a stick.

"It looks like this one's been set off by someone poking it with a stick."

"Don't be daft, lad; moles don't poke sticks into traps. They haven't got the brains."

Dave pulled another trap up from the ground.

"Well, I'll be buggered this one's been set off too. It can't have been a person doing this the ground wasn't disturbed."

Dave extracted the final trap. This one had actually caught something but the thing in the trap was no mole.

"Bloody hell, what's that?" asked Colin.

"I'm damned if I know." He held the trap and the dead animal up to examine it closer.

The animal was larger than a mole by far. It was as big as a good-sized rabbit. At first it might have been mistaken for an outsized rat but a closer inspection showed it was something quite different. Its head look more like that of a small dog than a rat, but the large chisel-like incisors showed that it was *some* kind of rodent. Its front paws were spade shaped and equipped with impressive claws, obviously for digging. The hindquarters resembled a large rat, save for the bushy tail.

"Do you think it might be something that has escaped from a zoo?" asked the vicar.

"Well, it don't look like any animal I've seen knocking round Scotland," replied Dave turning the corpse over.

"Hang on," said Colin. *"The nearest zoo to here is in Edinburgh; that's about 80 miles away. I can't see something getting this far."*

"Maybe it's something that has escaped from a private collection?" suggested the vicar.

"Or something new to science. Imagine if they name it after me, I'd be the most famous rat catcher in the world!"

"What are we going to do with it?" asked Colin.

"We usually bag vermin up and burn them back at the plant but this is something special. I'm going to send it down to the Natural History Museum in Edinburgh and see what they say."

"How about the churchyard?"

"Sorry, Reverend, I think we need to hang fire on this until we know what we are dealing with. These things might be endangered."

"They don't bloody well look endangered to me." Colin remarked looking again at the legion of mounds in the graveyard.

"I'll see what the experts say and be back in touch."

Dave got one of the plastic bags they used for carrying rat carcasses in and carefully put the creature's corpse into it.

Back at the depot he boxed the body up. After a quick look online he wrote a covering letter explaining where the creature had come from, and went to the post office and sent the specimen off to Professor Duncan James, head of Zoology at the Natural History Museum.

Two days later David received an e-mail from Professor James. If e-mails could sound breathless this one did.

> Dear Mr. Carling
>
> Many thanks for the specimen you sent to me. Most people, especially those in your profession would have just thrown this animal's body away without a second look. Thankfully you had more intelligence and foresight.
>
> The creature matches no known species of mammal known to be native to the UK. Neither does it match any known species of mammal on earth! It is clearly of the order Rodentia. Physiologically it most resembles the Siberian Zorkor *(Myospalax myospalax)* of the mountains and steppes of Eastern Kazakhstan, south western Siberia, and the, southern and western Altai. Though it seems to be of the family Spalacidae, it is clearly a new species. My colleagues are currently examining the animal's DNA.

The creature seems to differ from most other members of Spalacidae in its larger size and in the structure of the head and jaws. The almost dog-like shape of the skull, taken with the shape of the molars would argue for a mainly carnivorous diet, rare in rodents. This seems to be backed up by the guillotine-like incisors that recall some of the extinct flesh-eating marsupials of the Australian Pleistocene epoch, a bit on a much smaller scale, of course.

I cannot emphasise the importance of this find. If confirmed it will be a zoological bombshell. That a vertebrate of such size could have eluded discovery on a tiny, overcrowded island like Britain almost beggars belief. As this new species finder, Mr. Carling, you will personally gain quite a bit of fame!

If I may I would like to examine the area in which you captured the animal. Would it be alright with your employers if I accompanied you to Radan Cladhiac? I am keen to try and capture a living specimen for the Zoological Society of Scotland.

All the very best,

Prof Duncan James.

"Look at this," said Dave, calling Colin over. *"I don't understand half of what he's banging on about but it looks like I've found a new species. He wants to come all they way up from Edinburgh to check out the churchyard."*

"Do you think the council will be OK with that, Dave? Should you ask them first?"

"Ask the council? Screw that! Opportunity only calls once, Col. I could get on the telly with this. I wonder what they'll name it, Rattus carlingi, *Carling's rat?"*

He strode over to the office 'phone and picked it up.

The next day they stood waiting with the vicar for the professor outside the church in Radan Cladhiac. If they had been expecting a tweedy little man in specs they were wrong. The professor's car drew up and he emerged, a tall burly man with a beard like a spade. He was dressed in boots and overalls and carrying some strange contraption. He walked over and gave each of the men a bone-scrunching handshake.

"Delighted, delighted, I'm Professor James but call me Duncan. Gosh, I never thought I'd be hunting new mammal species in Banffshire. The Amazon, yes, the Congo, yes, Indonesia, yes, but dear old Scotland? Never in a month of Sundays!"

"What's that?" asked Colin, pointing to the Heath Robinson-type device the professor held.

"Ah this!" He held the wire cage trap aloft. *"It's my own twist on the Longworth Mammal*

Trap. Larger, of course. I want to catch a live specimen."

"What are you using for bait?"

The professor fished in his overall pocket and produced a lump of meat wrapped in paper.

"I took the liberty of dropping by the butcher's this morning. I doubt our little friends will be able to resist three pounds of rump steak."

"They'll be eating better than me!" snorted Dave.

"You think they are carnivores then?" The vicar sounded vaguely worried.

"Oh yes, or at least omnivores. Their dentition shows this. As I mentioned to David their incisors recall some of the extinct flesh-eating marsupials of prehistoric Australia. The formation of the skull argues for a predatory lifestyle as well. The dog, or rather wolf-shaped, skull has a sagittal crest in order to anchor large jaw muscles. They have a more powerful bite than most other mammals of the same size."

"Have we really found a new species of animal right here in my churchyard?"

"Yes, indeed we have. This is a creature never formally recognised by science. It is not totally unknown, however."

The quizzical looks on the faces of the others showed the professor he would have to elaborate.

"There is a tradition in Banffshire dating back to the 19th Century of creatures known as 'earth hounds'. They were supposed to frequent graveyards and burrow into coffins to feed on corpses. There are a number of accounts of earth hounds being seen, and even killed, in archives of the Department of Natural History of the Natural Museums of Scotland. The stories of them seemed to drop off in number after the First World War. There have been, however, alleged sightings as recently as the 1990s. No one really took them seriously until now."

He strode through the long grass and leaning tombstones.

"Careful, many of the graves have fallen in," shouted the vicar

"I see what you mean."

The professor had stopped by a yawning grave and peered in. The earth had fallen in and the coffin was clearly visible. The casket's wooden lid had been shattered and it seemed empty. The professor put down the trap and leapt down into the hole.

"Look," he motioned for the others to come over then pointed. *"See, in the side of the grave there are burrows leading off. These creatures have broken into the coffin and fed on the body within. Even the bones are gone. A lot of rodents gnaw bones for the calcium in them."*

The vicar looked unwell.

"If it's all the same to you I'm going to check up on the church."

The professor hauled down the trap and placed the bait inside. He set it up at the entrance to one of the burrows.

"Look, there are other passages leading off from this grave. I shouldn't wonder if every grave in this churchyard is connected via these burrows. The whole place must be like Swiss cheese."

He took out a small digital camera and took some shots. He scrambled back out, Dave giving him a hand. *"The little bastards triggered two of my traps using sticks,"* he said.

"Tool use. Incredible, but not unprecedented. Did you know there have been cases of migrating rat colonies using sticks to lead old blind members to the new burrow? Sighted rats would hold one end and the blind rat the other."

"I had no idea rodents were so intelligent."

"Rodents are the most successful and widespread of all mammals. We underestimate them at our peril. There will be rodents on earth long after mankind is extinct, believe me."

"There's something here I think you need to see, professor." The vicar had re-emerged and was looking pale.

"Here, in the church." He motioned for them to follow and turned back into the building. He led them across the stone flags and the pews to a set of worn steps at the back of the church.

"It's down here in the vault. I was worried about them undermining the church and I was right."

He flicked a light switch. The single bulb threw a wan, yellow light over the empty vault. At the far end was a gaping hole. Masses of earth were piled up on either side.

"They have burrowed up into the church searching for food."

"Do you have torches?" asked the professor.

Colin ran to retrieve them from the van. *"Sorry, only two."*

"Reverend, could you light a couple of candles for me as well?"

The four approached the hole.

"Are you sure earth hounds did this?"

"No doubt, look closer, claw marks in the earth."

The vicar shook his head in wonder.

"But why dig a burrow so wide? These things are only the size of rabbits."

"I have no idea. I've never seen rodent burrows this size before. Maybe it's to do with ventilation. Termites build great shafts to control air temperature and circulation in their nests."

He shone down the beam of a torch.

"It goes down deep but the gradient isn't too bad. Anyone coming in with me?"

"You're actually going down there? Are you mad?" The vicar sounded appalled.

"They're only rodents you know. I'm sure one could give you quite a nip it you grabbed a hold of it but they shouldn't be a danger."

"It's not the earth hounds I'm worried about. What if the tunnel collapses?"

"Health and safety would have a fit," added Colin.

"Health and safety are not here, are they, young man? Come gentlemen, science is calling and discovery awaits. Are we going to sit here like little girls or are we going to see if we can track down the legendary earth hounds?"

"Well I'm sure it's against regulations but screw regulations this is bloody fascinating, real David Attenborough stuff." Dave seemed keen to join the professor.

"OK, just so long as we don't get into shit with the council for this," mumbled Colin.

"The council will never know. You're all right with this, aren't you, Reverend?"

"Well, I can't say I really like the idea."

"Look," the professor appealed, *"you stay up here and if we are not back in an hour then 'phone the emergency services. Are you OK with that?"*

"Well, I suppose. But I'm allowing this under duress and against my better judgement. I thought we would just be laying a couple of traps not embarking on some Jules Verne style underground adventure."

"You're not. You're staying here. Anyway just think about the publicity the church will get when this new species is confirmed."

"I suppose you're right."

"That's the spirit. Well lads, Geronimo!" With that the professor leapt into the tunnel.

By torch and candle light, the three proceeded down the tunnel. It was large enough for a fully-grown man to walk upright. Occasionally a smaller tunnel, like the burrows they had seen in the graves would lead off from the main shaft. Every so often the Professor would stop to take a photograph murmuring excitedly under his breath.

Ahead the tunnel split two ways. The professor stopped and sniffed the air then turned left. The beams illuminated the rounded and surprisingly smooth walls as they walked. Thus far there was no sigh of the earth hounds themselves.

Suddenly the tunnel widened and a foul stench filled their nostrils. *"Euuh, what the hell is that?"* Colin was almost gagging.

The beams fell across several deep alcoves excavated in the wall. They were crammed with a jumble of human and animal remains. Some were bare bones, femurs sticking out at odd angles, others were decaying limbs, heads and torsos.

"It looks like some kind of storage area," said the professor striding over. These are the carcasses they have pilfered from the graves. There are sheep carcasses too. Maybe they hunt live prey as well as scavenging. He prodded a leg bone jutting from the vile-smelling collection of flesh.

Something burst from the mass, emitting high-pitched yapping sounds. It was followed by several more. The creatures toppled to the floor amidst bone and flesh scraps. They stood jaws agape, yapping and spitting like little balls of fury.

"Good God, live ones! They must be guards of the food store." The professor began taking snaps of the creatures. The earth hounds shrank back whining from the flash of the camera. Down along the corridor came a soft pattering sound like the noise of rain falling on leaves.

As the four men turned, a living carpet of earth hounds came oozing round the bend in the tunnel their little eyes glittering and slicing incisors snapping like a legion of man traps. Some of them seemed almost twice as big as the others with wider jaws and bigger teeth.

"There's thousands of them!" screamed Colin.

"The calls of guards alerted them," shouted the professor above the clattering of jaws and incessant dog-like yapping. *"Use your torches, they can't abide bright light."*

The mass of rodents shrank back from the beams, but did not fully retreat.

"Look, there is a more robust morph among them. No doubt fighters bred to defend the colony. Perhaps they have several morphs like naked mole rats in Africa."

"Now's not the time for a bloody lecture. I thought you said they weren't dangerous. Well they look bloody dangerous to me."

"No need to panic, David, stay calm."

"Stay bloody calm, he says. Have you noticed they have moved round and blocked off the way we came in?"

"Then we will just have to go another way. I'm sure there are other large exits to the burrow."

The men backed off further down the corridor as the mass of earth hounds swarmed and screeched just beyond the reach of the beams. As they moved back the creatures followed.

They were backed around a bend into another chamber. There in a nest of dry grass lay a gigantic earth hound the size of a Labrador dog. It was some kind of bloated female. At its distended teats, numerous blind, naked young suckled. In a circle about her were more of the impressively jawed fighting morphs.

"A queen, they have a queen!" breathed the professor.

At the mouth of the chamber, the earth hounds squirmed in like a shaggy tide. Colin became hysterical as they tumbled and frisked closer. *"GETMEOUTGETMEOUTGETMEOUT!"*

The sound seemed to infuriate the earth hounds who redoubled their ear splitting yapping. More of them sprang out from a hive-like network of burrows that dotted the walls of queen's chamber. One sprang upon the professor clamping its shearing teeth into his arm. He dropped the torch will a scream and in an instant a dozen more snapping beasts were upon him.

Dave rushed to his aid, swinging his torch like a crude club. The tide of rodents swarmed up him tripping him up face first into the dirt. As he looked up he caught a brief glimpse of Colin. He seemed to be doing some kind of weird, frantic dance with a number of earth hounds clinging to his arms, legs and body. Sharp pains exploded in Dave's own limbs as the earth hounds bit. The torch rolled from his grasp in the spinning light he saw many gaping jaws and sharp teeth scampering out of the dark towards him.

In the deep darkness below, Dave could not move. He reasoned that there was some kind of chemical in the earth hound's saliva that caused paralysis. His whole body was rigid as the rodents swarmed across him as if he were Gulliver. It was dark, the most profound blackness he could imagine. Without the torches he could see nothing but he felt the little horrors pulling and hauling his body as a team. With agonising slowness his helpless but conscious body was pulled back along the tunnel until he could smell a horrifyingly familiar smell. He felt his flesh pressed up against soft, cold, rancid flesh as the earth hounds pushed him bodily into the meat pile in their store. The flabby tissue flopped about his face and body. It seemed that sometimes the earth hounds like fresh game for a change.

In the church vault the vicar had paced up and down for a while and glanced at his watch every five minutes. They had been gone less than half an hour. There was probably no need for concern. He sat with his back to the tunnel entrance and mused on how he had not become a member of the clergy in order to hunt mutant rats in underground labyrinths. From behind him he heard something. It was a soft pattering, like rain on leaves.

THE VISITOR

We moved into Hollyhock Farm in the summer of 1977. My Dad was an author and my Mum a painter. We had lived in central Birmingham and both my parents wanted to get out of the city. Hollyhock Farm seemed ideal. It was in a rural area, but not too far away so that we could visit both sets of grandparents and various aunts and uncles who lived in the Black Country area.

The farm was set back off Penkridge Bank Road, right in the heart of Cannock Chase. I suppose I'd better tell you a bit about Cannock Chase. The Chase is a large track of ancient woodland and lowland heath in the English Midlands. Back in 1958, it became designated as an area of outstanding natural beauty. Several areas within it are classed as Sites of Special Scientific Interest. The Chase covers around 26 square miles and was once a royal hunting ground, hence the name. Now it is co-owned by Staffordshire County Council and the Forestry Enterprise.

The farm was a rambling three-storey building with a conservatory and various out-buildings such as barns and a derelict piggery. It backed onto the deep woods of the Chase. Mum and Dad fell in love with it a first sight. I can recall us driving out to see it as a family for the first time, Mum, Dad, my brother, my little sister, 'Buster' the dog and me. Us kids got excited about living in such a big house. We thought it was some kind of mansion! The idea of living next to the woods was appealing to us as well. Growing up in Britain's second city as we did, the closest thing you get to nature is the Birmingham Ship Canal, and in the 1970s, there was precious little wildlife in it, I can tell you.

The current owner was a little grey haired man with spectacles, called Mr. Bennett. He once farmed the land, but his wife died several years ago and his children, who had all grown up and moved away, had no interest in keeping the farm going.

"They think it's too much like hard work," he had said. *"And these days I'm inclined to agree with them."*

He wanted to retire to Southend-on-Sea where his sister lived. Dad was surprised at how little he was asking for the place. Mr. Bennett told us that its upkeep was too much of a job for one man. He just wanted a quiet little bungalow now.

We looked round inside. It was a little down at heel but nothing a lick of paint wouldn't fix. There was nothing wrong with the farm structurally and no rising damp or anything like that.

Mr. Bennett and his wife had moved in after the Second World War. It had been owned by a very old man who had passed away leaving no family. The house itself was from the late 18th Century.

One funny thing I did notice about Mr. Bennett is that he kept glancing back towards the woods. He seemed a little restless, almost agitated. But he was pleased to see us. He invited us all in for tea, petted the dog and talked at length with Mum and Dad. He was sorry when we had to go. I thought that he might have been lonely after his wife had died.

It didn't seem that long until we were moving in. Money paid, paperwork done. I can recall very little about the actual move except for big lorries, and men carrying furniture.

It was during the summer holidays so us kids had a wonderful time playing hide and seek round the house and the spooky old out-buildings and walking Buster in the woods. It was one of those endless summers you seemed to get back then, week after week of sunshine. We missed our old friends, but some of them came to visit at weekends. We made a few new friends, but as the closest neighbours were miles away we didn't see them very often. So usually it was just me, my brother and my sister in the big old house and the deep dark woods.

The only odd thing I can recall in the early days is just after we moved in. Between the house and the woods was a field. It had lain fallow for a long time and was now overgrown. I think I was on our first day there. I looked out of the living room window and saw what looked like a large tree stump in the field. About half an hour later, I looked out of the same window and the tree stump had vanished! I told myself I must have been mistaken but I was sure I had seen it.

As the night began to draw in, both the house and the woods took on a different character. They seemed stiller and moodier. It was early September and my brother and I were out in the Chase walking Buster. We had gone somewhat further than we normally did, maybe a couple of miles from the house. We were walking along a bridle path when we came out into a small clearing maybe fifty-feet across. We stopped for a while whilst the dog ran round sniffing. Suddenly he stopped; ears erect and looked straight into the woods. My brother and I had both noticed how quiet it had suddenly become. There were no birds singing and it was as if the whole woods were holding their breath for some reason.

The silence was suddenly broken by what sounded like ticking. The noise was coming from the trees and seemed to be mobile. It sounded like it was coming closer. We wondered what it could be. It sounded more like a metronome than a clock. It seemed to leave the tree line and come out onto the grass but there was nothing there; we could see nothing. As the noise drew nearer, Buster started to snarl. He was a friendly dog and I never knew him to act like this before. His hackles drew up.

The sound, or rather whatever was making it, apparently passed in between us. We were standing about ten feet apart at the time. As it came close it brought with it a horrid smell, like rotten eggs. The sound and the smell drifted between us, paused for a moment, then went on and apparently re-entered the woods at the far side of the clearing.

Once it was gone Buster seemed fine again and carried on where he had left off, sniffing about the clearing. My brother and I just looked at each other, totally baffled. We didn't tell anyone.

A few days later my sister came running into the house and told Mum that there was a big man watching her from the woods as she played in the garden. Mum went to look but couldn't see anyone. My sister said that he was very big and dark; she couldn't see his face well. Mum explained that Cannock Chase was a popular place for people to walk and that the man was probably just a member of the public. But she warned her not to talk to strangers anyway.

One evening the 'phone rang and my Mum answered it. The voice on the other end seemed to be spouting gibberish. She called for my Dad and he listened too. I heard it as well. It sounded like a speeded up record played backwards. These calls would happen two or three times a week. We had the BT engineer out but he said that there was no fault on our line. It seemed that they couldn't trace where the calls were coming from either.

I think that it was on the same night as that first odd 'phone call. I was looking out of my bedroom window at the woods. I had turned my light off and it was a clear night. I often did this as sometimes you could see foxes, bats, badgers and owls. I noticed something in the woods. It was two points of red light about eight feet or so off the ground. I watched them as they moved around in the woods. I thought that they might be fireflies but they both seemed to move together and stay exactly the same distance apart.

It was early October when the rabbit incident happened. My little sister had a rabbit called Mittens. Mittens was kept in a hutch with a large chicken wire run in the garden. One morning my Dad found that Mittens was gone from her enclosure. The chicken wire had been ripped apart and the wooden frame broken. My sister was hysterical. Dad tried to explain that when you live in the countryside these things sometimes happen. A fox from the Chase had gotten in and taken Mittens. Dad promised to get my sister a new rabbit and build a more secure enclosure.

There were some things about this, though, that made me think that it was not a fox that had taken Mittens. The ground was hard so there were no tracks but there were several strands of long black hair on the chicken wire. It didn't look like fox hair; that was red and fairly short. Mittens herself had white hair. Then there was the stink, an acrid, sulphurous smell like bad eggs. It was just the same as the smell my brother and I had experienced in the woods. Buster went berserk when he smelled it. He ran round and round barking for half-an-hour.

About a week later we saw the light in the sky. Dad saw it first. It was about nine in the evening and he was looking out over the Chase. He shouted us to come and look. He thought it might be a meteor burning up in the atmosphere. We all rushed upstairs too see it from Mum and Dad's bedroom window.

It was a glowing red sphere. As soon as I saw it I knew it was not a meteor, it was moving far too slowly. It seemed to be just above the treetops and meandered to and fro. Slowly it descended into the field behind our house and in front of the woods.

Dad had changed his mind. He thought that it might be ball lightning. He told me to grab the camera I had got for my birthday earlier in the year. We all ran out of the house into the field, except for Buster who flatly refused to leave the house.

As we approached the field, we could see the object was about twenty feet across. It was a bright, incandescent red and seemed to pulse. It made a crackling sound like electricity. I felt my hair standing up as we drew near to the field. It was like the time I touched a Van Der Graaf generator at school. It seemed like a light with no solid object behind it.

At the same time we heard a crashing noise from the woods as if something big was moving around in there. There were other noises too; odd electrical sounding noises, like someone badly strumming an electric guitar.

I began to take shots of the light with my camera not knowing how well they would turn out. Suddenly the light changed from red to a blinding white. Then with a noise like a champagne cork popping, it seemed to explode. The object was gone but it left a circle of luminescence on the grass.

We all walked back up to the house in bewilderment. Had we seen ball lighting or even a UFO? I didn't know what ball lighting was. Even Dad couldn't explain it properly. The thing had seemed like a light rather than a craft so I didn't think it was a UFO, well not in the traditional sense. When we got up to the house we were amazed to find out that it was midnight. It had been a whole two hours since Dad had called us up to his room after first seeing the light. If felt like we had been out of the house for less than half-an-hour but the clock insisted it had been almost two hours.

You must understand that at this point none of us was scared. We had been a little baffled by some of the events that had happened since we had moved into Hollyhock Farm, but we never felt threatened. All that was to change soon.

One Saturday morning my brother and I were sitting in the living room watching *Tiswas*. Dad was in the garden somewhere and Mum had taken my sister into town. We were both laughing at the antics of Chris Tarrant and The Phantom Flan Flinger when we heard the sound again. We both stopped laughing. It was the ticking, metronome noise we had heard in the woods, but now it was in the house... with us!

It seemed to start by the window then meander across the room. The stench was there too, it made us gag. As whatever was making the noise moved around the room, it seemed to affect the objects around it. A pile of magazines was thrown up from a coffee table and scattered across the room. A clock fell from the mantelpiece and a chair was pushed over. Then suddenly it seemed to exit the room. Before that we had felt safe but now the thing, whatever it was, had entered the house. Once again, we both decided to keep it to ourselves.

I got my pictures back from the chemist. They were very disappointing - just over-exposed blurs. Not one of them showed anything worthwhile.

Mum brought my sister a new rabbit. She called it Pongo and Dad built a secure hutch and run with heavy metal bars. No fox was going to get into that he said.

One night we had some of our old friends over from Birmingham to stay for the night. We were playing hide and seek round the grounds. We were looking for a place to hide and a group of us went into one of the old barns. As soon as we opened the door the smell hit me again, like rotten eggs. Some of our friends wrinkled their noses and asked what was causing the smell. I answered truthfully that I didn't know. Then over in the far side of the barn, in a great pile of old hay, something growled.

We saw something stand up. It was so dark that even against the blackness of the inside of a barn at night we could just about make out its outline. It stood up on two legs like a man but it was taller, much taller, maybe eight feet. I saw two points of red light and realised that what I had seen in the woods weeks ago were eyes; two red shining eyes.

We all screamed and ran like hell. Dad got a torch and an old cricket bat and returned to the barn. He thought there might be a prowler out there. He found nothing in the barn, not even an odd smell. Dad thought it was our imagination running away with us. He said we had been watching too much *Doctor Who*.

Three days later something took Pongo. The bars to the enclosure had been twisted in a way that no fox could. There was no sign of the rabbit but this time there were tracks. It had rained the night before and the ground was muddy. There was a set of tracks leading from the wood to the hutch then back into the wood. They were not the tracks of a fox. They looked like human footprints but far, far bigger than any I had ever seen. They were 14 inches long by 5 inches wide. The heels looked very thick and the toes, especially the big toe, looked very large.

Buster went absolutely berserk when he saw them; he barked and shook and snapped, then ran whining back into the house. He acted like he did when we had heard the sound in the woods, only more so.

Needless to say, my sister went into hysterics again. She refused to go out after dark from then on.

Dad ordered us back into the house and 'phoned the police. I snuck back out and took some shots with my camera. I put a ruler beside them for scale.

The police arrived and asked questions. They looked at the tracks and a photographer took more pictures and measured them. They looked around the garden. Dad asked them what they thought. One officer said that there had been a number of accounts of small animals like cats, chickens, guinea pigs and rabbits vanishing from back yards of homes in or near the Chase. He thought that some vagrants might be camping in the woods. He told us that there had been trouble with gypsies about ten years before. He thought they were stealing livestock to eat. He had no idea why a big vagrant might be walking around bare foot. *"Maybe he can't get shoes in his size,"* the copper had joked. Dad didn't find it very funny. He didn't allow us to play outside after dark any more.

One evening he had to go up to see his agent in Birmingham, and had stayed later than he had intended. When he finally got back it was 11:00pm. He looked pale and shaken. He slumped down into a chair and shook his head. Mum asked him what was wrong. She thought that he was having problems with his agent. But that wasn't it at all.

He said, *"I was driving home along Camp Road. I'd just got to the turning near the old German war cemeteries, and as I slowed down this thing ran across the road!"*

"What, a deer?" asked Mum.

"A gorilla!" he answered.

He must have seen the looks on our faces because he got quite agitated.

"I swear to you I saw a bloody gorilla, a great big hairy thing. It charged right across the road from one side to the other. It looked like it came out of the cemetery. The headlight lit it up and it kept running until it reached the woods on the other side. I've got to 'phone the police. It must have escaped from a zoo."

Dad 'phoned the police. He said they didn't believe him at first but they finally came out in the wee small hours. They drove to where he had seen the 'gorilla' and walked around the area shining torches. They found nothing. One of them suggested that it might have been someone in a costume playing a prank, after all it was nearly Hallowe'en, but as my Dad put it, *"Who the hell would be hanging around in an ape costume at a remote place like that at 11 o'clock at night?"* They promised him that they would 'phone all the local zoos in the morning to check for escapes.

The next day the police 'phoned back. They had checked all the local zoos, Twycross Zoo, West Midlands Safari Park, Drayton Manor Zoo and Dudley Zoo. Only two of them kept gorillas and they had never had an escape. The police said they had checked with the council and there were no exotic animal licenses in the county so no one was keeping wild animals, at least not legally. They reiterated the idea that it was someone in a costume, students perhaps.

That afternoon Dad drove into Stafford and bought a shotgun. He apologised to me for not believing my story about the thing in the barn. He told us never to go out after dark again, and he brought new locks for the doors and windows. He even suggested that it was the 'gorilla' that took my sister's rabbits. But gorillas don't eat meat do they? From then on Mum drove us to and from school instead of us taking the bus.

A week later Dad saw it again, this time outside of the house. He came running in shaking and grabbed the gun. He said he was pulling into the drive when the thing moved out of a stand of trees. He said it was eight-feet tall and stood on two legs. It was covered in black hair but he didn't get a good look at the face. It had run away from the car's headlights and he was sure it was the same creature he had seen crossing the road near the cemetery.

Both my brother and I were now having doubts about the thing being a gorilla. We had seen gorillas in zoos. They walked on all fours and they didn't eat meat.

Dad 'phoned the police again, and they came out begrudgingly and found nothing. I think they were losing patience with Dad for 'wasting police time'.

It came back the next night and this time we all saw it. It started with the noises, the weird sounds like an electric guitar being strummed discordantly. It was a drawn out wailing screech that set your teeth on edge. It didn't sound like an animal; the noise sounded artificial. The sound came from the Chase and seemed to come closer and closer. Buster was going insane, whimpering and shaking. The thing started to bang on the doors of the barns and the old piggery. It sounded like it was circling the house.

We looked out of the windows, but the creature remained in the shadows, just out of reach of the lights from the house. Dad went upstairs to a third storey window and shone a torch down into the garden and there it was. All of us saw it. It was a huge ape-like thing. It was head and shoulders taller than a man. It had shaggy black hair that looked matted. The head seemed to come to a point. Its face looked more like a gorilla than anything else I can think of. I could understand how Dad thought it was a gorilla, but it wasn't. Its eyes shone red, not reflecting light but luminescent of their own accord. It moved with a strange rolling gait, rocking from side to side almost like a teetering bowling pin. It threw back its head and let out the electronic screams. Even from the house we could smell the overpowering odour. It didn't like the light and seemed to shrink back towards the woods, but we could still hear it screaming.

Dad called the police and was told that if he 'phoned them again he would be arrested. The whole family spent the night huddled together in Mum and Dad's room. The screams continued until dawn.

I remembered I had taken photos of the huge tracks in the garden. We had them developed the next day. They showed the big prints clearly. We talked for some time over what to do. It was clear that the police didn't believe us. Finally Dad decided to contact a newspaper.

The following day a reporter and photographer from *The Daily Mirror* arrived. We showed them the photographs of the footprints. They asked if they could use a couple in their story. They talked to us all and photographed us, as a family and individually. They looked around the garden and saw the remains of the rabbit enclosure. They took pictures of the barn doors where the thing had hit them and broken some in places. They wandered into the woods for a while. We stressed how scared we were of this thing and how the police didn't want to help. The reporter said that the paper would run the story the next day and that then people would have to listen to us.

We brought the paper the next morning. On page seven the headline ran: **"MIDLANDS FAMILY TERRORISED BY YETI!"** The story took up a whole page and was accompanied by a picture of our family outside of the house and one of my photographs of the tracks. It told of us living in fear of a monster that killed family pets and wandered round outside the house at night. *"The police refuse to help,"* was a sub-heading. On the whole, the story was true but it was written in a very lurid way with irritating tabloid patois. We never called the thing a 'yeti'. We never really had a name for it other than the 'creature' or the 'thing'. I had heard of the yeti and bigfoot. But how could something like that live in England? Cannock Chase was 25 miles square. It wasn't the Himalayan forests or the wilds of Canada.

As it turned out having the story in *The Daily Mirror* didn't help us at all. In fact it made things worse. At school we were mercilessly teased as the 'monster kids'. I got into trouble for punching a boy who said my family were liars. I know Dad lost some work because people thought he was making the whole thing up as some sort of publicity stunt.

For several nights afterwards carloads of people turned up ay Hollyhock Farm. Some just sat outside in their cars honking their horns and shining the headlights about. Others came walking right across our property with torches, looking into the barns and even through our living room windows. Dad had to throw some of them off the farm. The one good thing was that the creature stayed away. I don't think it liked the crowds. I sometimes wonder what they would have done if it had turned up. I'd have loved to see the looks on their faces.

The BBC 'phoned us and asked if we wanted to be on *Nationwide*. Mum and Dad turned them down as we had seen what exposure to the media had done.

Gradually the fuss died down and people forgot about the story. The visits from cars full of drunken youths, or earnest looking men tailed off and finally stopped. Then it came back.

I knew it was coming. I just got this bad feeling at dusk and it grew and grew inside me. The first thing we knew about it was when Mum screamed. She was doing the washing up in the kitchen and we heard her cry out and drop a plate. We came running into the kitchen and found Mum on the floor white as a sheet and shaking.

She told us that she had looked up from the washing and right into the creature's face. It had been standing outside the kitchen window just feet away from her. It must have crept up quietly, no electric shrieks this time. Mum said it was so tall that she couldn't see the top of its head through the window. When she screamed it had moved away.

Then we heard it begin to pound on the side of the house. The whole building seemed to shake. The thing was terrifyingly strong. It began its screams as well. It was circling the house screaming and banging on the walls. We knew that even a bolted oak door wouldn't stop it if it decided to smash its way in.

Dad said we needed to make a run for the car. We were scared but he said that the thing would find a way in eventually. He got the torch and the gun and I put Buster's lead on and held him tight. He was foaming at the mouth as if he had rabies, and shaking violently.

We waited until the pounding sounded like it had reached the back of the house then we unlocked the door and hurried out. Mum had the car keys and Dad had the gun and torch. We made a run for it when the thing loomed up from the shadows. It must have been waiting for us, pounding on the back of the house then creeping to the front to catch us.

Up close it was even more terrifying. It bared yellow, saliva-flecked fangs in a face contorted with malice. Its leathery facial skin twisted in mask of hate. In its right hand it held a crude club. The air was full of its acrid musk. It charged right at us with its synthetic scream. Dad gave it both barrels. We were no more than twenty feet away from it. I knew that he didn't miss. I heard the thud as the shot peppered the thing's chest. But there was no blood, no sign of pain. It paused momentarily then kept coming. Dad swung up the torch and shone the beam directly into its red eyes. It let out a long wail that sounded like feedback and staggered to one side.

Mum got to the car and unlocked it. Dad kept the beam focused on the creature that was staggering about blindly. My brother, sister and I got into the back seat with Buster across our laps. Mum got into the driver's seat and turned the ignition. Thankfully it worked. Dad leapt into the passenger seat and slammed the door.

The creature came out of the shadows again but the headlights drove it back screaming into the shadows. The car span round and we pulled out of the drive onto Penkridge Bank Road. Mum put her foot down and we accelerated. I turned to look out of the rear window and saw the thing chasing the car. It seemed to be running impossibly fast. Mum must have seen it in the mirror as she forced the car faster still. Finally, the thing was lost from view. Despite it being left behind I still felt scared, almost as if its hateful presence was still with us. I kept looking back half expecting to see it still trailing us. I didn't feel safe until we reached Birmingham.

We stayed with our aunt that night - and for the following days - until we found some accommodation. Dad sold Hollyhock Farm for a very low price not long after and we brought a modest house in Dudley.

I heard that Hollyhock Farm had caught fire and burned to the ground a few years later. Maybe the new owner burnt it down himself for the insurance. I have never been back to the site or even to the Chase. Now, all these years later I will still drive miles out of my way to avoid being anywhere near Cannock Chase after dark.

To this day I don't know what that thing was, where it came from or what it wanted. I don't know what connection it had with the weird light or the ticking noise. But I do know something; it wasn't a flesh and blood animal in the sense you or I would understand.

THE ONE THAT GOT AWAY

The old Afanc floated lazily among the reed beds. The diffused sunlight played over his mottled back creating strange patterns on the green skin. He hung in the shallow water like some awful cross between a crocodile and a shark. His small, amber eyes scouted his realm unblinking, hunting for the slightest movement.

The Afanc had the patience of Job. He had swum these waters for over one hundred summers. His size and strength made him master of all he surveyed. The prey would come to him eventually. It always did.

"Come clean with me, Owen; is he really as big as you say? I've heard stories like this before."

Bryn sipped his pint of bitter and stared at the old man across the nicotine stained table.

"Would you have driven all the way up from Cardiff if you thought I was a liar?"

Bryn shook his head. Even here in the snug the old man was keeping his voice down.

"He's a secret, my secret. I only reveal him to those who I think will truly appreciate him." He paused momentarily than added: *"And those who won't go blabbering about him. If this fish and its location were to get out we would have every angler and reporter and naturalist in the country crawling all round Llyn Mawdryn."*

Owen slurped his own beer and eyed Bryn suspiciously.

"Look, you know I'm on the level. I just want to catch him, measure him, photograph him and then put him back unharmed. I'll not reveal the location or even which part of Wales the lake is in. A pike of his size is a real rarity."

"Rarity? Rarity! I'll guarantee you he's the biggest northern pike in the world. There's no other fish like him. We are talking about a living legend."

Owen glanced around as if worried he'd been overheard. But the few other patrons of 'R 'N Goch Ddraig were otherwise engaged in drinking, talking or half heartedly throwing darts at the antiquated dartboard.

"I first knew there was something odd in Llyn Mawdryn ten years ago. I was fishing out there and I was watching a big mute swan paddling across the water about forty feet out. Then WHAM! He's just gone. Something came up out of the water, grabbed him and pulled him under in one motion. Just like that."

He slammed his hand down on the table with a bang, causing several people to glance over. He waited for the prying eyes to turn back to their own business then lowered his voice almost to a whisper.

"It was like one of those crocodiles you see on them wildlife programmes. You know, when they grab a wildebeest?"

Bryn nodded.

"Well a few weeks later old Tom Evans from the village was out shooting ducks. He backed one over Llyn Mawdryn and in goes his retriever to get it. Just as the dog collars hold of the duck the waters beneath him heave up and this great monster bites into him and drags him under. Never found a bloody trace of the poor thing. Old Tom, he goes to the police but they just think he's been drinking, see?"

"So how big do you think he is?" asked Bryn.

"Well, I've got no photos of him but my mate Rhys says he was out fishing on his rowing boat and the thing surfaced alongside him. He says it was bigger than the boat."

"And how will we find him? Llyn Mawdren is not a small lake."

"Oh, I've got that sorted. I know where he lurks. I've been feeding him offal and chunks of waste meat for weeks so that he stays in the same area."

"So tomorrow it is then Owen?"

"Yes, I'll be here at dawn, don't be late. Angling glory awaits you."

The bed at *'R 'N Goch Ddraig* was not the most comfortable Bryn had ever slept in but then what could he expect? The pub was the only place for miles around where he could stay. He cast his mind back recalling when he had first heard from Owen Thomas. The letter written in that crabbed spidery hand on old note paper. The fantastical claims of a giant pike terrorising a remote lake in Gwynedd. He almost screwed the letter up and threw it away. It had to be nonsense; the dimensions the writer had stated were beyond belief.

But he hadn't thrown the letter out. Perhaps it was because it was handwritten. Surely a hoaxer would have just e-mailed him. Bryn Jones was well known. He had the nickname of 'King of the Pike-men'. He ran a website on pike fishing and edited a moderately successful news-stand magazine on the subject. He had fished pike everywhere from Russia to Canada. According to

Owen that's why he chose him to reveal his secret to. A pike as big as car! It was, of course an exaggeration but very big pike had been recorded in Wales before. Hopefully, this one would turn out to be a seven footer.

He had struck up a correspondence with Owen via the old man's PO Box. He refused to give his address. Finally, after weeks of exchanging letters they agreed to meet. The place was a tiny village in Gwynedd that Bryn had never even heard of.

Andras s Bwll was a tiny collection of houses with one small shop and one pub. And so he found himself here in the arse-end of nowhere on the trail of a legendary monster pike. Well if it all turned out to be rubbish at least he'd have a good story to write for the magazine.

In the cool air of dawn Bryn waited for the old man. He arrived in a battered old brown Ford Anglia. He pulled over and wound down the window.

"Get in boy, we've not got all day."

Bryn deposited his tackle and rig on the back seat and climbed in beside Owen.

"Is it far?"

"A few miles, have you got your camera?"

"You bet I have," Bryn patted his breast pocket. *"And I've got a tape measure too."*

"I don't know if he'll stay still long enough to measure."

"If we get him up on land we should be OK."

"Well don't ask me to get near the head end, boy."

The car bumped and jogged its way through country lanes and over hills. Cattle grids made the car vibrate so much Bryn was worried bits would fall off. It seemed to be held together by rust, as it was. Some twenty minutes later Owen drew up near a rusty old gate. He opened the gate and then they drove down a rough dirt track. Then Llyn Mawdryn came into view.

It was a large expanse of slate grey water surrounded by hills that obscured it from view to the passer-by. A few stunted trees were scattered around its shore. The rising sun was slowly turning the grey water to gold then red. Steam rose up as the sun's rays struck the lake.

They got out of the grubby car and trudged down towards the water, Bryn carrying his equipment.

"Sure you've got enough there, boy?"

"Well, I've only got one chance to catch him; I'll need all the help I can get."

The old man shrugged and walked on. Bryn thought the place had a ghastly atmosphere. It seemed as if they could be at some remote lake in Siberia, hundreds of miles from the nearest other humans, rather than in north Wales. There was something about Llyn Mawdryn that made a man feel small, insignificant. He felt that it was not a place he'd like to be if he were alone.

Owen walked across the shingle beside the lake to where he had tied up a rowboat. He climbed in and took up the oars. Bryn deposited his tackle then untied the boat and pushed it out. He felt the cold of the water even through his Wellington boots. He jumped in as Owen began to stroke taking them further from the shore.

Owen began to unpack his tackle basket and fix up his rod.

"Look at that," he announced proudly. *"Harrison Ballister slim blanks, three fully corked handles with Fuji screw winch reel seats and silicon carbide Fuji rings."*

Owen looked at him as if he were speaking Chinese.

"Sorry, I'm a bit of a geek when it comes to pike fishing."

"What you got for bait? Mackerel, rudd, eel?"

"I usually use dead bait but I had to come a long way for this. No way of preserving it. It would have gone off by now."

He reached into his basket and pulled out a silvery doubled headed lure.

"A spinner, it emulates the movement of fish."

He busied himself attaching the spinner to the fishing line.

"He's usually lurking over by them reed beds." Owen nodded towards a vast stand of reeds across the lake.

"Like I said, I've been feeding him. He associates that area with food now so he shouldn't be too difficult to find."

The little boat drew closer to the reeds.

"We'll troll up and down. If you row the boat slowly it should be ideal."

Bryn cast off and the spinner shot through the air with a satisfying whizz and plopped into the water a few feet from the reeds.

"Not using a float then?" Owen enquired.

"No, I'm dragging the spinner along the bottom, about a foot from the lake bed. If he grabs

the lure I'll feel the pull on the rod. I just need to be sure that I don't snag anything."

"He's big and strong. Don't let him pull that fancy rod straight out of your hands."

They moved slowly back and forth along the reed bed for almost half an hour. Nothing had stirred, not so much as a bird amidst the reeds.

Suddenly something massive surged in the shallow water. Bryn caught a glimpse of a back above the surface that looked like a tree trunk, it was so broad. The waters churned as the huge fish snatched the spinner and made off. Bryn let the line spool out before taking the strain. He was almost jerked out of his seat by the force.

"God, he's strong!" he managed to gasp.

"I told you he was a big one. There's ten feet of him if there's an inch."

The boat lurched to one side and then span around.

"God, he's pulling us."

A wake appeared on the surface of the lake. It suddenly swung round and came straight back at the rowboat.

"Jesus, he's coming back, what a fighter."

Both men were almost flipped from their seats by the impact of the great fish as it slammed into the side of the boat.

"I've never known a pike do that before."

"You've never met a pike like this one, boy."

"I think the cunning devil is under the boat."

Bryn started turning the reels as quickly as he could.

"I'll see if I can pull him up."

A greenish bulk rose up beside the boat. Bryn saw a gleaming eye, rows of crocodile-like teeth and a pale underbelly before it dived again.

"He's longer than the boat! I can't believe it! We'll never land him!"

The pike took off again and the reel was spinning like a Catherine wheel. When he tried to stop it Bryn almost broke his thumb. He stood to struggle with the fish as if pulled the reel away. The rod was wrenched from his hands and shattered leaving his palms bloody.

"A pike can't be that big, it just can't."

Suddenly Bryn felt something slam into him. The old man had barged into his back with his boney little shoulder. The blow did not carry much force but in the rocking boat it was enough to force Bryn off balance and send him crashing into the water. He surfaced spitting water. The cold had robbed him of words for the moment and it was all his numbed limbs could do to keep treading water.

"What the hell did you do that for?" he finally managed to gasp. *"Are you mad?"*

He reached up to take hold of the side of the boat, acutely aware that he was bleeding and thrashing in the presence of a very big predatory fish.

Owen brought the end of an oar down on his hand, breaking the fingers. Bryn screamed and the hills threw his scream back at him.

"This isn't any pike, you idiot. This is an Afanc, *a devil-fish, a monster written of by Welsh bards for hundreds of years. This* Afanc *is over a hundred years old. I am his keeper as was my father before me and his before him. We keep the* Afanc's *secret and we feed the* Afanc.*"*

The old man's last words struck home and Bryn began to scream again. Looking back across the grim waters he saw a wake heading for him like a torpedo. He struck out for the shore but his clumsy flounderings could not out pace the great fish.

The Afanc dived then hit him from beneath lifting him bodily from the water as the great, flat jaws encircled his body. The impact knocked what little breath Bryn had from him. Hundreds of razor teeth were opening up his stomach and piercing his spine. Predator and prey crashed back down into the water. The monster fish shook the man side to side, the teeth shredding flesh.

The Afanc knew its victim was dead and began to devour him at its leisure swallowing the main body whole then swimming back and forth to hoover up scraps of meat that floated in the water.

Owen watched from the boat. He knew he was in no danger; the monster had sated its hunger. All that was left of Bryn now was a rapidly dispersing cloud of red water.

It was better this way. Not like in the old days when they chose one of their own number to sacrifice to Afanc. No one could trace this man to this lake and even if they did no trace of him would be found. It would have all been long since digested.

The old Afanc, its belly full, returned to the reeds. It would be weeks before it needed to feed again but it knew the prey would come to him eventually. It always did.

Skull of a huge pike found at Llangorse Lake, Wales (CFZ Collection)

THE YELLOW MONK

The monastery, or what was left of it, sat atop the thicket-choked hill above our village. The grass never grew too hearty or hale about it. It always seemed to have a yellowy, dry look to it, even in spring. Sheep seldom grazed there, though they were plentiful in the surrounding fields. It stood on land owned by an old family called the Mortimers. They had never attempted any kind of preservation of the building. The age-battered ruin was a landmark visible for miles around. On a clear day, you could see it from Ripon. Abandoned since the days of the Civil War, the building was now home only to rooks and bats; oh and the Yellow Monk.

My Granddad first told me the stories of the Yellow Monk, the ghost said to haunt the ruins. Look in any pre-War book on ghosts and you will find it listed. 'The Yellow Monk who walks in Battersly Monastery, Yorkshire'. There is seldom any detail to the accounts; just vague twice-told tales of a yellow hooded figure. There was a path that led down from the ruin to a copse in a neighboring field that was known as 'The Monk's Walk'.

My Granddad said that one of his friends had seen it as a boy. He had been sent to look for a lost sheep in the wood, when he saw it. It was sliding along the path by moonlight. He said it had no face, just an empty cowl. The lad took to his heels and never looked back. I don't think my Granddad really believed him. He always said he was a one for yarns.

No one had reported the monk for years. The last sightings I had heard of were before the First World War. My Granddad's mate supposedly saw it in the 1880s. The Yellow Monk never frightened me or my friends. We didn't believe in the Yellow Monk. Why should we? I mean, the whole thing was rather stupid. Why would a monk be yellow? Anyhow even if there were such things as ghosts why would anyone be frightened of a ghost monk? Weren't monks supposed to be men of God?

There were three of us. Me, Bunny (Warren) Perry, and Clifford Till. We played up at the monastery as lads, back in the 1930s. I suppose parents today would have a dickie-fit at the thought of it. All that slippery, crumbling masonry. Even the idea of letting three ten-year-olds wander about on their own. You can't do that these days; kids miss out. It's a shame. Back then, during the school holidays we'd make a few jam sandwiches, and take a bottle of pop and be out all day. We'd spend hours up there in the long hot summers playing at knights and castles. Of course, when the summer's dying breath heralded the longer shadows of autumn the monastery became Dracula's castle or some such creepy place in our imaginations, but we were never really scared, not until 1938.

The previous winter had been a harsh one. There had been snow on the ground until April. The wind that came howling down off the moor could cut you in two, so we hadn't been anywhere near the monastery since October.

We climbed up there one bright morning and it seemed as if the grey, wet blanket of the last five months had been lifted. The sun was bright and the air fresh. As we reacquainted ourselves with our old playground we noticed that something had changed. A section of wall had collapsed. Perhaps it had been frost heave forcing the decaying old stones apart, but there was a great heap of them beside one of the larger walls inside.

The whole wall hadn't collapsed though. It was very odd. As we drew closer we saw that the section that had fallen seemed to be a secondary wall built over the first. We scrambled over cracked and scattered blocks to get a closer look. There was a door.

An archway was set in the stone of the first wall. It had been hidden behind the second as if deliberately bricked up. I recall Bunny Perry wondering why someone would block up a doorway like that. Cliff Till said something about walling up prisoners alive. Inside the arch were badly damaged blocks. It looked like whatever they had used as mortar back then had perished and when the water had leaked in and frozen it had forced the blocks apart like it had the wall in front of it.

There was some kind of markings on the stone. Very old and worn, they were hard to make out. I wish now that I had taken more notice of them or perhaps made a rubbing from the surface. I seem to recall a snake biting its own tail to form a circle, and what looked like an eye in the centre of some sort of star.

I walked up and pushed my fingers through one of the cracks. With a little struggling I managed to pull a chunk free. A fist-sized piece of masonry fell away and I peered into the darkness beyond. There was a weird smell, like stagnant water, that wafted out from the hole. Together we began to pull. More of the stonework fell away. Bunny found a rusty old iron bar and we improvised a crowbar to heave out the larger pieces.

It took us several hours but finally the archway was clear. Beyond was an inky blackness and the strange wet smell. I tossed in a stone and heard it rattle away down what sounded like steps. It made sense when you thought about it. The only place the doorway could lead was down; we had explored all the ruins above ground. Bunny ran home for a torch and Cliff and I waited staring excitedly into the dark; we had a new place to explore. When Bunny was back he shone his big bullseye torch through the arch. I was right; the beam fell on carved stone steps leading downwards. Bunny entered first with Cliff and me following. There was only enough room on the steps for us to walk one abreast. They led straight down for about thirty-feet, then came to an end in a muddy tunnel.

Shining the torch around it looked like some sort of natural cavern down into which the steps had been built. The pale walls looked like limestone. The floor of the tunnel was damp earth. The torch shone on until its beam dissipated, devoured by the dark. We walked on tentatively; the smell of rank water grew stronger. I suppose we must have walked about a hundred yards. It felt like longer but we were walking slowly. Then the light fell on something that glittered. It was water. The tunnel had widened out without branching and a pool of unwholesome green water filled the larger cavern. It smelled like the old water that sometimes builds up in cellars or in water butts left un-emptied over winter.

The beam did not reach the far shore of the pool so it must have been wide. Cliff bent down, plucked a stone from the mud and threw it into the dark, reeking waters. The mirror-still, moss-green water was shattered. The splash echoed un-unnervingly loud around the cavern. The concentric rings rippled across the surface and finally broke upon the muddy bank where we stood. We looked down and Bunny played the beam over the bank about us. The torch illuminated something glaring white against the dirty brown mud.

Not five-feet from where we were standing was a skull. It was some kind of animal, a deer, I think, its antlers long gone and bleached by time. It grinned up, regarding us with long empty sockets. After the initial shock, we were impressed. I bent to pick the skull up but it crumpled like dry dirt in my hands disintegrating into a white powder. Its age must have been immense.

Then, from out across the pool we heard a noise. It was like a wet sucking sound. Bunny said it must have been running water, maybe a subterranean spring that fed the lake. Then the noise stopped as quickly as it started. Cliff mentioned that it was getting late and we had quite a walk home. I agreed a little too quickly for some reason. The cavern and the pool had taken on a strange atmosphere. It suddenly seemed very cold. We left without looking back.

The odd feelings were forgotten the next day. We returned eager as ever to see more of our underground world. It seemed like it was ours alone; we discovered it like great explorers or scientists. We hurried down to the tunnel. On the way, Cliff noticed something in the mud. There was a sort of track, as if something wide and heavy had been dragged through the mud on the cavern floor. Coating the furrows was a sort of odd, clear slime. I lifted some up on a twig and Bunny shone the light on it. The stuff reminded me of the slime a snail or slug leaves behind. It stank as well. The same rancid water smell of the green pool. We followed the trail as it criss-crossed the tunnel and finally reached the steps. The same slippery goo trailed up the short flight of stone stairs.

We decided to play outside in the sun that day. Bunny suggested that we tried to build a raft to see if we could cross the pool and find what was on the other side. I didn't like the idea at the time, and I said so to the others, after all we didn't know how deep it was.

But Cliff and Bunny were taken by the idea and we spent the rest of the day searching for wood to build the raft. Our quest for timber took us away from the ruin and into the woods and the local tip. I felt a slight relief at being away from the monastery. Somehow it had become oppressive.

It was that night I overheard my Dad talking to my Uncle Bob. My uncle was telling him how Mr. Hogan, who farmed the fields beneath the hill that the ruins sat upon, had lost some sheep. Two ewes had vanished. They were too big to have been killed by a fox. My Dad thought it might be some feral dogs. The odd thing was though, there was no mess. Dogs are messy killers, bits of fleece and guts all over the shop. But Mr. Hogan's field was clear. Uncle Bob said that maybe the sheep had just strayed, and Mr. Hogan had been too idle to go looking for them.

We went back to the ruins the next day. It took several trips to cart up all the timber we had collected. Cliff had brought a hammer and nails and Bunny and I had got hold of rope to lash the raft together. We had started out on building the craft when a thought hit me, would we be able to get it through the archway? I decided to go back to the arch with some string and measure how wide it was so that we could get the raft through. I asked Cliff to come with me, to hold one end of the string, I said.

We almost fell over it. We were busy talking and didn't notice it lying among the rubble. It was one of Mr. Hogan's sheep. I knew the sheep hadn't been missing long but this one looked like it had been dead for days. It was a dry husk, its skin stretched out over the bones, the desiccated eyes staring in mute horror. The skin about its lips had been pulled back by the drying process, and seemed to be grinning inanely. As we bent to look closer, we noticed it was covered in circular marks. They were about the size of an old two-penny piece. Cliff said that it must have been some kind of disease that had killed the sheep and caused the marks. We showed it to Bunny then decided to go and tell Mr. Hogan.

Old Mr. Hogan followed us up the hill puffing and panting. When he saw the sheep he didn't think that it was his until he saw his own tag attached to the animal's ear. He said he'd never seen anything like it before and agreed with Cliff that it must be some kind of illness. He told us not to touch the carcass and that he would move it himself and call the veterinary to look at it.

We didn't go back up to the ruins for a few days after that. I saw Mr. Hogan in the village though, and asked about the sheep. He told me that the vet had said that he had never seen anything like it in thirty years of dealing with livestock. He said that it wasn't an illness but the sheep had been attacked by some kind of animal. The vet had no idea what kind of animal. He told Mr. Hogan that it had been exsanguinated. I didn't know what that meant at the time. I told Cliff and Bunny about what Mr. Hogan had said. They got all excited about the idea of an animal attacking the sheep. Bunny thought it might be something exotic that had escaped from a zoo or circus. I pointed out that the nearest zoo was in Scarborough and there hadn't been a circus in these parts for three years.

Bunny wanted to go and look for it so we marched up to the woods. We didn't find anything and after a while we got bored. Cliff suggested we resume work on the raft. We scrambled up to the ruins again and got back to work. We noticed that the hammer we had left there was missing and began to argue about who had the tool last. Finally, we all decided to look for it among the ruins. We should have split up really but we stayed together, I don't know why. It was then that we saw the Yellow Monk. Not by moonlight, not in the reeking tunnel, but in broad daylight on a bright spring afternoon.

We had been poking around the ruins for about half-an-hour without finding the errant hammer. We turned a corner in what was once a long corridor but whose roof had crumbled centuries since. There was something at the end of the passage. It was a crouched figure that slowly stood up. Perhaps 'unfolded' would be a better term. It was a dirty yellow colour, and must have stood head and shoulders above the tallest man I'd ever met. It looked like a mass of filthy sackcloth. It had its back to us and we didn't know what we were looking at until it turned round.

As it slothfully turned it revealed itself to be a shape like a monk's habit, save for the size and the sickly yellow colouration. Where the face in the cowl should have been there was only a suggestive blackness. Where hands should have protruded through the arm-holes of the habit there was the same inky darkness. We realised that we were looking at the Yellow Monk.

All of us froze like rabbits caught in a lamper's light. I didn't know how I had expected a ghost to look. I couldn't see through it. It was not wispy or light, it seemed bulky and ponderous. As we watched something moved beneath the cowl. A mass of writhing feelers slipped from the hole where the face should have been. Wet brown tentacles, as long as a human arm. They all ended in a kind of tooth-fringed sucker like a lamprey's mouth. A wet sucking noise, the one we heard in the tunnel accompanied their snaky dance. Two more clusters of these drooling, mouthy tendrils emerged from where the hands should have been.

It dawned on me that what I was looking at was no ghost. What, at first, had looked like cloth was folds of slimy yellow skin. This was some kind of animal. The holes were mouths and the feelers feeding apparatus. Apparatus that now stretched and slavered as the form began to glide forward on a slime coated, ragged base.

We ran, the three of us. I don't mind telling you, I pissed myself. Bunny and Cliff did as well. We charged headlong down the hill falling into a sodden ditch and grazing ourselves on barbed wire. I felt that the thing was following us, slipping along like a ghost on a trail of slime. We told our parents nothing of what we had seen. We just said that we had fallen in a water-filled ditch, which wasn't a lie. That night I couldn't sleep. It felt as if the thing were watching me from the ruins atop the hill. The three of us didn't talk much about the Yellow Monk after that. We realised that it must have come up out of the pool in the tunnel. Maybe it had been walled up for a reason years ago and we had set it free, whatever it was. We never went back to the monastery.

Mr. Hogan lost more sheep. I heard my Dad saying that he was going to talk to Mr. Mortimer the landowner. Mr. Hogan was a tenant farmer on his land.

Sometime after this, World War Two broke out and everything else was forgotten. Battersly Monastery was hit by a German bomb and raised to the ground. It's funny but on the night of the bombing we all heard the air raid sirens and the explosion, but no one recalled hearing the high pitched drone of the German bombers.

I suppose that whatever had come up from those tunnels had been sealed back in again. That is, unless, the tunnels had more than one entrance. That is something I can do without knowing.

WALKER ON THE WINDS

When the 'phone rings at 2.30am in an asylum it is seldom good news. It rang when Alan Dodds was on duty, early that bleak, dark January morning in 1949. On the other end of the line was Superintendent Derek Hopper. His first words were: *"All hands to the deck, it's a bad one."*

It transpired that they were bringing in an incredibly violent individual who had been found roaming the desolate lanes of the North Yorkshire Moors. Police patrolmen had come across him squatting naked in the middle of the road, in a snowstorm eating the carcass of a roe deer, raw. He had been caught and sedated after a terrible struggle and was being transported back to Burntwood Asylum. A secure cell needed to be prepared post haste.

Dodds looked out into the night from the little golden portal of his window. The wind whipped up sending snowflakes swirling and rattling the glass. He waited with the other wardens. The cell was ready for whatever they were bringing back off the moors.

Across the white expanse of the grounds he saw the gates in the tall surrounding wall swing open and the black Maria plough its way in through the snow. It spun around and backed up as orderlies opened the door to the building and cleared the way. Dodds was glad he was not qualified or cleared to handle 'patients'. The back doors of the Maria were flung open and three burly officers emerged. Between them, with the use of catchpoles, they held the prisoner. The catchpoles were secured around his neck and the officers stood as far back as they could from the man, if you could call him a man.

He was tall and gaunt. His long matted hair fell down to obscure his face. His body was splattered with filth and mud. If he felt the biting cold, he certainly didn't show it. The sedative seemed to be wearing off as he suddenly jerked into frantic activity. Shrieking like a wildcat he lashed out at the officers not with fists but with hands curled into claws, the long, jagged nails caked with filth and gore. The three men struggled to hold him and keep out of range of his raking hands. He seemed devilishly strong.
As the man thrashed his wild hair flew up and occasioned Dodds a glimpse of his face. He wished it had not. His mouth was fixed in a leering grin, teeth still redly wet. His sunken eyes

---

rolled and flashed about. They were bright with an animalistic lustre. He threw back his head and let out a long, inhuman cry. Working in a madhouse one hears some horrific screams, but Dodds would not have credited that human vocal chords could have created the sound that emanated from the naked man in the asylum yard. The ululation echoed around the grounds and off over the snow blanketed moors as if he were calling out to 'something'. No answer came.

"Get the Doctor out here now, he needs another sedative!" one of the struggling men shouted. Dr. Silas Farrimond emerged from the front of the vehicle, his long, black coat standing stark against the white. He held onto his hat with one hand as the wind tugged at it. In the other, he carried a long thin object. The officers wrestled the naked man into a crouching position; their faces were reddened by the struggle. Farrimond lunged forward and jabbed the man's thigh. The device he was holding was akin to those used by zookeepers when sedating dangerous animals from more than arm's length. A syringe fitted to a hollow metal pole.

The prisoner surged to his feet with a scream and reached for Farrimond who shrunk back horrified. It took the combined strength of the three big men to stop his dirty claws ripping into the physician's face. They manoeuvred the man towards the doorway. There was no question of attempting to put a straitjacket on him yet. His frantic movements seemed to Dodds almost like watching a speeded up film. What in God's name could have affected the mind of a human being to turn them into *this*? Then, he reasoned, nothing in *God's* name.

As the sedative finally took effect the man began to sag. At last he collapsed to the floor his body twitching with muscle spasms. Two orderlies gingerly approached. When they saw the man was unconscious they quickly strapped him into a straitjacket. He was transferred to a padded cell and watched round the clock.

He awoke at 11:00am the next day and tore free of his straitjacket as easily as if it had been an old cotton shirt. He then embarked upon hurling himself around the cell like a demented chimpanzee uttering inhuman squeals of fury. The patient went through cycles of frantic activity, clawing at the padded walls and leaping around his cell, then falling into a deep sleep.

In the days that followed it became apparent to Dr. Farrimond and the Burntwood Asylum psychiatrists that the man was unlike any other patient they had ever come into contact with. He was far too violent to be approached and food was left in his cell when the patient had been moved into an adjacent cell via a sliding door. He refused all food save for raw meat, which he devoured with relish. He took no water and the only liquid he imbibed was the blood from the flesh he was given. The man made no attempt to communicate nor did he indicate anything other than animalistic intelligence and unreserved violence. At night he would set upon wailing and moaning as if he were calling out to something the doctors couldn't see.

A week after his arrival a breakthrough was made: the man's identity was discovered. The police contacted Superintendent Hopper with some grisly details. Friends had noticed the absence of an elderly couple from Hebdon Bridge. Ron and Eileen Meeker had not been seen for several days and a friend had contacted the police. After a forced entry the remains of the couple had been found. What was left of Ron and Eileen Meeker was little more than skeletal remains. Forensic examination of the bones revealed tooth marks, human tooth marks.

When a neighbour had said that he had seen their son Clive with them, the police tried to contact him. They had no luck. It seemed that Clive Meeker had vanished. A check on dental records had matched the marks on the bones with Clive Meeker's teeth. The police had not released any details yet. The Meekers were a well-to-do couple and very much respected in the town.

Clive Meeker, 42, had trained and worked as an engineer before the war. He joined the army and served in Burma reaching the rank of Major. After the war, he had spent a number of years travelling the world and had only recently returned to England.

A photograph sent to Hopper was clearly the same man as he had in the cell. Despite the long matted hair and facial features twisted by madness, Hopper knew that it was Clive Meeker who was pounding and screaming and gorging on raw meat. At least here he was away from the public. Burntwood had been built in 1824 to house the most dangerous and disturbed patients far from where they could do harm. Situated on the North Yorkshire Moors it was miles from the nearest town or village. Here he could harm no one; at least that's what Hopper thought.

To the doctor's continued amazement and concern, Meeker's condition grew more bizarre. The man began to sweat and pant profusely. He seemed on the edge of collapse through heatstroke until the heating to his cell was stopped and he made a full recovery, swiftly reverting to his cycle of raving, gorging, wailing and sleeping. Despite the amount of food he ate, Meeker seemed to be becoming emaciated. His ribs showed clearly through his skin. It was almost as if the man were growing tall, stretching out. His limbs and digits seemed longer and more spare by the day. His skin took on a pallid, sallow appearance and the mane of hair about his head grew a silvery white. Strangely he grew no body hair or facial hair. After a while they stopped thinking of the patient as Meeker. He now seemed barely human. They were already referring to him as a 'creature'.

Dr. Farrimond was thinking of calling in some colleagues from London to examine the patient under heavy sedation. He suspected that the patient had contracted some foreign pathogen whilst on his travels. Something new to science. He needed to find out exactly where the man had been. That might give him some clue as to the nature of his weird condition. As it happened, he never had the chance to invite his peers to look at the patient. The events of the night of February 19th saw to that.

The patient had been particularly violent on that night. His teeth and nails had become more like fangs and claws and he had managed to strip away the padding on the cell walls. This triumph seemed to spur him on and he set up a frenzied pounding on the cell door. It would have reduced a normal man's fists to a bloody, broken pulp but not so this patient. He belayed the 3-inch thick steel door with gorilla-like strength until after an hour it gave way.

There was a screeching of tortured metal and a splintering of plaster as the door began to yield under the super-human onslaught. The alarm was sounded just before the door was smashed from its hinges and tossed into the corridor. Three guards had arrived and set about Meeker with lead-loaded nightsticks.

He turned on them, a rabid dervish of teeth and claws. Nightsticks were snapped like twigs, their bludgeoning having no effect on the feral thing that had once been Clive Meeker. The guards fell back, one dead, two more with arms and faces shredded as the thing shrieked in demented glee. The creature bounded up to one of the windows and twisted the iron bars from it like so much tinfoil. He shattered the pane and leapt from the third storey window in a cascade of broken glass, landing with cat-like grace on the ground thirty-feet below.

Without a breath, he was bounding across the grounds towards the wall, sometimes on two legs sometimes loping on all fours like a beast. An armed guard pumped four bullets at the receding figure. To his dying day, he swore that at least one found its target. Yet the thing never once flinched and there was no blood on the snow.

It reached the high wall about the asylum and scaled it like a vast, ghostly spider, its talons finding easy purchase in the brickwork. The barbed wired coils at the top didn't even slow it down. By the time the outer gate was opened, the creature had vanished, its pale form being lost in the deep snows of the moorland.

A search party was organised within minutes and armed men with searchlights drove out into the dark. Whatever tracks the thing had left were swiftly becoming obscured by the snow. Three teams split up to cover more ground whilst Hopper informed the nearest police station at Rosedale. The icy roads made driving treacherous and slow. Finally they proceeded on foot searching nearby woodlands and out-crops of rock around which the wind seemed to sing and howl. The tracker dogs whined and hid their tails between their legs refusing to follow any spoor there might have been. Finally the elements forced them back.

"Not even that thing could survive, naked, out here in these conditions," Hopper had said.

The men returned to rest, planning to resume the search in the morning. Most felt that they would now be looking for a corpse.

It was the following morning that the asylum had a visitor. It seemed he must have walked through the waist deep snow from the nearest village, and appeared unperturbed by the weather. The man at the heavy gates 'phoned through to the Superintendent's office and Hopper was about to tell the man where to go when the stranger said he knew Clive Meeker. The man who entered Hopper's office and warmed himself by the fire was one of the most unusual visitors Burntwood had ever had. He was old and short. His weather-beaten face had copper skin and dark eyes. He wore what looked like eagle feathers in his white hair. He was dressed in hiking boots, jeans and a jacket decorated with beads. A rucksack was thrown across his back.

The man introduced himself as Kaneonuskatew, a Cree chief from Ontario, Canada, and his story was a strange one.

"I met Clive Meeker early last fall," he said slipping off his rucksack and settling into a high-backed leather chair.

"He was travelling the world, said he'd been to Africa, Asia, Australia, South America and he wanted to see the wilds of Canada. He hired me as a guide for his expedition and some of my people to help carry supplies. He wanted to go into the wild interior of Ontario. We went by canoe along the Bloodvein River. There's no roads up there, not even logging roads.

He wanted to see some ancient petroglyphs that were on cliff faces up river. He said he wanted to see wild bears and wolves as well. We stocked up with supplies for two months and set out in early September. The weather was fine and we made good headway for a number of days. But the weather can change quickly in Canada. The storm came out of nowhere. It was one of the most savage downpours I have ever seen. There was a flash flood and our canoes were swamped. We lost our supplies, guns, tents, radio, equipment; the lot went to the bottom of the Bloodvein.

It was lucky that none of us were drowned, or so I thought. I came to question that later. We were soaking wet and with no shelter or food. But I knew of a cabin some ten miles upriver that was stocked with dried food. There are a number of these cabins set up. If someone is lost and hungry they can use them.

The walk there was arduous. We were soaked, hungry; some of us in shock and it was bitterly cold. Every damn step felt like a mile. And all the while the rain lashed down like a whip in the face. Finally we got to the cabin. To our horror we found that a grizzly bear had broken in and eaten the whole stock of dried meat and fish. I think it was looking to put on extra fat before hibernation. Not a scrap of edible material was left in the cabin. We managed to gather a few berries before it got dark but that was all. We got a fire started in the cabin and huddled round it, mentally and physically exhausted.

During the night the temperature plummeted and the rain turned to snow. It was a white out and the snow piled up around the cabin. In the morning it was decided that some of us should try to find food. We had no guns but two of my people had their bows and arrows. Others would set snares. For three days, we tried to find food but there was no game. We swiftly ate the few berries in the area but you cannot sustain eight grown men on berries alone and the snow had shrivelled most of them to nothing. Have you ever been hungry? I mean truly hungry? Somehow I doubt it. Here you live from your hand to your mouth. In the forest, if you do not hunt and kill you starve. We were reduced to boiling leather and chewing on that. They say that the most civilised man is only a few meals away from becoming a savage.

And every day more snow.

We tried to look further afield, but we were weak from hunger. One day we walked too far from the cabin. There was an avalanche. At first a roaring like a great beast then tonnes of snow crashing down towards us. It snapped great pines like so many matches, a wall of white that swept everything in its path away. I thought the time had come for me to meet my ancestors but the wave of snow snatched me up and carried me on top of it. It was over in seconds.

I found Meeker clinging to a tree, shivering and blue. We searched for the others, digging in the snow until our fingers were numb, but we could not find them. Twilight was upon us and we had to turn back to the cabin.

That night as I sat shivering by the fire I heard the wind piping through the mountain passes and shaking the trees. The wind seemed to howl about the cabin and I fancied I heard something else with it. Meeker just sat staring into nothingness, still, silent as if he were listening.

In the morning I set out to try and find the bodies of my friends. Meeker was too weak to come. I found one man. I could not bury him as the ground had frozen like iron. I covered his body in stones and made my way back."

I fell asleep through sheer exhaustion. It was an uncomfortable slumber, haunted with bad dreams. When I awoke, Meeker was gone. Searching outside I saw his footprints in the crisp, hard snow. I followed them all the way back to where I had buried my friend the day before. Meeker had removed all of the rock and was eating the man's corpse. He had already eaten his buttocks and part of one of his legs. I should have killed him then, as soon as I knew he was going Wendigo."

Kaneonuskatew looked at the blank faces of the Superintendent and the other men in the office.

"Going... Wendigo?" asked Dr. Farrimond.

The old Indian nodded.

"The Wendigo, the Walker on the Winds. It is an evil spirit or Manitou. It is known to all the northern tribes, the Cree, the Ojibwa, the Maliseet. The Wendigo is the personification of hunger and winter. It lurks in the eternal cold of the far north and comes down to hunt men in the winter months. It is a giant made of ice, rage and unsated appetite. Not only does the Wendigo feed on men but it can posses them. If a man is forced, by hunger, to eat the flesh of another man, then the Wendigo can enter him and posses him. The victim goes insane and will take no food other than human meat. He becomes an insane cannibal whose lust for man flesh is never sated. If someone with this curse is captured in the early days then the spirit can be melted from his body. The Wendigo has a heart of ice and frozen water in its veins. The victim's heart will freeze until it is a lump of ice in their chest. If this can be melted then the person can be saved. If the possession continues then the victim transforms into a smaller version of the Wendigo and it will kill and kill until it is stopped, because its hunger never ceases.

I struck Meeker on the head with my hatchet, knocking him out. I tied him up as best I could and dragged him back to the cabin. I sat him close to the fire and stoked it up making him breath in the smoke. He screamed and raved for hours before he vomited up the human meat and lumps of ice."

Outside the wind grew into a great storm that shook the cabin like a toy. In the wind I could hear a howling, screaming noise and I knew it was the Wendigo. I dared to peek out of the window even though I should never have. The clouds were racing across the purple sky and when the fat moon shone down from between them I saw it as it circled the cabin."

"What did it look like?" asked Hopper.

"My hair was black before. Now it is white. The Wendigo was a towering shadow surrounded by a maelstrom of wind. One moment it seemed to be composed of nothing more than columns of icy fog, the next it seemed to be a skeletally thin giant caked with hoar frost and with a mouthful of icicles. The one constant were the eyes that burned like two indigo stars.

I chanted the songs of my ancestors and prayed to the Great Spirit. I am no medicine man but I did what I could. Meeker vomited up more ice and the storm seemed to abate. The howling of the Wendigo faded. I collapsed and slept.

Next morning Meeker seemed to be himself again. I felt strong enough to go and check the snares. I found that I had caught a beaver. I prepared and cooked the animal and we both ate. Meeker had no memory of digging up the carcass and feeding from it. I thought it as well not to tell him. I said he had fallen and cut his head. That was where my hatchet fell on him. The beaver meat did us both good and we grew stronger. The snows melted in a couple of days and we set out to find help.

We walked for many miles along the riverbank and by good fortune were picked up by some Indians and taken back along river to the nearest town. Meeker spent a week or so in hospital but he seemed to have fully recovered. He flew back to England a few days later.

Over the last few weeks I have been having bad dreams, dreams about the Wendigo. The dreams told me that a tiny piece of ice had remained in Meeker's heart. Like the smallest piece of a weed, it would begin to grow back again until it possessed him and turned him Wendigo. I knew then that the Great Spirit had charged me to hunt down and kill the Wendigo spawn. I found out where Meeker lived and took a boat across the Atlantic to Liverpool. Then I journeyed here, the Great Spirit guiding me."

Hopper rose from his desk. *"If I had heard this before last night I would have been inclined to keep you here in the asylum. But after what occurred last night I'm willing to believe just about anything now."*

The old Indian's eyes narrowed. *"What happened last night?"*

"The man you were hunting, Clive Meeker, who had apparently killed and eaten his own mother and father, was being detained here. He tore a 3-inch thick steel door right off its hinges, clawed a man to death, tore metal bars from a window and then jumped thirty-feet to the ground before scaling the outer wall under gunfire from crack shots.

Forget your guns, Mr. Hopper. Bullets will not harm him. His skin is as hard as stone now. Clive Meeker has turned full Wendigo. His hunger will be never-ending. He will devour anyone he comes across. We have only one recourse and that is to kill him. Have you begun to search for him?"

"All last night till dawn. We found nothing, the dogs refused to follow the trail but after a night out on the moors in this weather he will be dead."

The chief shook his head. *"You're not listening. Forget Clive Meeker, he's gone. The thing out there on the moors is a Wendigo, a cannibal monster that exists only to kill and feed. It is impervious to cold or fatigue. Now, where is the nearest settlement, he will have headed for there in search of food?"*

"Rosedale, it's about thirty miles from here." Farrimond answered.

"That will be no distance to him. He has the blood of the Wind Walker in him now."

"There's somewhere closer," said Hopper. *"Bennett's Farm, it's in almost a straight line between here and Rosedale but it's only about twenty miles."*

"Well, gentlemen, that will have been his first port of call. If we are lucky he will still be there."

"How are we going to kill him?" Farrimond looked more than worried.

"You fight ice with fire. We need to burn him, the whole of him, to ashes. Now collect as many flammable liquids as you can. We need to be fast. Wendigos are slower by day but at this time of year, the sun is low in the sky and has little power. We need to leave soon."

The thing that had been Clive Meeker had no memory of the man. It did not feel the biting cold of the winter wind or the deep snow about its legs. It was colder by far than the land about it. The only pain it felt was hunger. A deep, burning, maddening hunger. It ran swift as a caribou across the frozen snow away from the building, the bright lights and the men whose sticks spat fire.

It reared up, its eyes gave it night vision like an owl but its main sense was smell. The slits that were its nostrils widened and twitched. It caught a scent on the air. A sweet, intoxicating scent; the scent of life. The thing bounded off on its pale, spare limbs in the direction of the smell.

Eventually it came upon a lonely grey building. Small out-buildings were scattered around it. From one of these the smell came. The creature's vision picked up on heat as well as light. It saw many small, warm-bodies tucked up inside the little wooden structure. Hooked, icy talons ripped away the wire surrounding the enclosure and splintered the wooden door. Drool fell to the floor in frozen pools.

"You hear that, Mavis?"

Roy Bennett sat up in bed and groped for his glasses. Beside him his wife rolled over.

"Hear what, love?"

"Out in the yard. The chickens are going mad."

Indeed, a frantic squawking could be heard together with muffled crashing sounds.

"It's that bloody fox again. I'll blow his bleedin' head off this time". He fiddled with a box of matches until his bedside lamp was lit. Putting on his slippers he headed downstairs.

"Be careful, love, its awfully slippy outside," Mavis cried after him.

He retrieved his gun from its case and loaded it. *"Right you red-furred bastard, let's see how you like these apples."* He unlocked the door and stepped out into the moonlight. Turning a corner he saw the yard splattered with blood and feathers, but it was no fox that rose up out of the chicken coop. Instead a bone-white, man-like thing stood up like some long-legged insect unfurling. Its white face was splattered with blood that showed in stark contrast against the pale skin. Gore hung in strands from its teeth and steam rose from the sundered breast of the fowl it clutched, forming serpents in the cold night air.

Burning indigo eyes regarded Roy from beneath the shock of silvery hair. The thing's distorted mouth seemed to turn up in a gleeful smile. It dropped the tattered chicken as it saw better fare.

Roy whipped up the gun and gave it both barrels. There was a flash that temporarily blinded him and a boom as the shotgun discharged. It was followed by a high-pitched whistling cry from the creature. As his eyes refocused, Roy saw the thing was un-marked. He was standing only fifteen-feet away from it, how could he have missed? But the creature showed no sign of a wound on its ivory torso.

The Wendigo screamed in joy and leapt towards Roy, its arms stretched out as if to embrace him.

When her husband did not return, Mavis became worried. She had heard the retort of his shotgun. Had the old fool slipped up and hurt himself? She pulled on her slippers and hurried downstairs.

"Roy, Roy, are you alright?" She turned the corner around the house to where the chicken coop was.

Roy was being held by something in the manner a child holds a doll or teddy bear. The tall, white, utterly inhuman thing was clutching her husband's body like a toy whilst biting his face with a mouth so wide that it covered all of his features. On the floor beside them was Roy's shotgun, twisted and bent like an old pin.

The beast looked up, taking Roy's face with it, clean away from his head. The hot flush of her own urine against the cold of her legs stopped Mavis fainting. Before she had time to scream it was upon her, a living mass of greed and hunger that ripped and tore like a rabid baboon.

It was hours later when the vans from Burntwood arrived. Kaneonuskatew climbed out and sniffed the air.

"He's been here. I can smell him, the smell of corruption."

"Look at this, sir." One of the guards had found frozen blood on the ground; lots of blood. Hopper strode over and an examined it.

"There's chicken feathers here, but too much blood to be from chickens."

The men looked up and their eyes followed the trail of iced viscera to a large barn whose doors hung half open.

"Careful," warned the old Indian. *"He'll be as dangerous as a grizzly bear if you corner him."*

They gingerly crept into the barn. A vile stench met their noses. Hopper played the wan light of his torch around the interior. Amidst bales of hay was a pile of bones. Gnawed clean of flesh, even the marrow had been sucked from them. He bent to look.

"Sheep, chicken and human." He prodded a femur with his boot.

"The Wendigo is using it as a store house," said Kaneonuskatew. *"If he finds no more meat he will come back and eat even the bones. The curse of the Wendigo is that the more he eats the hungrier he becomes. The more he eats the larger he becomes. He can never be satisfied. He will be out now hunting but we know that this is his lair and we can trap him. Mr. Hopper, get your men to bring some of the petrol and paraffin in here."*

They soaked the bales of dry hay with paraffin and petrol and threw some around the wooden walls of the barn. The vans were driven out of sight and the men sat in the bitter cold and waited, thinking about what Kaneonuskatew had told them to do if the creature returned. The old chief had strung his bow.

For an hour, shivering and cramped they waited until finally it came. It strode across the white fields dragging something wet and red behind it. As it drew closer they could see it had one of its talons fastened around the head of a deer.

Hopper and his men were surprised at how much bigger the thing seemed. It was close to nine-feet tall now but slim and gaunt. The ivory skin seemed be stretched across sinew and bone. Its face was almost skull like, the lipless mouth a rictus grin of teeth. Little spirals of wind seemed to jump up around it making the snow dance and stirring its mane of silvery hair.

It paused by the doors of the barn and seemed to sniff the air. The men thought for a horrible moment that it had caught wind of them. They soon realised that it must have smelt the fumes from the paraffin and petrol but not realised what they were. After a few moments hesitation it entered the barn.

Kaneonuskatew waited a moment then stepped from his hiding place. He lit the oil-covered rag he had attached to his arrow then notched it and fired. His aim was true. The arrow flew in a burning streak right between the doors and into the hay bales.

There was a boom as the hay ignited. Four burly guards ran forward, and slammed the barn door drawing the bolt across it and trapping the Wendigo in the burning barn.

The wail that emanated from inside the burning barn seemed to scratch at the minds of the men like nails behind their eyes. The barn doors shook as the Wendigo hurled itself at them causing the whole structure to rock. Thick black smoke was now billowing from the roof and from under the doors.

The doors bulged outwards as the screaming monster hammered them again.

"Pour more petrol on the ground!" shouted Kaneonuskatew.

The men upended more canisters forming a pool outside the barn as the old man notched another flaming arrow. Seconds later the barn doors splintered apart under the super-human onslaught. The Wendigo leapt out, flames already eating at its mane of hair and shoulders.

The Indian shot his burning arrow into the pool and it ignited in a ball of blue flame surrounding the creature. Chattering wildly and clawing at the flames, the Wendigo tried to roll on the floor. This only caused the flames to leap higher. The men fell back as the creature swiped blindly at them but it was now a staggering, clumsy mass. Semi-liquid tissue fell bubbling and fizzing from its body. It looked like some twisted ice sculpture melting in the summer sun. Finally it fell forward motionless and the watchers crept nearer.

The body was falling in on itself. Consumed by the flames, the matter that composed it fell away in hundreds of rills that flowed across the cobblestones of the yard. Soon all that remained was a greenish object like a stone. *"The Wendigo's heart of ice,"* mumbled Kaneonuskatew.

The green mass of ice shrivelled and vanished leaving a smell like stagnant water. Suddenly a wind seemed to whip up from nowhere, screaming about the house and fanning the flames of the burning barn. It buffeted the men, almost knocking them off their feet. Then, as soon as it came, it was gone, whirling out across the moors to be lost in the frozen vastness.

Kaneonuskatew watched as the wind receded.

"The Wendigo taking back his own," he whispered.

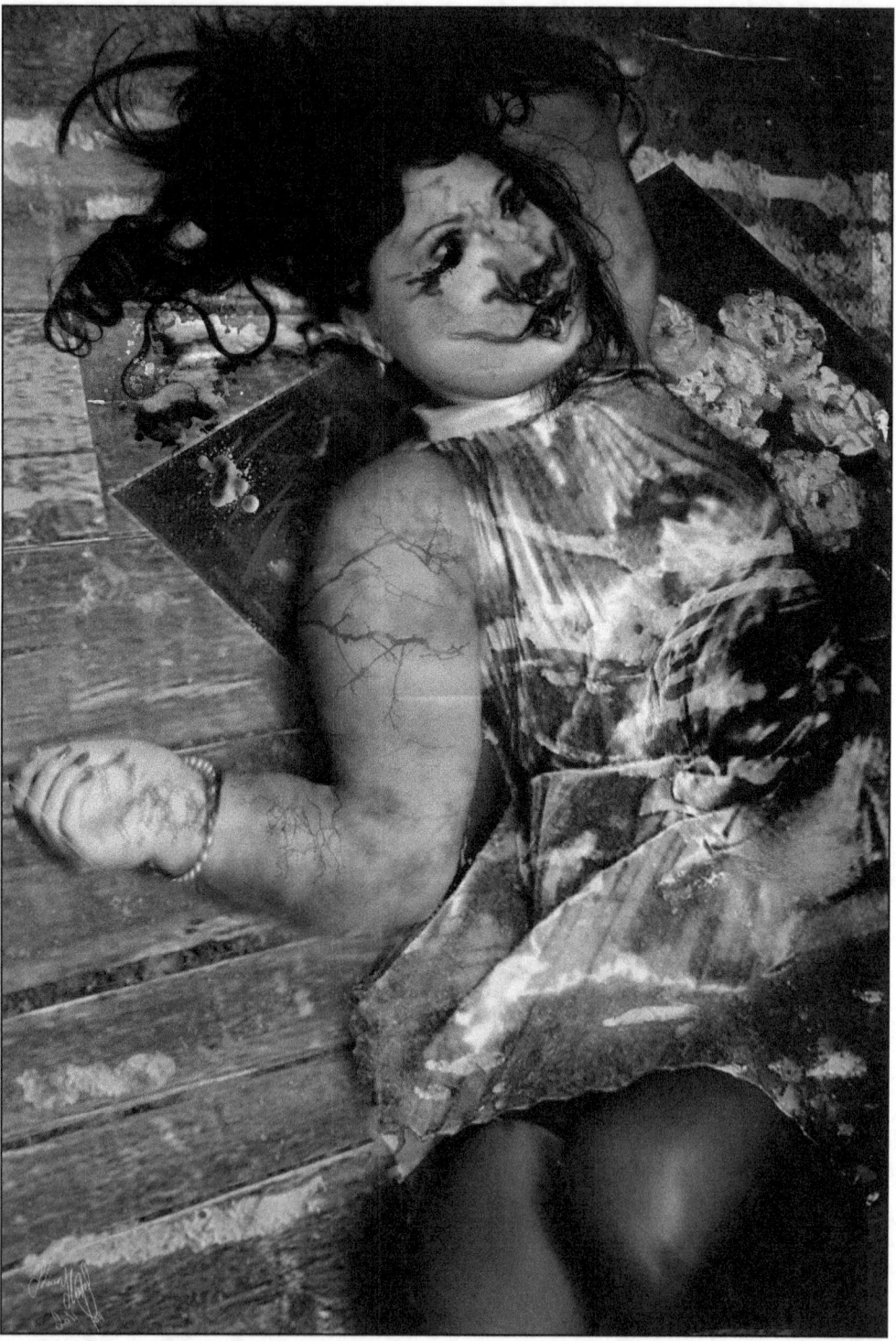

INCARCERATION

The gallery was not an old building, not one of the rambling heaps that generally spring to mind when the word 'gallery' is mentioned. Rather, it was - like its contents - a piece of modern art. Bright, new, white, outwardly almost featureless, and hexagonal in shape.

It stood out like the proverbial sore thumb above Milford Haven harbour.

The gallery had been erected in '88 with a government-aided grant from the Welsh Arts Council. It was meant as a forum and showcase for up and coming artists in Pembrokeshire and neighbouring counties. Its current flagship was a piece by Lydia Whittal. Local girl made good, Lydia's work had won national prizes and had been exhibited in London, Paris and Prague.

Current darling of the art world, she had a workshop above the gallery in order to be closer to her work and on certain days to allow the public to see one of Britain's most renowned artists in her element. As yet, fame had not spoilt Lydia Whittal and she welcomed the public attention (that in summer could prove a distraction) with admirable good grace.

'The Warp' was the collection's centrepiece, which Whittal had completed two years earlier when it had won both prizes and the national attention. The Warp was a cast of a whole room in plaster of Paris. It measured eight feet by sixteen by seven and weighed twelve tons. Its mould had been the living room of a condemned house in Camden, North London.

The council had allowed her three weeks to complete her work before pulling the said house down. Size alone had made the distance from London to Milford Haven almost impossible for the piece to be transported. For a while, it seemed destined to stay in the Tate Modern. But money was made available and The Warp was moved by road and air to its current resting-place, a process that involved removing the gallery's sky-light.

Everything in that room had been caught and held just as it was that day, two years ago. The furniture, books, threadbare carpet, pictures on the wall, all frozen in time, caught like flies in amber, hence the title. But Lydia had caught something else in that room, something that should not have been there. It had been resting, sleeping in the room when The Warp was created.

It awoke, confused and alarmed in a cold, dark prison and began to seek a way out. Yet the fabric of the plaster in which it was trapped was like a maze. It cast out tendrils of itself, probing the calcified matrix, particle by particle, each like another room, another twist in the labyrinth, for whilst in The Warp it had little conception of relative size. Emotionally it was a base thing, driven by base feelings: hunger, anger, hate, revenge.

Lydia had changed her style, as artists are wont, several times since The Warp. She now used oils and was currently painting a life-size portrait of her two favourite artists, Richard Dadd and Arthur Rackham. They were collaborating on a painting inside her painting (despite being separated from each other by a lifetime). She was working late in her studio hoping to finish 'Beyond the Fields we Know' before dawn.

An exit at last. It had taken two years of constant searching but now it finally knew the patterns of atoms, the chains of particles, and the pores in the material. It began to ooze like molten wax from the sculpture. Flowing in rivulets at first, then in folds from the plaster. It reached the tiles on the floor and felt the first new sensation in two years. It saw the moonlit hall with whatever in its nebulous mass passed for eyes and then, with liquid swiftness swept across gallery like an icy tide. It reveled in its freedom; it ached with a new need, a greed for sensation and retribution.

Pausing in its rush, it reared up and poured like quicksilver into an ornamental carpet, hung up on a wall. It slipped with ease through the carpet's weave and its curling patterns. It flashed across an abstract in green and violet watercolour before tasting the cold bitterness of a Punch and Judy man sculptured in bronze. Scattering the shells of a collage like fallen chessmen, it swept on towards the door.

It fumbled at the lock: another cold, alien thing, with something that was a stage-way between clammy flippers and jelly-like fingers. It finally oozed through the wood when it found the grain easy to navigate. It ran like a reversed waterfall up the spiral staircase, leaving a crust of frost on the thick pile like a slug leaves a trial of slime. Its form pulsed and changed, sometimes without substance, sometimes with, sometimes a wispy in-between like a frosty gas.

It flashed between states of being like an angry cuttlefish as it changes colour. Other emotions now lost or forgotten, it existed to slake one need alone. Half-mad with rage, it swept through another door and at last saw its tormentor; a soft pink thing. Her back tuned, Lydia was unaware of the aggressor's entrance.

It gathered up its unwholesome mass, rearing up like a striking cobra, then it fell in the fashion of a breaking wave. The pink thing was poorly constructed; soft damp redness draped over brittle, white rods.

The death of Lydia Whittal was the strangest on police record in the whole of Wales, if not nationally. The caretaker has unlocked the gallery in the morning and found a trail of frost leading from the main gallery to Lydia's penthouse workshop. Frost in June! Words like 'killed', 'murdered' and 'butchered' seemed to lose all meaning compared to what had been done to Lydia's carcass.

She became the painting she was working on. She was unrecognisable at first; in fact it was the dental records that confirmed that the distended, discoloured corpse belonged to her.

The body and face were tattooed with fronds of frost that blackened the swollen skin. Her face, torso and limbs seemed monstrously fat, as if inflated. And most bizarrely of all, the body had no blood. Yet the vessels had been filled to bursting point with oil paint.

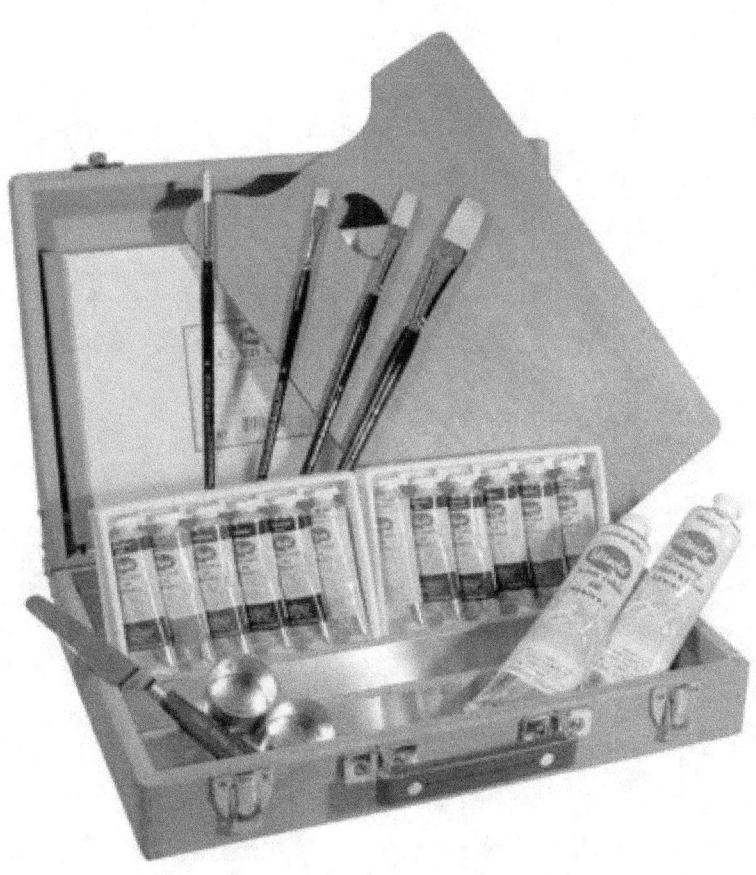

I CAN SEE YOU

Who really notices when a homeless person disappears? By their nature many are vagrant. Perhaps they just move on to the next town. But when several vanish over a short period it seems strange, especially if they were people you knew, people who were, by and large, sedentary.

Kim Miller worked in a soup kitchen along Brick Lane near Spitalfields in the East End of London. She had got to know the faces of the people who came there. Some just passed through, others were 'residents' of the streets around Brick Lane, as much a part of the area as the Brick Lane Market, the Black Eagle Brewery or the Bangladeshi restaurants. But then, many of those faces were not showing themselves lately.

The missing people had something in common, they were all reasonably young and able-bodied. The elderly or disabled turned up as usual. At first Kim put this down to them having found work or a home or simply that they felt life might be easier elsewhere. But it was strange that none of them had dropped by to say goodbye.

There was Carol, a 30-year-old schizophrenic who always stopped to talk with Kim. Bobby, a youth of indeterminate age addicted to crack cocaine was another, as was Mandy, a 16-year-old who had run away from an abusive stepfather and a mother who wouldn't face the truth. And there were many more, more than Kim cared to think about. It was amazing how many young people ended up on the streets, forgotten. Kim knew she couldn't solve their problems, but at least she could get some food inside them and give them someone to talk to.

One by one the familiar faces vanished. She asked some of the older people if they knew anything. Violet Tibbins, a bag lady who was always to be found in the park or round the market, said she saw Mandy get into a car with a white-haired old man who walked with a stick. That was the only clue she had. Violet couldn't recall the number plate or even the make of the car. *"It was silver,"* was all she remembered.

No one knew anything else or had seen any of the missing people in weeks. The police were of little use. Kim recalled what one sergeant had told her. *"The thing about the homeless is we don't know who most of them are in the first place. They don't carry I.D., they often use assumed names and unless we have some kind of records on file there's not much we can do to help find them. It's like looking for the invisible man."*

That last phrase had stayed with her. To all sense and purposes, these people were invisible. With no families or families that did not give a damn, there were few people to miss them. If they disappeared, who was to know?

The charity 'Missing People', did what they could but there were no photos of the missing people to put on their website and precious few details of who they were and where they came from.

In frustration Kim decided to take matters into her own hands. She booked two weeks off work and went onto the streets undercover. She knew full well that what she was doing was dangerous, foolish even, but she could think of nothing else.

Dressed in old clothes from charity shops she selected a doorway of an abandoned newsagents and settled in with a piece of cardboard on which she had written 'homeless and hungry'. Kim sat day after day watching all humanity go by. Occasionally she asked for spare change.

Seeing the world of the homeless from the other side was a shock. Working in a soup kitchen she thought she might have some idea of what it was like. She didn't. She was sworn at, spat at, even kicked once. But she found that those who just ignored her were the worst, those who looked through her or stared blankly ahead, pretending not to see her.

Kim felt bad about the duplicity, pretending to be homeless weighed on her conscience. She felt the wallet and phone in her pocket, she knew at night she could just go home to a hot meal and a warm bed. The real homeless could not. But, she told herself, she was doing this for a purpose. At the end of each day, after she had been home and tidied herself up, she returned to Brick Lane and gave the cash she had made begging that day to the first homeless person she saw.

It was halfway through the second week that the elderly man with the stick approached her. She had been daydreaming when the sound of a handful of coins landing in her upturned cap jolted her back to reality.

"Thanks," she said, eyeing a number of pound coins that were shaming the coppers around them.

"My pleasure, have you been on the streets long?"

He was about 75-years-old with silvery white hair and a little, neat, pointed beard.

"Not too long, thankfully, under a fortnight. But that's long enough; it's not an easy life here."

"I don't doubt it, my dear." He leaned on his walking cane. He looked rich, dressed in tweeds, a waistcoat and dicky bow. He had the demeanour of a retired schoolmaster. He looked over his pince-nez glasses at her. She wondered if she looked too well nourished to be homeless.

"You look like you could do with a good hot meal inside you."

She knew he must have been the man with whom Violet saw Mandy. Her heart was in her throat but she nodded.

"Yes, yes I could."

"Then come with me. I can help you."

He leaned over and offered her his hand.

"It's alright, I don't bite"

He helped Kim to her feet and still holding her hand, shook it.

"I'm Dr. Marcus Whitelocke, glad to meet you."

"I... I'm Kim."

"Well, follow me, young lady."

He walked to a large, silver Jaguar that stuck out like a sore thumb on Brick Lane. He graciously opened the rear door for her and allowed her to slide inside onto the leather seats. He then got in beside her and closed the door.

"Home, James. Ha, ha, ha, I never get tired of saying that."

The peaked capped chauffeur made no answer but started the car and pulled away.

"Where do you live, Doctor?"

"Oh, I have a place near to High Wycombe. It a big old pile, gets a tad lonely at times."

"There wouldn't be anything I had to do in order to get this meal would there, Doctor?"

The old man looked confused for a moment until it dawned on him what Kim had meant.

"Oh good lord, no! I'm just trying to help someone down on their luck, my dear, nothing else."

He seemed genuinely hurt so she quickly changed the subject.

"What are you a doctor of?"

"Botany, me dear," he grinned. *"I used to work at Kew Gardens as a collector. They sent me all over the world looking for rare specimens for their collection, not just the plants themselves but the seeds. They have a vast ark of plant seeds, three quarters of all known species. I found a number of plants new to science."*

The drive across London and out to High Wycombe was a long one but Dr. Whitelocke kept Kim entertained with his stories of plant collecting expeditions in far off places. At one point he rolled up his trouser leg to display a line of vivid, circular scars.

"Bloody crocodile in the Congo. I thought they were going to have to amputate but a tribal witchdoctor saved my leg from infection with herbal potions. You know most of our modern medicines are derived from rainforest plants. Anyhow, I was off my feet for weeks. I retired after that. I couldn't get around like I used to. Luckily for me I had an inheritance from my Uncle so I brought a place in the country and started my own collection. It already had an orangery so I expanded it into a series of hothouses. I've been running it ever since. Tropical plants are my obsession."

The journey took them up through North West London and finally out along the M40. Before they reached High Wycombe proper, they left the motorway and traversed a number of smaller roads.

"The area was called Blooms Wood once, appropriate for a botanist don't you think?"

Finally a track took them to a modest mansion hidden from the road by trees. Behind the building, large greenhouses were clearly visible. They parked up and the driver saluted and strode away. Dr. Whitelocke opened the large oak doors with a brass key and they entered an impressive hall. Kim was shown to a room up several flights of stairs.

"There is a shower just across the corridor. If you look in the cupboard you will find a dressing gown. My daughter is about your size; I believe I have some of her old clothes you can change into."

"Thank you. You didn't tell me you had a daughter."

"Oh yes, but she emigrated to Australia some time ago. I only see her once or twice a year these days. Now, if you'll excuse me I'll go and prepare dinner. I'm a pretty good cook if I do say so myself and it's so seldom I get guests these days."

With that he took himself off back downstairs. Kim looked around the room with its faded old sepia photographs, paintings of plants and four-poster bed. She could easily 'phone the police now, but what would she tell them, a kind old man offered a homeless girl a meal? No, she needed to find out more. She took the nightgown from the cupboard and crossed the corridor to the shower.

It had been a long hot day in dirty clothes and Kim had taken longer than she had meant to in the shower. When she returned to her room she found a dress, slippers and undergarments neatly folded on the bed. They more or less fitted her and she was grateful to be wearing something clean.

Shortly there was a knock at the door.

"Dinner is ready when you are," called the Doctor.

Kim walked down the stairs and into a spacious dining hall with a large table. The Doctor had pulled two chairs to one end of it. On the table a sumptuous meal had been laid out. They dined on smoked goose and papaya salad followed by a beef Wellington in exquisite puff pastry washed down with glasses of the Doctor's home-made blueberry wine. The dessert, that he presented with some pride, was a black cherry soufflé with white chocolate sauce and shortbread.

"Doctor, that was amazing, I don't think I could eat another thing."

He grinned proudly. *"Well, I like to see you're well fed."*

"Where did you learn to cook like that?"

"Well, when you are as well travelled as I am you get to pick things up."

"So you live alone then?" She was fishing for more information, hoping he would let something slip.

"Well, my dear wife departed five years ago and as I said my daughter left for Australia. I have James to drive me but he's hardly the world's greatest conversationalist."

"So you're looking for company?"

The old man smiled and held his glass of wine up regarding the dark liquid.

"Yes, to a certain extent, but there's more to it than that. I'm looking for someone to help me. You see I'm in my seventies now and having a gammy leg doesn't help matters. My plant collection is quite large and it's getting to be a handful."

"Why don't you advertise for help?"

"Oh, I've tried that. All I get is disinterested youths forced to come here by the benefits office. None of them were of any use. Most botanists have full time jobs in research or teaching so I thought that I could approach homeless people. You see, I would then be helping my fellow man and getting a hand in hothouses to boot."

Kim knew she was onto something now. She kept calm and asked more questions.

"Have you asked any other people off the streets?"

"A few but none wanted to take me up on the offer. I think they didn't want to be tied down to one place so I just gave them a decent meal and a bed for the night then dropped them back off in the Old Smoke.

Would you be interested in helping me here, Kim? I can give you a home, feed you and pay you a wage. Of course you would be free to leave at any time if the work didn't suit you."

"Goodness me, thanks Doctor. But I know nothing about plants. What would the work consist of?"

"No need to worry about that, I can easily train you, it's not rocket science. You would be assisting me in things like pollination, cultivation of seedlings, maintenance of the heating and sprinkler systems, the potting of rhizomes and so on."

Kim decided not to ask what a rhizome was.

"Doctor, will you show me your collection please?"

The old man beamed like schoolboy who had been asked to show off his collection of toy cars.

"I thought you would never ask! I never get tired of showing off my children. Come with me."

He led her out of the dining room and through a library. Bookcases that reached the high ceiling covered the walls. All were full of leather-bound volumes that reeked of antiquity. She noticed a fancy stepladder folded up in one corner.

"I'm quite a bibliophile my dear. Next to plants, books are my greatest passion. You can learn anything from books, the amassed knowledge of generations. It's like a kind of magic really."

They left the library and the Doctor opened another door. A wall of heat struck Kim as the Doctor reached for the light switch. The florescent tubes flickered and crackled before illuminating the first hothouse.

The atmosphere was thick and muggy. Steam rolled and curled as condensation misted the glass panels. Water dripped down onto Kim's head causing her to flinch.

"Sorry about that but we have to keep it hot and steamy in here. I specialise in tropical plants. My collections come from places like Indonesia, Malaya, Central Africa, South America, New Guinea and so on. I have to maintain conditions akin to those in a tropical rainforest in order to cultivate these species."

As they stepped into the hothouse the mists parted to reveal a riot of colour. Vines and creepers hung from a canopy of palms and cycads. They were strung with swathes of damp moss like green bunting. Dotted along them were green leafed plants whose flowers were masses of red and purple spikes.

"Eye-catching aren't they? That's Billbergia pyramidalis, *a species of bromeliad from South America. Bromeliads use their scaly leaves to catch and store water at the bottom of their stem. Many small animals live in the mini ponds the bromeliads create. Their excrement goes to providing the plant with nutrients. The stuff hanging down from the creepers is Spanish moss,* Tillandsia usneoides, *which of course is not a true moss at all but another species of bromeliad."*

"Of course," nodded Kim

She walked over to examine some clusters of flowers that were striped in red and yellow like old-fashioned candy.

*"*Acampe rigida, *an orchid from Malaya. Orchids are one of the most successful and abundant plant families. There are four times as many species of orchid as there are mammals."*

Another orchid species with huge white and gold flowers was growing near by. Kim took a closer look.

*"*Dendrobium formosum, *" said the Doctor. "The beautiful giant-flowered dendrobium, found only on the island of Formosa."*

"Don't you mean Taiwan?"

"I'm an old fashioned sort of chap, my dear. To me Sri Lanka will always be Ceylon, Thailand will always be Siam, Myanmar will always be Burma, and Taiwan will always be Formosa."

Kim turned back to the orchid and smelled its scent.

"You won't want to do that in the next hothouse."

She gave him a puzzled look but he just beckoned to her as he moved into the next vast conservatory. Following him through she almost gagged as the stench of rotting flesh filled her nostrils. Her mind briefly swam with visions of the decaying corpses of the homeless taken from the streets.

"What the hell is that stench?"

"Ahhh, the heady bouquet of the world's largest flower." He gestured to an outlandish bloom that towered in the centre of the greenhouse.

It stood full eight feet tall and consisted of a thick green stem that supported a purple bloom that recalled a Spanish flamenco dancer's dress. The fleshy yellow spadix sprouted up like a surreal phallus from inside the flower.

"Amorphophallus titanum, *commonly know as the titan arum. It is found only in the jungles of the island of Sumatra in Indonesia where it comes into bloom only once in its lifetime, then dies. You are indeed lucky to see it."*

"But why does it smell like rotting meat?"

"It is pollinated by flies. It smells like that specifically to attract them. In fact all the plants in this section are pollinated by flies. Over here we have Rafflesia arnoldii *from the jungles of Indonesia, Malaya and the Philippines."*

He pointed to a group of equally strange flowers. They grew low to the ground and were three feet across. They had broad, fleshy leaves and bowl-like centres, which were a rusty red spotted with white.

"This species is called the corpse flower by natives because of its cadaver-like aroma," he beamed.

"I never knew plants were so interesting," admitted Kim.

"Everything about the plant kingdom is fascinating. I could talk for hours about the wonders of the rainforest. But I have something special in store. Would you like to see my most prized specimen?"

Kim nodded, *"Yes please."*

"It's the rarest plant in my collection. It's the only one in cultivation anywhere in the world. Not even Kew has one of these."

With a triumphant grin, like a boy who has found the largest beetle, he opened the next door and threw the light switch. She followed him in.

There was only one plant in this tall hothouse and it was stranger than any that had come before. As the mist cleared Kim got her first good look at it.

The plant was around 30-feet tall and had a fat gnarled trunk with grey/brown bark like ironwood. Twisted roots ran from the bottom of the trunk and seemed to claw at the earth. In lieu of branches the plant possessed innumerable elongate tendrils that spilled from the apex of the trunk recalling the hair of a gorgon. The tendrils were flattened and fringed along both edges with long, sharp thorns. Despite the dead stillness of the air, Kim thought she saw the tendrils stir slightly as if moved by a breeze. The plant un-nerved her. It looked, well, un-natural.

"W-what is it?"

"That, my dear is a *ya-te-veo*. In the language of the natives who venerate it. The name means 'I can see you'."

"Where did you find it?"

"I brought this one back as a sapling many years ago. I found it in the remote jungles of eastern Honduras. They are so rare that the natives look on them as gods. You see the ya-te-veo *belongs to a group of plants most of whom died out long before the dawn of man. It is a living fossil. The discovery of this plant is the vegetable equivalent of finding a living dinosaur. The* ya-te-veo *is found only in undisturbed rainforest in Central and South America. There is an even rarer species in south eastern Madagascar."*

Kim gazed in wonder at the horrid looking thing, could it really be unknown to science? She certainly could not recall ever seeing a picture of a plant like this before.

"Why haven't you shared this with your fellow botanists, a discovery like this would make you famous?"

Dr. Whitlocke scowled. *"Fellow botanists,"* he snorted. *"A bunch of ignorant fools. I told them of my discovery, even showed them photographs of the* ya-te-veo. *Do you know what they said, do you? They said I was mad, that the tropical heat had got to my head and I was believing in native fairy tales! They said I hoaxed the pictures, they laughed at me after all my years of service to the Royal Botanical Society."*

"But couldn't you take them part of it, some bark or a leaf or a seed?"

"And have them steal my glory, claim that they identified it, have them give it a Latin name? No fear! You are indeed privileged. Kim. Few westerners have ever gazed on the ya-te-veo.*"*

"No offence, Doctor, but it sort of gives me the creeps."

The Doctor laughed out loud.

"It won't win any prizes for being pretty I'll grant you that but it has the most exquisite aroma of any plant on earth. The scent of the ya-te-veo *is to die for. If you go closer you will smell it yourself."*

Kim hesitated for a moment but then moved closer; after all it was just a plant, what harm could it do?

The smell was indeed intoxicating, a deep, cloying, sweet smell somewhat like lavender mixed with over-ripe peach. She drew closer and found her head spinning as if she were drunk. The scent was making her woozy. She stumbled against one of the finger-like roots.

Instantly the tendrils whipped down and coiled about her. It was so fast she didn't know what was happening. At first she thought she had fallen over and hurt herself as the world tripped upside down and sharp pains shot through her side and legs.

She saw the Doctor's grinning face from an odd angle and realised that she was being hoisted up and held aloft. As her head cleared she realised that the plants thorn lined tendrils had coiled like vegetable pythons around her body. They were swiftly tightening, forcing the dagger like thorns deeper into her flesh. She tried to scream but a questing tendril had fastened itself round her neck.

The Doctor was smiling up at her as he approached the foot of the ghastly plant.

"The ya-te-veo *is a flesh eater. Its roots act like trip wires that trigger the predatory members. In the wild they mainly eat birds, monkeys and other animals that blunder into them. The plant produces a scent that causes dizziness and clumsiness.*

An adult nearly got me once, that's what caused the scars on my leg. I managed to hack myself free before it got a decent grip. The native tribes make human sacrifices to these plants, they force the victim to trigger the roots and then go wild with ecstatic rites around the ya-te-veo whilst it kills its victims. Here in England, you homeless types make ideal victims; no one misses you."

The tendrils pulled her higher still. As she was swung over the top of the plant she looked down to see a hungry, gaping maw at the centre of the nest of thorny vines.

The members tightened further like huge hands wringing out a damp cloth. Her punctured, crushed, twisted body was squeezed dry of blood. Her bodily fluids cascaded down into the waiting mouth. Finally the tendrils loosened and Kim's tattered remains tumbled into the hollow trunk splashing audibly into the digestive fluids therein. Slowly the fibrous tentacles returned to their natural place, hanging limp beside the trunk.

Dr. Whitlocke was pleased. The plant would not need to feed again for another six weeks and soon it would be old enough to reproduce. Soon it would be budding off dozens of tiny reproductions of itself. The new hothouse was ready for them. As shoots they would make do with rats and mice. And when they were bigger, well there were an awful lot of homeless people in London.

THE YA-TE-VEO, OR CARNIVOROUS PLANT.   476

CUTTY DYER

"Don't go down to the riverside
Where Cutty Dyer do abide
Cutty Dyer ain't no good
Cutty Dyer will drink your blood"

Traditional children's rhyme.

More rubbish is written about vampires than almost anything else. How they are portrayed in books, films and television as ageless, beautiful, sexual predators is utter nonsense. Fear of daylight, crosses and garlic, all rubbish as well. Forget everything you think you know about vampires. Forget all the dross spouted in teen pseudo horror drivel like *Buffy the Vampire Slayer* or *Twilight*. Reality is somewhat more unpleasant. A vampire is an ugly, foul smelling, disease-spreading monster. If they ever were human, which I doubt very much, they are not now. I should know, I saw one.

I grew up in a little town on the edge of Dartmoor called Ashburton, in the 1950s. There were only about 2,000 inhabitants and back then motorways had not reached their asphalt tentacles down into Devon so it was a quiet place. It had the cosy, small town feel that has largely been lost now. In the days before easy excess and e-mail we were largely cut off in winter.

We liked it like that though. It wasn't that we disliked or mistrusted strangers, it was just that we were a close community. We had everything we needed. The influx of tourists in summer was negligible back then. Nowadays the 'grockles', as we call them, flock down here in their thousands.

It came as a shock to me then when they found old Silas Beer. Silas was a tramp who lived in some woods on the edge of town. He had a little camp there with a shack he had built himself. He frequented the pubs in town, and in summer we would often see him in the town square or the park. He never caused any trouble, even though he liked his drink. In fact, the village children were fond of him. He would tell them jokes, give them sweets and chat with them. There was nothing sinister about Silas; he just wanted company. The kids thought he looked like a rather scruffy Father Christmas with his tatty white beard. Another thing about Silas is that he never begged. He did odd jobs around the town like painting fences and mending things. Silas was a great handyman, and could fix just about anything. He would lend a hand on farms at harvest time as well. He scraped together just about enough money to get by and have his beer. We thought his name was quite appropriate considering how much he drunk, but then again Beer is a common family name in the West Country. There must have been a dozen families called Beer in Ashburton.

I had been walking to school through town with a group of my friends one morning when we saw a crowd of people near King's Bridge. We went running down to see what had happened. *"What's going on?"* I asked.

"Someone's drowned in the river," a man answered. *"A man saw the body on his way to work. The coppers have just pulled him out."*

Sergeant Pomroy was there with PC Tuttle. They had a stretcher covered with a damp blanket between them. As they manhandled it up the slope, PC Tuttle slipped and the body flopped out from beneath its cover. It was old Silas, wet and pale as a ghost. There was a ragged gash in the side of his neck. Sergeant Pomroy swore at Tuttle. *"Jesus, what's happened to his throat?"* one of the crowd gasped.

"Must have been a big eel had a go at it," said Pomroy. *"We all know what a drunk he was. He must have had one too many at the Exeter Inn and fell off the bridge. Then an eel's started to eat him."*

The weird thing about it was that there was no blood on the wound. *"Where's all the blood gone?"* I shouted.

"It's ran off into the river ain't it?" snapped the sergeant. *"And what kind of question is that for a kid to be asking anyhow? Now clear off, we need to get this body out of here. It's not a sight for kids."*

They bundled the poor old man back onto the stretcher and my friends and I walked on to school. We couldn't believe it. I'd only been talking to Silas a few days ago. He had been clearing out some weeds from my aunt's garden. He sat drinking tea with me.

It's the River Yeo that runs through Ashburton. It's usually quite slow and fairly shallow but when it's in spate it can be dangerous. There is an old Devon saying that the Yeo must take at least one victim every year. The weather had been good though. It was early summer and there had been no rain.

At school the playground was buzzing with the news. All the kids thought they knew just what had happened, old Silas had been killed by Cutty Dyer. Cutty Dyer was a local legend, a sort of water spirit or river monster. The story went that he lurked in the Yeo and drowned his victims before drinking their blood.

No one could agree on what Cutty Dyer looked like. Some said he had green skin and was covered with waterweed. Others said he had horns and a long green beard. All the accounts said he had long, sharp teeth.

"It 'ad to be Cutty Dyer, we all saw that bite in his neck," said Sally Brewster.

"Yes, it didn't have any blood in it!" piped up Tony Danks.

"That's cos Cutty drank it all," Sally answered.

"I bet it was 'im that got that kid last year," added Brenda Collins.

The year before a boy in a class two years below me disappeared down by the river. They never found his body. The children of Ashburton blamed it on the river monster. *"Someone ought to deal with that monster. Then us kids could play on the river and never have to worry,"* said Simon Rodgers.

"Yes," I said, nodding my head slowly. *"Yes, they should."* And it was then that the germ of that fateful idea began to take form in my head.

That night I was lying awake in bed. I couldn't sleep. It was a hot night and I had my window and bedroom door open. I could hear my parents and grandparents talking downstairs. I caught snatches of their conversation. *"I saw it years ago when I was a boy and my bloody hair stood on end."* It was my Granddad's voice.

Then I heard my Dad say, *"What's made it leave its territory?"*

"I don't know but I hope it goes back upriver or wherever it comes from." That was my Mum's voice. *"Just thinking that it might be watching us from the water even now, ugggh, it makes me shudder."*

"A person a year, the old saying goes." That was my Gran. *"That's what they say. Well, maybe the river's appetite's got bigger."*

It sounded as if they were talking about something dangerous, something that scared them. It sounded like they were talking about Cutty Dyer. I don't think they would have said anything if they knew I was awake and listening.

After school the next day, a group of friends and I got together and I told them of the idea I had been mulling over for the last 24 hours. *"We build our own raft and go off down the Yeo on it looking for Cutty Dyer."* The other kids were silent.

"We could do it. We could get a gun and a net. Knives and other stuff and tie 'em to broom handles. We could make harpoons." A murmur ran through the boys and girls who had assembled at our traditional meeting place on the edge of town.

"I have a pen knife," said Archie Baker.

"That won't do," Brenda cut in. *"You'll need something longer than a pen knife."*

"My Dad's got a shot gun. I could try to nick it for a bit when he's at work." It was Colin Haley. He was a good friend of mine from school and always up for anything adventurous. I remembered that a couple of years before he had almost got us lost down an old tin mine on the moor.

Most of the kids let out an awed gasp.

"Not everyone can get a gun," said Sally Brewster wiping her specs.

Another lad, Tony Danks, put in his four-pennorth. *"No, but we could get garden forks to use like tridents and spades to use like axes. We could cut him to bits."*

"You're all nuts!" It was Alan Baker, he was two or three years older than most of us and he had only tagged along because his mum had asked him to keep an eye on his little brother. *"There's no such thing as Cutty Dyer. No more than there is Father Christmas. He's just a monster made up by adults to stop kids going too near the water. Good thing too, I say."*

"There is a Cutty Dyer! Who do you think killed poor old Silas?" snapped Tony.

"Himself, you idiot. He got pissed up and fell off the bridge."

"Then what ripped his neck open and drank his blood if it weren't Cutty Dyer?"

"An eel, didn't you hear what the Sergeant said? An eel started to eat him after he died. Eels eat meat and that's all you are after you're dead: meat. Come on, Alfie, we're going."

Alan grabbed his little brother and pulled him away.

"So are we going to do this or what? Alan's a coward, that's why he doesn't want to come. Who wants to come with me and hunt Cutty Dyer?"

The others all nodded and there was a round of "yes". I think some of them were afraid but they were more scared of what their friends would think if they said no. *"What we need first is a raft. We need to get as much wood as we can, planks, pallets, old doors and stuff to help it float."*

Over the next couple of weeks we dragged together begged, borrowed and stolen wood. I'm not sure what the other kids told people but I told my Mum and Dad that we were making a camp in the woods. None of us knew a damn thing about making rafts. I got a book from the library and tried to follow the pictures as closely as I could. We lashed together doors and pallets. We tied an old, empty oil drum at each corner. We purloined them from the garage. No one seemed to notice, or if they did, they didn't mind. We named our raft *The Otter* and toasted her in ginger beer.

Most of us had got some kind of weapon or at least something that could be doubled up as a weapon. I had a garden spade that I could swing like a battle axe. Sally had got a long garden knife that she had bound to a broom handle with string and wax. Simon had got his dad's old rusty hatchet and sharpened it up on the quiet. Brenda had a garden fork she was waving about like a pitchfork. Tony Danks had a bow and arrows he had borrowed from his cousin. But Colin, oh Colin, he had stolen his father's shotgun along with a pocketful of cartridges. He had slunk it out of the shed when his dad was down the pub and carried it out in a rucksack. He told us he knew how to use it because his dad had taken him clay pigeon shooting.

Looking back then it all seemed so innocent. But those were different times back then. Kids often carried knives, but no one got hurt by one, not like today. It also seemed innocent that we thought we could just drift down river, find the monster and kill it. We had even brought packed lunches as if we were on a picnic or a school outing. How I wish to God I had never come up with that idea.

We waded out carrying the raft and dropped it in the water. It seemed surprisingly sturdy. The hardest part was actually getting onto *The Otter*. Some of us had to hold it steady whilst the others climbed on, then they dragged us onto the raft. We had long sticks to punt with, like gondoliers. We manoeuvred the raft out unsteadily into the middle of the Yeo and let the current take us. The children with the improvised poles looked out for rocks, logs, sandbanks and the like. The water in the centre of the river was quite deep and raft moved along at a steady pace. It bobbed and lurched occasionally when caught in an eddy but we all kept our balance.

So there we were: a handful of children with improvised weapons on a home-made raft. We were floating downriver to hunt... *what*? None of us even knew what Cutty Dyer was. It was a lovely summer's day and I recall the light reflecting off the waters of the Yeo like molten gold.

The sluggish river wound its lazy way through the countryside. As the time passed, I think some of us even forgot what we were supposed to be doing, until we got to a certain bend in the river.

There was a sharp bend, after which the river got broader and slower. The section seemed clogged with masses of waterweed. Great patches of hundreds of lily pads and masses of floating duckweed made the surface of the Yeo look almost like solid ground. Strands of waterweed tangled the poles and the raft slowed down as it began to push its way through the lily pads.

We hit something with a jolt and most of us fell down. It was pure luck that none of us tumbled overboard. *"What happened?"* shouted Sally.

"I think we must have hit a rock or a tree stump. We can't see them because of the weed," I said.

No one was hurt and we all got back to our feet. Tony and Colin began prodding the water with their poles, trying to find the obstruction. They poked at nothing but water and weeds. The raft began to move again. *"Whatever it was, we're free of it now. It must have been roots or something under the surface."* Colin began punting once more.

"What's that up ahead? An island?" asked Brenda. Something protruded from the water. It looked like a small, light-coloured sandbank, perhaps six feet long. As we slowed, the 'sandbank' suddenly sunk in a swirl of green water.

"Did you see that?" Simon shouted. *"It dived under the water."*

It dawned on us that what we had seen was not a sandbank at all but the back of large creature. Looking back now it reminded me of films I have seen of hippos diving.

We all stood gawping as the trail of bubbles came towards the raft. And then the thing hit.

The raft was lifted bodily out of the water, sending us reeling across it. Three of our number were pitched into the Yeo's slothful current. They arose spluttering and spitting out river water. I noticed that the water around us had an oily film on it.

About ten yards from the raft something heaved itself from the water. It looked as large as a haystack, and was swathed in weed that gradually flopped back into the river as the thing began to move towards us. We screamed, both girls and boys, as the tumbling weed revealed the thing beneath.

None of the children's stories or rhymes or the legends and folktales ever did the awful thing justice in its sheer repellence. It was a pallid, greasy, hairless hulk whose form vaguely recalled that of a man. A flabby body the size of a cow. Fat arms with sausage like fingers ending in filthy hooked claws. We never did see the legs or lower half of the creature. The round head sat upon the body without benefit of any visible neck. The head, though as large as a pumpkin, seemed small on the titanic, corpulent, body. It had tiny, black eyes. I recall thinking that they looked like raisins in dough. The nose was broad and flat, the ears tiny. The creature's lipless mouth was so wide it seemed to bisect the head. It had no elongate fangs like the Hollywood vampire, but row upon row of small triangular teeth like a shark. A purplish tongue lolled from the mouth, in the manner of a panting dog, like a fat worm. It looked like some monstrous out-sized, deformed baby. And God how it stank, like an open grave full of shit and fishguts. This thing was Cutty Dyer.

It paused for a moment making a gurgling sound. Then with a high-pitched shriek, it lunged at us. Some panicked and jumped back into the river. Colin raised his dad's gun and gave it both barrels. The shot slapped into the rolls of ivory fat. Where the skin broke a clear liquid oozed out. The gun had no effect. Cutty Dyer did not even register the hit.

Moving faster than such a bulky thing had any right to, it was upon us in seconds. Before we could think it had snatched up the gun and twisted it as if it was a piece of wire. It tossed the mangled weapon aside and snatched up Colin in its flabby claws. It hoisted him aloft and seemed to stare into his eyes for second. A large wet patch formed on his trousers as his bladder gave way in terror. Then the wide, toothy maw was clamped to his neck with a vile sucking sound. The elongate wormy tongue seemed to writhe and probe with a life of its own.

I lifted the spade I was holding and swung it down violently with a primal, terror driven scream. The metal thudded into the white blubber and bounced back so violently that the spade almost struck me. Without detaching its mouth from Colin's neck or even looking my way, the monster swatted the spade from my grasp with an open-handed slap that sent it sailing across the river.

Colin's body was as limp as a rag doll by now. The colour had drained from him leaving his skin as pale as snow. By contrast Cutty's flesh was gaining colour and was now a light pink in hue from the blood it had drained from the boy.

Sally was suddenly at my side thrusting her home-made spear at the horror. The rubbery meat of the creature would not yield. It dropped Colin and shattered the spear with a casual swipe of one of its claws. Then Sally too had been scooped up to the greedy mouth and wriggling tongue. The colour of the monster's skin was growing more flushed as it gulped down more blood. It seemed as if the whole body was a sack, a massive, translucent stomach for storing and digesting blood.

I leapt off the raft and swam for the shore, adrenalin lending me speed. I heard it drop Sally's empty body and the splash of water as it turned and dove to pursue me and the others. I kicked and flailed madly expecting to feel the slime coated claws rip into my back at any moment.

Suddenly I felt the river bed at my feet and staggered up the bank. I chanced a look over my shoulder. There was nothing there. Cutty Dyer had dived back into the green, weedy deeps and vanished. I collapsed on the grass and passed out.

The next thing I recall was waking up in hospital. Apart from shock and swallowing water there was little wrong with me. The police asked me a number of questions. I told the story as it happened. I expected them to get cross and shout at me, call me a liar but they didn't. They just took notes and frowned. They told me not to speak to anyone else about what had happened and then went away again. Colin's body was never recovered. His family buried an empty coffin. They found poor Sally a few miles down stream. The coroner said she had drowned and her body was partially eaten by fish, possibly eels.

The whole event was written up in the papers as a tragic accident stemming from the foolish behaviour of children. It was used as an example of why children should never play near the river.

My family moved away from Ashburton later that year. I have never been back but I hear that the River Yeo still claims at least one victim every year.

HOUNDED

N o Milk Today' by *Herman's Hermits* was playing loud on the jukebox. It rang out into the street as Dawn Boswell left the youth club on Pike Road. She wouldn't let those pair of bastards see her cry. She had more dignity than that. She slammed the youth club door behind her and marched off down the road.

How could he? she thought. With that slut Tina Greaves, everyone knew she would drop her knickers for any boy who asked. She was 13 the first time with that boy from the fair that had stopped in Pickering the year before last.

"You can fuck yourself, Terry Jackson," she yelled out loud, the tears stinging in her eyes.

More like 'Terry CACKson', she thought, and that cheered her up a little but she was still angry. He was supposed to be her boyfriend. They had been seeing each other for six months now, sneaking out to kiss and cuddle in barns and under trees, dancing together at the Pickering Youth Club. Then she finds him kissing Tina Greaves round the back of the youth club, his hands were down her knickers. I hope he gets crabs, she thought.

Not only had this ruined her relationship with Terry, it had also ruined what very little social life she had. There was not much for a fifteen-year-old girl out here in the backside of nowhere. She lived in the hamlet of Riseborough Hagg and she thought that it was as bad as it sounded. There was no shops, no pub, nothing save for a handful of houses and farms.

The youth club had been a blessing. It was run most evenings by Mr. Bradshaw, the music teacher from school. He was a nice guy, young, friendly, into pop music, not like most of the teachers. Mr. Bradshaw, or Phil as he insisted the kids call him, and now she had that taken from her. She couldn't go back to the club, not with Tina and Terry together. God, she would be glad when she was old enough to get out of this hole and start living, start to see the world outside of this insular, dull little backwater. Dawn marched off into the night. She was so angry that she wasn't really looking where she was going. She walked and walked, swiftly leaving the orange glow of the streetlights behind her.

It must have been a good ten minutes later that she realised she had been walking the wrong

---

way. Instead of following the High Street she had wandered away from the town and along Marton Lane. The narrow, unlit road would lead her back to Riseborough Hagg but it would be a walk of four miles. Dawn shook her head. She didn't mind, she needed a walk, it would do her good. It was early October and still quite mild.

She wandered onwards unworried. Marton Lane was a pretty straight road. At the end, just before it branched off into Gallows Lane she would turn left, another half a mile after that and she would be home.

A breeze stirred the grasses in the fields making them ripple like water. It rolled the clouds across the sky sending a moon shadow sweeping the land. Somewhere a tawny owl hooted, declaring its territory or attracting a mate. Out here, away from the town and all its noises, it seemed that her hearing had become unnaturally acute. In the hedgerow some small animal scurried. She wondered if it would make it 'til the morning alive. Dawn pulled her cardigan on and carried on down Marton Lane.

As she walked on a new sound seemed to rise above the other small noises of the night. Unlike the others it sounded hard, unnatural, metallic. She paused again and the sound became more acute though it still seemed a long way off. What was it? It sounded almost like chains. Yes that was it, chains being dragged along the rough, pot holed tarmac of the lane. She chided herself as the childish image of a bed sheet ghost rattling its chains popped into her mind. She turned and looked back along the moonlit lane. She could see nothing to account for the sound.

You're being an idiot, she told herself. It's just the wind blowing through old farm machinery or rusty gates. The sound, whatever it had been had now ceased and the clouds rolled over the moon again. Dawn turned back and walked on. At least the odd little event had taken her mind off Terry and that slapper Tina for a bit.

She had walked no more than a couple of hundred yards further up the lane when an acute feeling of dread sprang up in her from nowhere. It began in her stomach where it wriggled about like a living thing then crawled up into her chest where her heart began to race. Finally it scurried up her back with thin, icy legs. There was a palpable feeling of being watched, watched by something hostile. The thought 'some*thing*' stuck in her mind. She had never felt like this before. It took all her self-control to turn around and look back along the lane. Nothing. There was nothing there except darkness and silence. Dawn shook her head and carried on, though she was aware she had picked up her pace a little.

She had gone but a little further when the wind once more unwrapped the moon from its wrapping of clouds. Though she knew she shouldn't, Dawn glanced behind her again. The lane was empty but then a blob of darkness seemed to pull itself from the shadows of the hedgerow like a blob of ink in water. Whatever it was stood in the middle of the lane and Dawn had the feeling that it was looking at her. Was it a trick of the light or did she see two dots of red light in the dark mass? Red lights like two eyes shining in the darkness.

It began to move slowly up the lane towards her. It was some kind of animal. It must be a dog from one of the farms. Some of the guard dogs could be aggressive to trespassers. She knew that running was a bad idea, it might trigger an attack. She began to walk calmly away. She was in the lane and not on private land and reasoned that the dog wouldn't consider her a threat. It had probably just strayed too far from its home. It would go back soon and if it followed her home she would just get her dad to 'phone round the neighbours to see if anyone had lost it.

She walked on, straining to stay calm. She heard the noise again, the sound like dragging chains. She thought that the dog must have been chained up somewhere on a farm and had pulled free taking its chain with it. She looked back once more. The clouds had hidden the shape in the lane but deep in the dark she could see the two red dots that bobbed up and down as the animal moved. Red eyes that glittered like distant embers. What would make a dog's eyes shine like that? The eyes seemed closer than they had before meaning that whatever was behind them had drawn closer too.

Maybe if it was lost she could help it, take it home or something. After all it hadn't barked or even growled.

"Here boy, good doggie." Dawn bent down and called along the lane. The animal was moving slowly closer, never breaking into a run but not stopping either. As it came closer the shape resolved itself into a dark, canine form. It seemed at first to be a big farm dog but then it drew level with a gate post. The creature stood as tall as the gate post. No dog was that big, not even a Great Dane. That sound came again the dragging clanking noise like chains. The thing seemed to be looking at her with those eyes like liquid fire.

A memory came to Dawn, of her grandfather and a story he had told her as a child.

"Me an' Edward Riley saw him one night back in 1920. We were walkin' down Gallows Lane when he leaped over the hedge in front of us. He just stood there glowering at us with them big red eyes like burnin' coals. Big as a donkey he was and black as sin. It was the Barghest, the black dog, the hound of hell. We ran home like beggary, and all the ways back we could here this noise like chains clankin'. A week later Eddy was killed when he fell under a plough. They say the Barghest is a harbinger of death. He only appears when someone is going to die. I never saw him again and I thank God above for that. I was only 25 at the time but afterwards me hair had turned white as a swan."

Dawn thought it had just been a scary story to stop her wandering off to far as a child. Now she realised that her grandfather had been telling the truth. The dog just stood and gazed. Its eyes seemed to flicker like embers. The most primal instinct, self-preservation, released a mass of adrenaline into her system. She flung herself over the tall hedge in one bound. She would never have believed that she was capable of such a leap.

She landed with a crash in the corn, rolled and stood up running. The corn was at its tallest, just before harvest. It was almost as tall as her. She ran blindly into the field smashing a path through the waving stems as she went. The fear was an ally; it covered the pain in her lungs and the stabbing of the stitch in her belly brought on by the exertion. She almost tripped twice but carried on running, never looking back. She expected to feel the dog's jaws ripping into her calves at any moment.

Suddenly Dawn exploded from the forest of corn. She couldn't stop herself and her momentum took her flying out onto the road. There was a screech of brakes and a blinding light. She instinctively fell and rolled into a ball with the smell of burning rubber in her nostrils.

She heard a car door open and slam shut.

"You idiot, I nearly killed you!"

Dawn uncurled and through her dizziness saw a figure approaching, backlit by the car's headlights.

"Dawn?"

She recognised the voice but in her state it took her a moment to remember who it was.

"Mr. B- Bradshaw?"

"Thank God I found you. One of the other kids said they had seen you run off crying. I didn't want you walking home in that state in the dark; anything could have happened."

She stood up on shaky legs like a new born foal and looked round nervously.

"Mr. Bradshaw..."

"Call me Phil."

"Phil, we have to get into your car, quickly, now!"

"OK, OK, calm down, I'll take you home."

Dawn scrambled madly into to Phil's Volkswagen Beetle and slammed the door. She was still scanning the countryside. He saw she was shaking wildly.

"Looks like I gave you quite a shock. What where you doing in a field of corn anyhow? I'm sure the farmer won't be best pleased."

"Lock the doors, please."

"It's OK we're..."

"Just lock the doors, it still might be around."

"What might be still around?"

Dawn looked at her feet. *"You'll think I'm mad if I tell you."*

He put his hand on her shoulder. *"No I won't, I can see something's really scared you."*

She looked up realising that she was crying for the second time that night.

"The Barghest, I saw the Barghest."

"Dawn, that's just a story, a legend from centuries ago."

Dawn felt the fear give way a little to anger. *"There, I told you. I told you that you would think I was mad!"*

"I didn't say I thought you were mad."

"Look I saw it; I saw it along Marton Lane. I was so upset by what happened tonight that I walked the wrong way so I ended up walking along Marton Lane. Then I heard something following me, a noise like dragging chains. It got closer and then I saw this black dog. It was huge, Phil, huge like a donkey! I jumped over a hedge and ran across the field. I was scared it was coming after me."

Phil shook his head. *"Look, I know what happened with that little twit Terry at the youth club. You were upset, it's only natural. Your emotions were running high. What you saw was probably a big farm dog. I know Mr. Bainbridge from Primrose Farm has got a big black Labrador-Alsatian cross called Prince. He'd scare the pants off anyone if you saw him down a dark alley at night. Soft as a brush though."*

"But the noise, like dragging chains. I heard it."

"And that's exactly what it was. The dog was probably dragging his leash behind him and you heard it rattle. He's just gone for 'walkies' without his owner."

"But its eyes were glowing red."

"They were just reflecting the moonlight, that's all."

"It was massive, as tall as a gatepost."

"Everything looks bigger at night."

Dawn had calmed down a little and her breathing had slowed to a normal pace. Here in the car she felt safe. Suddenly she felt silly as well. Of course Phil was right. It had just been a big farm dog dragging its chain. She had acted like a kid. Her face flushed with embarrassment.

Phil leaned over and opened the glove compartment. He took out a torch.

"I'll have a little look round if it will make you feel any better."

She nodded and he opened the door and got out. He strode confidently across to the field of corn and switched the torch on. Its yellow beam swept the waving ears several times, reaching as far as the hedge Dawn had jumped over at the far side. He could see the path of flattened corn where she had ran. There was only one path, nothing had followed her. He returned to the car.

"There's nothing out there. The dog's probably gone back to whatever farm he came from for a bit of supper. I saw where you ran through the corn, you left quite a track. But it was the only one. There was nothing following you through the field."

"You must think I'm stupid, Phil." She hung her head.

"Of course I don't think you're stupid. I remember when I was your age I was walking back from a friend's house one night when I thought I saw a ghost. A great, white, shapeless thing it was. Seven feet tall if it was an inch. I ran all the way home and hid under my bed! Next morning I went back to look again in the daylight. I found out that my 'ghost' was nothing but a sheet that had been blown off someone's washing line and had got tangled in a tree. There is always a rational explanation for what people call the 'paranormal'."

"Can you drive me home?" she asked.

"Of course I can. You were lucky you didn't twist an ankle running across the field in the dark like that."

He turned the ignition on and started the beetle. The car moved off into the night. As they drove on Dawn noticed that they had passed by the turning to Riseborough Hagg.

"Phil, we've missed my turning."

He smiled. *"There's no need to go back home right away. You've had a nasty scare and you need to calm down a bit. You don't want your mum and dad to see you shaking like a leaf, do you?"*

"No, I suppose you're right."

"It's a lovely night and I thought we could go for a little drive till your nerves settle."

She smiled. *"Thanks, you're so kind."*

"If you open up the glove compartment you will see something that might help you feel better."

She opened the compartment up and felt around. Next to the torch and some driving gloves her hand fell on a bottle. She took it out. *"Whisky?"*

"Nothing better for calming the nerves. That's why Saint Bernard dogs used to have little barrels around their neck when they went out looking for avalanche victims. Go on, try a nip."

She gulped back a mouthful then gasped. It tasted bad but there was a warm afterglow.

"See what I mean?"

She nodded. *"I didn't think a teacher would encourage under-age drinking."*

"It's purely medicinal, besides I'm sure you're mature enough to handle it. Have another swig."

Dawn took a second gulp, larger than the first. The whisky warmed her stomach and she had stopped shaking. The incident with the dog in the lane seemed so distant now as to be almost unreal.

"Did you mean what you said about me being mature?"

"Sure I do, you're far more grown up than the other kids at the club. You're not really a kid anymore, you're a young lady."

She smiled; no one had ever called her 'grown up' before. She took another swig from the bottle. *"It sort of grows on you this stuff."*

"That's what I mean. The others would have just taken one taste then said they hated it. You gave the drink a chance."

He pulled over into a lay-by.

"I know about what happened with Terry tonight. I wouldn't waste any tears on him if I were you. He's not worthy of you. He acts like a child because that's what he is. As I said before, you're not a kid, you're a young lady. You don't need a boy in your life you need a man."

"How do you mean?" Her head felt a little fuzzy.

"You're a woman now, Dawn, with a woman's needs that only a mature man can satisfy."

"I still don't understand."

"Then let me show you." He lent over and kissed her full on the mouth.

Dawn pulled away. *"You're my teacher!"*

"Does that really matter? I've been watching you develop for a while now, you can't deny it, there's something between us."

"Yes there is, twenty-odd years!" Suddenly her head was clear. She knew with alarming clarity why Mr. Bradshaw had brought her out here. The feeling was more horrible than when she had seen the dog. She felt his hand groping at her leg beneath her skirt.

"This is wrong!" she yelled and pulled away, fumbling with the door handle. Twisting sideways she jumped from the car before he could grab her.

"Don't be silly, Dawn; we could have something special here."

She backed away as he left the car and walked forwards slowly, hands held out in front of him.

"I'm not going to hurt you, Dawn."

"Like hell you're not!"

Suddenly he was running at her. She tried to run as well, but his long legs caught up with her in a few strides. They fell over together on the ground. Dawn felt him on top of her. She felt his beard in her face and his hard crotch thrusting against hers as his rough hands pinned her arms down.

"Relax, you'll enjoy this. You'll thank me later."

Behind them the headlights of the Beetle came on. The car's wireless sprang into life with the sharp hissing of static between stations. Bradshaw paused and turned his head for a moment. Dawn struggled violently again.

"Lie still," he snapped. *"I don't want to hurt you. I'm not a brute."* He lent forwards again and began to kiss her neck. As she turned her head in disgust her eyes focused on something over his shoulder. Something moved around the side of the car, something so big that its head was clearly visible over the bonnet. There was a sound, like dragging chains.

She screamed wildly.

"I said be quiet, damn it!" It looked as if he was going to strike her but then he realised her eyes were focused on something behind him. He slowly turned round.

Padding slowly towards him was the Barghest. Phil rolled off Dawn and stared at the great dog in mute horror. It was the size of a small bear. Its pitch black, shaggy hair seemed to stand on end as if it was electrically charged. The beast seemed to be all predatory muscle. As it moved, the sinews in its legs and haunches bulged beneath the hairy coat. Its sloping back gave the Barghest an almost hyena-like outline. The ears were wolfishly pricked and its upper lips twisted back to show sharp white teeth flecked with foam and drool. Where it fell to the ground it sizzled. The eyes were the worst thing. Burning ruby orbs that flickered and danced.

It made no snarls or barks but was accompanied by the sound of dragging chains, despite the fact that no chains were apparent upon it. Another noise mingled with the metallic rattling. An electrical crackle like that of a Van Der Graaf generator. The very air around the monster seemed charged like the air before a storm.

Bradshaw was back pedalling on all fours whilst babbling like a child. The Barghest plodded on unhurriedly. It paused momentarily beside Dawn and swung its great head round and looked at her from a couple of feet away. The red eyes regarded her unreadably but the black, ragged lips seemed to twist into a nasty smile.

Then it moved on towards the prone teacher. He somehow managed to stagger to his feet and continued to back away as the beast almost lazily approached. It suddenly broke into a loping run. Within an eye blink it was on him. Paws the size of boxing gloves rested on his shoulders as the slobbering jaws clamped about his neck. Man and dog fell backwards and the hound continued to worry his face and throat. If he screamed at all, the hound's maw muffled the noise.

She didn't look back. She walked away not ran. She knew the Barghest hadn't come for her. She didn't tell her parents what had happened that night. Indeed she never did tell anyone about what occurred that night.

A newspaper article some days later told how the popular teacher and youth group leader Philip Bradshaw had been found dead near his car in a remote lay-by. He had apparently been killed by a massive electric shock. It was theorised that he received the shock whilst fiddling with the car as it too had suffered electrical damage. No one could quite explain why his body was so far from the vehicle, though.

OLD BONELESS

Well I suppose it's better than the last place. A council flat, I ask you, could anywhere be less spooky?"

"We wanted to go for a gritty, realist feel, you know, down to earth. Not every programme can be set in some stately home or castle."

"But that family, Yvonne, they were just ghastly. At least no one lives here."

Darren Asquith patted his bouffant hairdo and gazed into the mirror, apparently satisfied with the job the make-up girl had done. Though how long it would last whilst he was gallivanting round a dusty old mansion was debatable. Waving the make-up girl away he swivelled round in his chair to face the executive producer, Yvonne Meadows.

"Yvonne, Manifold Manifestations *is a TV success story. It's bringing down an audience of millions. Don't you think the likes of me and you should be benefiting more?"*

Yvonne sighed internally. Darren was in one of his 'difficult' moods. The filming session had not gone well at all.

"You get paid well, don't you?"

"Sometimes I wonder, love. It's not so much the ghosts that bother me, it's the people."

"Well, the ghosts wouldn't bother you. We've never found any."

"The public don't know that," he smirked.

Darren Asquith had made a career out of 'speaking to the dead'. After a stint in drama school he had discovered his true talent. He was psychic. Or rather he found out how gullible the general public was. A bit of background research, putting on a funny voice in a darkened room… money for old rope. He had started with séances and progressed to stage performances. Yvonne had seen him in the summer season at Blackpool and offered him the part of *Manifold*

Manifestations' resident psychic. That had been ten years ago now. He had become a major TV personality.

"Then don't rock the boat. This nonsense is a great gravy train for all of us. Just you keep those spirit possessions coming. Have you read the background notes on this place?" she motioned to the folder on the desk beside him.

He picked it up and leafed through it.

"Oh yes, Smedly Hall, fairly interesting story. I think I might just pick up one of the workers who died in the tunnels or even Sir Marcus Smedly himself."

Yvonne beamed.

"Good to hear it. The viewers will be expecting something dramatic after the last episode's wash out. We need more than a few bumps in the dark this time."

"Oh, don't worry you'll get that." He stood up and screwed his face into a mask of pain whilst holding his fingers to his temples.

"Ohhhhh, the dark. The dark, it's so heavy, so cold. The weight in the dark, it's crushing me. My wife, my children, who will provide for them?"

"OK, Laurence Olivier, don't over do it. Anyhow, the others should be about ready by now."

"I wonder if we'll see another of Harriet's performances? She's the biggest medium I've ever seen."

Yvonne stifled a giggle.

"Oh, Darren you are rotten at times."

"Did you see her try to produce ectoplasm back at Marsden Grotto? It was just spit and snot. At least I can act."

"Never mind, the others will probably be waiting now so shake a leg."

The two of them walked out of Darren's trailer and into the night.

The crew had already set up lights for night filming. Smedly Hall loomed darkly behind them. The small crowd included Alan the soundman, and Bob and Terry the cameramen. Resident sceptic Dr. Sam English and parapsychologist Carl O'Leary were standing next to several men Darren did not recognise. Carl seemed to be holding some Heath Robinson style device.

"What the hell has he got this week?" mumbled Darren under his breath. *"Looks like some-*

thing off Doctor Who. "

"You know Carl and his gadgets, I'm sure he will explain."

Yvonne approached the group smiling and addressed the three strangers.

"Hi guys, thanks for coming. This is Darren Asquith, our psychic, I'm sure you'll recognise him from the show.

There was a round of 'hellos' and Darren gave his best smile, shaking hands with each of the men as Yvonne introduced them.

"This is Mr. Pickering," she said, indicating a bespectacled, balding man. *"He's the caretaker and historian here. He'll be making sure we're safe down in the tunnels as well."*

"Oh I'm glad to hear that. I get on well with ghosts but I don't want to be one just yet!"

They all laughed, Darren already had them eating out of his hand.

"These gentlemen are Mr. Cornell and Mr. Brandon. They are both witnesses."

"Oh wonderful," Darren beamed, *"I can't wait to hear your stories."*

"Good evening, dear hearts, sorry I'm late." A high, shrill voice pierced the air.

Out of the dark, a fat, middle-aged woman in a voluminous dress came swanning in. Her bell-shaped gown reached the ground hiding her chubby legs and gave the impression that she glided along rather than walked.

"I'd rather be a tad late and look good than be on time and in a two and eight," she giggled, her painted face cracking into a toothy smile.

"Harriet de Lange," she said, proffering a meaty hand, whose sausage-like fingers were adorned with large garish rings and purple nail varnish, to the newcomers.

"Harriet is our physical medium," explained Yvonne.

The historian and the witnesses gave blank looks that prompted Harriet to give more detail.

"My body is a conduit between two worlds."

"More like the Watford Gap," said Darren under his breath. Yvonne stifled a giggle and kicked his shin.

"I produce ectoplasm," Harriet continued, *"a substance from the ethereal world that allows*

spirits to take form on our plane."

The three listeners seemed none the wiser.

"OK guys, let's make a start," piped up Yvonne. *"Darren, if you could stand alone and give us your first impressions; a cold reading as usual?"*

Alan fitted a mike to Darren's lapel.

Darren walked away from the main group and stood alone and backlit. As the cameraman shouted "speed" he began his monologue.

"I sense a great weight here. I don't mean in a spiritual way but in a physical way like ton upon ton of cold hard rock crushing down on me."

He creased his brow and brought one hand up to his forehead dramatically as he paced up and down.

"The feeling is not coming from the house itself but from beneath it. It feels like there is some-thing trapped deep in the earth below the house."

He turned and looked directly into the camera.

"Something is calling for help and reaching out to me from underneath this very house!"

Perfect, thought Yvonne as she called "cut".

Next she interviewed Mr. Pickering who fidgeted as his mike was fitted.

"Mr. Pickering, you're the caretaker and historian for Smedly Hall, can you tell us a bit about its history?"

He adjusted his glasses and nervously cleared his throat.

"Well, what Darren has detected is quite interesting given the history of the area. Sir Robert Smedly of the British East India Company built the hall in the 1780s. Smedly had made his fortune importing spices from the East Indies and India. He died of malaria in Padang, West Sumatra, in 1808 leaving his wife Maria and son Marcus.

Marcus tried to carry on the family business but the trips abroad took their toll on him. He disagreed with the hot, humid climate and after several trips to the tropics he decided to put his family's money into a new venture, coal mining.

The North Somerset Coalfield had been in use for a number of years when Marcus Smedly opened the Puxton Colliery in 1830. Marcus always seemed to have an affinity with the earth.

His mother's diaries tell us that as a boy he was forever digging holes in the grounds of Smedly Hall, much to the consternation of the ground staff.

As a man he was known as a kind and generous employer who was well liked by his workers. The Puxton Colliery was a success until the cave-in of 1848, a disaster that took the lives of 53 miners. Marcus closed down the mine and refused to let any repair work be done on it for fear of more people losing their lives.

Marcus took the disaster very badly and blamed himself. He gave away a lot of his fortune to the families of those who had died. For a while he became a recluse. During this period he began his own excavations in the cellars beneath the hall. Finally, he began to employ local people, including some of those who once worked in his mine. As the years passed, the excavations became a network of tunnels. Marcus seemed to be obsessed with digging. Some said he was searching for buried treasure, some said he was trying to dig down to hell itself.

Marcus used up his entire fortune digging those tunnels. His wife left him and finally in 1860 he was committed to the asylum at Taunton where he died just one year later. The tunnels undermined the whole structure of the hall making it unfit for habitation."

"Can you tell us something about the ghost that is supposed to haunt the area?"

"Ahh yes, Old Boneless, the locals call it. You see, soon after Marcus began his digging in the cellar of Smedly Hall people began to report seeing a strange, white entity in the grounds of the hall and along the road outside. It was dubbed Old Boneless on account of its shapelessness. Witnesses said it looked like a cloud or a great blob of white mist."

"Some said it was the ghosts of the dead miners combined into one mass, others that it was something that Marcus had accidently set free as he burrowed."

"That's an amazing story and now we are going to hear from some people who say they have actually seen Old Boneless with their own eyes."

Yvonne turned to the nearest man.

"Mr. Cornell, can you tell us what you saw?"

"Well Yvonne, it was my Granddad who saw Old Boneless first; this was back before the First World War. He was a bobby back then. He had a bike; there were no police cars then. His beat took him along Cowslip Lane that runs right past Smedly Hall. He always said that this stretch of road gave him the creeps. Anyhow, he was cycling along one evening when he sees this thing in the road in front of him. He said it was like a woolly sheep with no head and no legs, or a dense cloud. Then suddenly it slithered up and over him and his bike. He said it felt like a wet, heavy blanket being dragged across him and it had a terrible, stale smell. It carried on along the road leaving him lying there in shock."

"And when was it that you saw the ghost?"

"That was years later, about 1974. My girlfriend and myself were parked up in a lay-by about a mile or so from here. She won't mind me telling you as she's my wife now! It was a lovely, clear summer night, no clouds and a full moon, nearly as light as day. Well as you can imagine we were quite busy but then some noise disturbed us. Looking up we saw the cows in the field next to where we were parked had got very agitated. They were mooing like crazy and had all crowded up at the far end of the field.

Then we saw what had unsettled them so much. There was something crossing the field. It was about the same size as a cow but lower to the ground, sort of flattened. It was just a shapeless white blob. It seemed to move by stretching and contracting. It slid across the field and was lost from sight. As soon as it was gone the cows started to act normally again. We didn't lose any time in getting out of there I can tell you. We found other places to park up from then on."

"That's an amazing story, Mr. Cornell. Thanks for sharing it with us." Yvonne turned to the second man.

"Mr. Brandon, I believe you have seen the entity as well?"

The second witness smiled a little shyly, then began his narrative.

"It would have been around 1980 or 81. At the time I was working nights as a security guard on an industrial estate near West Hewish. It was a bit of a dull job as I spent most of my time looking at TV monitors that were rigged up to security cameras. Mostly we got foxes and badgers, once in a while kids mucking about or the odd vandal but nothing very exciting. Then this one night I recalled seeing this, well I can only call it this 'thing'. It came creeping around the side of one of the units. It reminded me of a mattress, white, flattish and sort of stretching out as it moved. There was a darker blotch in the centre of it. It was surprisingly fast. I suppose I had it on the monitors for no more than 30 seconds. It was picked up by several cameras as it crossed the estate from one side to the other. I was going to investigate but I thought better of it. Something told me I was better off staying inside.

One of the other guards said he had seen the same thing or another one like it about three years before whilst he was driving along Maysgreen Lane. He said it slithered across the road in front of his car and he had to brake to avoid hitting it.

I told my boss about it but he told me not to mention it to anyone. He seemed quite rattled by it. I know he took away the video tapes from that night which was strange as we usually re-used them, night after night."

"Thank you Mr. Brandon. Another strange story, let's see what our experts make of it."

The cameras swung around to the show's stars. Harriet was the first to speak.

"What these men are describing are clearly masses of ectoplasm, the spirit in question has been unable to shape the substance into a coherent form for some reason. Perhaps the ghost is in so much torment that it cannot hold its shape for any length of time."

"Rubbish," snorted Dr. English. *"Something like that can be explained by meteorological means. It sounds like some freak weather condition; an odd, low-lying mist or something. I think we have all seen clouds of mist that look like ghosts, its just simulacra."*

"Then why were the cows so scared by it?" asked Carl.

"They might have been frightened by something else that was totally unconnected to the shape the witness saw. Just a coincidence."

"Some coincidence, Sam."

"Well," Yvonne interrupted, *"shall we go inside and see what we can turn up?*

The group walked towards the crumbling mansion. Even by night they could see the state of disrepair the building was in. The windows were either broken or boarded up. The roof had collapsed in places and the walls cracked as if by subsidence. The whole place smelled of damp and decay. As Mr. Pickering unlocked the large double door with an impressive brass key, a flock of pigeons rose up from the broken upper windows and the holes in the roof.

"Jesus!" Darren jumped back in alarm.

"It's only pigeons, the place is full of them," smirked Mr. Pickering. *"Anyhow, I thought you weren't afraid of ghosts?"*

"Haven't English Heritage done anything about the place?" Darren answered, changing the subject.

"Well they have slapped a preservation order on it and that's about all. There's not much money about with all the cutbacks. It would cost millions to repair Smedly Hall and you would have to fork out millions more beforehand filling in the miles of tunnels underneath it."

They entered the dusty hall and Mr. Pickering handed out hard hats.

"Health and Safety I'm afraid. Amazed they even let you film here."

Darren and Harriet looked uncomfortably at the hard hats but said nothing.

"We want to concentrate on the tunnels," said Yvonne. *"The lighting technicians have run cables into some of them but they have left others in darkness so it will look suitably spooky."*

Mr. Pickering led them around the stairs, and through several more rooms and finally to another large oaken door that was stained with dampness. It was already open and beside it stood a small generator that the technicians had set up that afternoon. Cables snaked out of it and trailed off down a flight of steps. Yvonne was glad they were insulated as she could see pools of water on the cellar floor.

"This is the former wine cellar where Marcus began his excavations."

With cameras rolling, they descended into the dimly lit cellar, save for Carl who was busy at the generator. Several hand-hewn tunnels lead off from the main cellar. They were held up with supports of varying ages. None looked very safe.

A noise from the steps made them turn around. Carl was descending, holding his machine that he had now plugged into the generator. A long cable spooled out behind him, unwinding as he walked. He placed the strange device on a relatively dry area of the cellar floor. What looked like speakers and an outsized tuning fork rose up from a base that sported several knobs and dials.

"Well Carl, don't keep us in suspense any longer, exactly what does that weird thing do?"

Carl grinned, he liked nothing better than explaining his machines to Dr. English, who was the only one that really appreciated them.

"It's an infrasound machine. It produces sounds lower than 20 Hertz per cycle, lower than the human ear can detect."

"And what has that got to do with ghosts?" asked Darren

"Well, lots of animals, including elephants communicate in infrasound. There is a whole undiscovered world of noise that exists outside of the range of human hearing. I have a theory that low frequency sound waves can be used to attract and even communicate with the things people call 'ghosts' or 'spirits'."

Dr. English was quick to reply.

"There have been several experiments linking infrasound to supposed ghost sightings. Vic Tandy of Coventry University discovered that sound waves of 18.98 Hertz cause the human eyeball to vibrate causing illusions of grey blobs that the witness interprets as ghosts."

"I'm familiar with Vic Tandy's paper, 'Ghost in the Machine' and the work of Professor Richard Wiseman into the effects of sound at 17 Hertz. I'm using my machine to produce even lower sound waves. Besides I'm only using it here in this cellar, not in the tunnels below so you should be fine. Anyhow there was no infrasound when our witnesses saw whatever it was they saw."

Carl switched on his machine then fiddled with some of the knobs. A light came on but there was no sound. However, a subtle change seemed to creep over the cellar. Each person felt a slight pressure on their inner ear. It seemed to come and go, pulsing in a rhythm. The tuning fork-like device atop the machine vibrated noiselessly.

"Well, I'll stay here and see if anything turns up, and if it does I'll catch it on this." He held up a pocket camcorder.

The others turned and continued down the main tunnel.

"Where is the deepest part of the tunnel system, Mr. Pickering?" asked Harriet as she hoisted up the hem of her dress to keep it off the wet floor. *"I'd like to conduct my session where the caverns run at their lowest. That way I'm closer to the element of earth that seems to have trapped these poor spirits."*

"If we take a left off the main passage there is a tunnel that runs steeply down then meets with a natural fissure. It's unlit down there and there's nothing like a safety rail. It's quite dangerous."

"What do I care for danger when I can help trapped souls? Please lead us down."

They took the left-hand tunnel and followed its steep incline. Soon they were using torches to illuminate the pitch-black corridor. Finally, it levelled out over a wide crack that seemed to fall away into nothingness.

"No one knows how deep that is," mused Mr. Pickering. *"It's never been measured."*

He reached down and picked up a pebble.

"Listen."

He tossed it into the gully. There was no sound of it hitting the bottom.

"Christ, that's deep." Darren took a step back. *"Are you sure you want to stay here, Harriet?"*

"Of course, don't worry, dear boy, I'll be careful."

A little later, a stool had been placed in the cavern and Harriet's ample behind had buried it. Terry the cameraman had set up a small camera on a tripod. Harriet faced Terry and spoke as Bob adjusted the other camera that he erected on a tripod.

"As you know, I always work alone when I produce ectoplasm. Some spirits are shy, and besides, the production of the substance itself is a private act I must do unaccompanied. In case any of our viewers think I'm a fraud, we have an infrared camera being set up here to film me in the dark. It will soon detect any trickery."

"All done," said Bob, *"it's rolling now."*

Harriet turned and faced the camera as the others walked back up the tunnel leaving her in the dark.

"Remember, keep away from the edge, don't move when you're in the dark," Mr. Pickering *called back as they retreated.*

Back in the main tunnel they took another branch and Yvonne asked Darren to see if he could 'pick anything up'.

He ran his fingers along the damp walls and looked up into the mildewed cobwebs above him.

"They were scared when they died, those miners. Scared, but not for themselves. It was for their families. They were worried about who would provide for their wives and their little children. They were so grateful for what Marcus did, the way he made sure they were all looked after. But they can't move on. Something else is keeping them here, not in the old mine but here in the tunnels built by their employer."

He was giving a gala performance.

"What is it, Darren? What is keeping the souls of those dead miners trapped?"

"I don't know, they're scared to tell me. It's something to do with what drove poor Marcus insane. Oh, now it's fading. I think we will need to go further into the tunnels to maintain contact with them and find out what the mystery is?"

Yvonne stepped in front of the camera.

"Powerful stuff. Once again, Darren Asquith's remarkable psychic talents have revealed strange secrets. Will we be able to unravel the riddle of Smedly Hall and Old Boneless? Is it really the combined ghosts of all the dead miners still roaming the lanes of Somerset? Only time will tell."

She turned back to Mr. Pickering.

"Mr. Pickering, have you ever seen or felt anything odd in these tunnels or in the building above?"

"I've worked her nigh on thirty years, Yvonne, and I can honestly say I've never seen anything out of the ordinary. It's a little creepy down in these tunnels but that's only to be expected in the dark and damp."

One of the witnesses, Mr. Cornell piped up.

"If some money were spent on this place it could make quite the tourist attraction. There was a chap up in Liverpool, Joseph Williamson; they called him the 'mad mole'. He dug tunnels

like these. Employed hundreds of men and all for no apparent reason. Some of his tunnels have been cleaned up and the public can visit them. I've been up myself, there's a Heritage Centre and everything."

Mr. Pickering looked like he was about to answer when he was abruptly interrupted.

A long, whining scream echoed through the tunnels. It seemed to combine fear, revulsion and despair.

The crew and presenters looked at each other.

"Harriet!"

They ran back down the corridors falling over each other.

"I knew that didn't look safe," gasped Darren. *"She was sitting in the pitch black next to a bloody great hole. She's fallen over the edge, I know it."*

"Oh great, if she has that's the show finished and the company sued." Yvonne had turned noticeably paler.

"Nice you care so much about her," snapped Dr. English.

Mr. Pickering was shaking his head.

"I knew I shouldn't have said yes to this, I knew.*"*

They didn't stop running until they reached the steep incline that led down to the deepest part of the tunnels.

The torch beams shone down to show the stool on its side and the tripod and camera tipped over. Thankfully, Harriet seemed unharmed. She was standing in front of the fissure and seemed to be beckoning to them.

"Oh Harriet, thank God you're alright. We heard you screaming and thought you had fallen over the edge. What's wrong, love?"

Darren was picking his way down the rubble-strewn slope with the others close behind. As he drew closer he saw the strange lustre Harriet's skin seemed to have taken on. As the lights illuminated more of the cavern it became apparent that Harriet was coated in some translucent substance from head to foot. It seemed to be growing gradually thicker.

"Oh God, oh God! Yvonne do you see that? She's done it, she's actually done it. She's produced ectoplasm!"

Darren felt himself begin to shake. In all the years he had been claiming to be psychic never once had he seen anything remotely paranormal. Now, as it was unfurling before his eyes, he found it hard to take."

"I never thought... I never thought any of this was actually... could actually be..."

He caught himself in mid-sentence when he realised that the cameras were still running.

Harriet's hand seemed to be gesturing for them to come closer. As they did they realised that the apparent beckoning motion was a result of Harriet rocking back and forth on her heels as if something were tugging at her. The big woman's eyes rolled back in her head with a vacant expression. The translucent slime seemed to be taking on a pinkish hue.

Suddenly, violently and in total silence Harriet pitched backwards down the crevasse.

"Jesus, she's fallen!" Dr. English was first at the edge, shining a pocket torch down into the dark. Its wan beam did not penetrate far into the gloom. As some of the others, with more powerful lights leaned over they could see further down but make out little detail. Somewhere, deep in the hole there seemed to be a pulpy, whitish mass.

"Harriet, Harriet, can you here me?"

He received no answer.

"I'm calling 999." He whipped out his mobile phone and stabbed at it with a shaking finger. It remained silent.

"Fuck, no signal."

Several of them tried theirs with the same results.

"We'll have to get back to the surface and ring from there," he barked. *"Come on!"*

Darren turned back to the yawning hole.

"Don't worry, love. We've gone to get help. It won't be long. Try not to move."

"I'll stay here in case she comes round," said Mr. Pickering. *"Just go back the way you came. Stay on the main tunnel where the lights have been rigged up. Don't stray off or you'll get lost down here. One disaster is enough."*

The others scrambled back up the slope and headed for the well-lit main tunnel.

"Do you think it was the shock?" stammered Darren. *"I mean, of producing the stuff?"*

"We don't even know what it was," Dr. English snapped. *"She may have fallen down and got coated in the substance, whatever it was. I wish I could have taken a sample."*

As they turned a corner into the main tunnel, their eyes fell upon something ahead. It seemed to be slipping out of one of the side corridors and into the larger one. They all stopped.

It was a translucent, pallid mass the size of a double bed. It was compressed close to the ground and moved with a strange sliding, pulsing motion. At its centre was a black, circular blotch as big as a beach ball.

"That's it, that's the thing I saw on the security camera." Mr. Brandon pointed with a shaking finger.

"What the hell is it?" whispered Dr. English

"It's Old Boneless, that what it is!"

Yvonne found herself thinking that it looked like a giant fried egg with a black yolk.

The thing stopped. It seemed bereft of eyes or ears but somehow it had sensed them. It began to creep in their direction, sending out groping pseudopods.

"Back down the tunnel quick. We'll have to take another way."

Despite Mr. Pickering's warning, no one felt inclined to argue with Dr. English. They ran back the way they came and took the first left.

"If we keep turning left it should bring us round in a circle and back out onto the main tunnel behind whatever that thing was. I just hope there are left turns off the branch we're in."

Back beside the pit, Mr. Pickering's ears strained as he thought he heard a movement from the crevasse. Had Harriet regained consciousness and begun to feebly move? As he looked, something pale appeared at the lip of the hole. He moved closer to look, shining his torch at the glistening substance. It seemed to be the same stuff that had been coating Harriet before she had fallen. What was it they had called it? Ectoplasm? He had never heard of the stuff before. He gingerly reached out to touch it and then withdrew his hand from the stinging sensation. It was like touching nettles.

Suddenly a mass of it shot up and enveloped his forearm and the torch he was holding. He let out a yell and tried to pull away but he was held fast by the sticky, rubbery substance. Pain shot up his arm. He remembered being stung by a jellyfish whilst swimming as a boy. This felt the same but the pain was growing. Whatever it was, pulled him down to his knees. Another bleached mass rose and paused for a moment before coating his face and heaving him down into the blackness.

"That wasn't ectoplasm that was all over Harriet." Dr. English was striding ahead despite having the smallest and least effectual torch on the team. *"What ever that was back there, another one of them got Harriet. It covered her and pulled her back down the hole. That means there are two of them at least and possibly more."*

"They remind me of something but I can't recall what," Alan the soundman had hung doggedly onto his mike like a child's teddy.

"I know what you mean, but I just can't put my finger on it."

"Old Boneless is good enough for me," Mr. Brandon was shaking now. *"That first time I saw it I knew it was dangerous, I just sensed it."*

"We shouldn't have come here," whispered Darren. *"We've stirred them up, made them angry."*

"Get a grip on yourself," snapped Dr. English.

"Well what's your explanation now, Mr. Sceptic? You saw Old Boneless just like everyone else did."

"Well, I don't think it was made up out of the souls of dead miners for a start. Anyhow, look here is a branch to the left, with any luck it'll lead us back out."

The tunnel did indeed lead to the main, lit passage. Of the white thing there was no sign. They pressed on heading for the wine cellar and thence freedom.

"I hope Carl's all right," Yvonne whispered.

On entering the former wine cellar they found no sign of Carl. The machine was still connected to the cable and its fork like device silently vibrating as the speakers throbbed with a matching lack of audible noise.

"Carl! Carl!" Dr. English darted the beam of his torch into the corners of the cellar finding nothing but cobwebs and silence.

"Maybe he's headed back to the trailer. If he saw one of those things then perhaps he's gone to get help."

Yvonne was cut short by the sound of something falling. There was a soft, wet plop as something dropped into the centre of the room, close to Carl's infrasound machine.

When caught in a beam of light it turned out to be a fist-sized blob of clear, jelly-like matter. Something seemed to glean and shine within it. Dr. English bent to examine it. He found it contained an imitation Rolex watch.

Slowly he turned his eyes and his torch upwards to the vaulted ceiling. Carl hung there, suspended inside one of the creatures like a fly in amber. His features looked hazy, indistinct and the matter that composed the entity that surrounded him was a rich pink, darkening as they watched to a light red.

"He's dead. It's digesting him. Christ, look, his blood is being sucked out and into the thing's body, that's what's making it change colour. That's what happened to Harriet."

Yvonne started to scream and scream until Dr. English slapped her.

"Carry on like that and you'll have a dozen more of them down on us."

"We left Mr. Pickering down by the pit," she sobbed.

"We'll come back for him, but we need to get help now. It's too dangerous to go back now. God knows how many of those things are down there."

They ran up the steps from the cellar and out into the house proper. In the hall outside another one of the things lay, blocking the way to the still open doors that led out onto the drive.

Darren grabbed Yvonne's hand and squeezed.

"We're trapped, there's no way past it."

The thing seemed at first to be motionless but then it began to shudder. Dr. English edged gingerly closer. A large number of pigeons were visible inside the translucent mass that was already tainted with the colour of their blood.

"It's fed on some pigeons. It might be inactive for a while. We could try edging around the side of it."

"I'm not gong anywhere near it".

Yvonne's voice had an edge of hysteria.

What looked like a split had appeared along the centre of the entity.

"Look, at that, it's got a split along it. Has it been wounded?" asked Terry

Something clicked inside Dr. English's mind.

"No Terry, that's not a wound. The organism is reproducing. I've just realised what we're dealing with. These things are giant amoebas. Huge single-celled life forms!"

"But amoebas are tiny."

"This must be some gigantic new species. Some marine species grow as large as grapes but nothing like this. The dark shape at the centre is the nucleus. They must live deep under the earth."

"What's brought them out? Why are they coming here now?" asked Yvonne.

"Obviously the odd one has found its way to the surface in the past and created the Old Boneless ghost stories. It could be that they lie dormant for years. Normal amoebas form protective membranes called microbial cysts during adverse conditions. But now it seems they are coming up in greater numbers. It must be Carl's machine. The infrasound is attracting them.

This one has fed and now it's reproducing. It's splitting in half. It will be dormant until the process is finished. We can get past it and escape back to the trailer van. Do you gentlemen have cars?"

The two witnesses shook their heads.

"We came in a taxi from Minehead," said Mr. Brandon. *"The studio paid."*

"Then come with us. Who has the keys?"

Alan the soundman took them from his pocket and held them up.

"Ok follow me and just ease past gently."

Dr. English edged along the wall and past the recumbent amoeba. It made no attempt to attack but lay quivering as the parting in its body grew wider and the nucleus itself began to split.

"Come on quickly, the process takes about a quarter of an hour."

They all edged past and one by one emerged through the doors and into the night air. As Bob, the last man out stepped into the drive another of the organisms dropped down from the side of the ruined hall and fell on him with a damp, sickening thud. He was flattened under its mass and floundered like a man drowning in a vat of glue. They could see his mouth opening and closing but any screams were muffled by the thick cytoplasm of the huge amoeba.

Terry turned back to help his friend despite the shouted warnings. He tried to reach into the adhesive mass and grab Bob, but he was caught fast and he too was hauled into the shuddering, twitching pool of primitive, predatory life.

Looking up, the survivors saw dozens more of the creatures slithering over the walls and roof of Smedly Hall, their pseudopods groping blindly in search of prey. Others were now approaching across the unkempt lawns like huge silver slugs in the moonlight.

"There must be fissures all over the place. We need to get to the trailer van now."

They ran down the drive and found the van, doors open. Of Tina the make-up girl there was no sign. Most of them clambered into the back of the vehicle and pulled the doors shut. Dr. English and Alan leapt into the front and Alan turned the key in the ignition. Thankfully, the engine rumbled into life.

Alan backed the trailer out running over one of the slithering horrors in the process. As he accelerated away down the drive he looked in the rear view mirror to see the mass swiftly re-forming as if nothing had happened.

The trailer smashed into the gates of Smedly Hall, tearing them off their hinges, and sped away down the darkened road.

"What the hell do we say? Who is going to believe this?"

Alan was still struggling to control his breathing.

"Did you see how many of those things there were, Sam? It was a plague. And you say they can reproduce by just splitting in half? How often can they do that?"

"It depends on conditions. In some cases once per hour. There could be thousands of them soon."

Another thought struck Dr. English as they put more miles between them and the horrors at Smedly Hall. Carl O'Leary's machine had been left on.

WELCOME HOME GEORGE

Stony Road was always a funny little street. It seemed isolated from the rest of town. It was a row of ten grubby little houses that were constantly caked in dirt. It wasn't that the people who lived there were unclean. It was the location of Stony Road. It was at the bottom of Tuttle Hill, a busy main road that led into the centre of town. To the front of the road, as one came down Tuttle Hill towards the town, lay railway lines. To its rear was a polluted canal and beyond that Juddkins Quarry. To its right was the road, then another quarry. To its left was a cement works. The combined filth generated by these caked the houses on Stony Road and gave them a depressing air. Like a rotten tooth in a jaw, the furthest house on the left, the last in the row, was derelict. Glassless windows gazed down like the eye sockets of an ancient skull. The roof was missing a fair amount of the tiles and looked like it was sagging. Yet it was not these things that grabbed the onlooker's attention, rather what was written on the front of the house. In large painted letters, now faded, were the words 'Welcome Home George'. That house was haunted, everyone knew that.

Nuneaton is a dull, faceless little town in Warwickshire. Introverted, unimaginative and depressing, the town seems to actively sap ambition like a vampire drinking blood. It has no claim to fame and its few well-known sons were nothing more than 'z' grade celebrities or authors both boring and dead. Nuneaton does have two landmarks though. One is 'Mount Judd' the spoil heap from Juddkins Quarry, now covered in grass, which rises several hundred feet above the town. The other is the 'Welcome Home George' house.

It was Adrian Stephens who first suggested the idea of the Nuneaton Ghost Club. We were in the playing fields of Camp Hill Secondary School at the time. We all thought the idea was great. The summer holidays would be upon us in a few days and we had six weeks to kill. The Nuneaton Ghost Club had its first meeting in my Granddad's garden shed that doubled up as a gang hut that weekend. There were six of us, Mark Ward, Julie Timpson, Mandy Box, David 'Diddy' Quafe, Ann Styles and me. The subject matter was where to look for our first ghost.

Mandy had suggested Astley Castle. The former home of Henry Grey, the Duke of Suffolk, the moated castle had been a hotel in recent years. It had been burned out in a mysterious fire two years before. Mark had kept a scrapbook of the newspaper coverage at the time. There was one small room left unburned. The black and white photo showed what looked like an altar with knives, a doll and weird markings like back to front question marks. There was talk about 'black magick' at the time. The castle was left as a shell. Either Henry Grey or his daughter, Jane Grey, were supposed to haunt the ruins. No one seemed to know which of the two it was! One of the boys at school, a couple of years above us said he had seen the ghost, but no one really believed him. Everyone agreed that Astley Castle was a great idea but the ruin was some miles out of town and on private land. We would need to make a whole day of it. We decided to try that later in the school holidays. For our first investigation, we needed somewhere that was actually in town.

David came up with the idea of the 'Welcome Home George' house. The playgrounds were full of stories about what the writing actually meant. Obviously it was meant for someone coming back from WWII. According to the stories we had heard, the writing was painted by the wife of a young soldier who was due to return home. Just a couple of days before he left he was killed (the stories never did tell how) and his wife died of a broken heart. It was said that she still haunted the now abandoned house and the sound of her crying could still be heard.

Stony Road was within walking distance for everyone in the club so we decided that this would be our first 'case'. As it turned out, it would also be our last.

It was the first Sunday of the summer holidays. We had all met up having told our parents that we were going for a walk. Back in those days, before the media fuelled paranoia about paedophiles, people worried a lot less about their kids being out. I remember staying out for hours in the holidays. We brought torches and I had an instamatic camera with a flash. I had a copy of the Usborne book '*Mysteries of the Unknown: Monsters, Ghosts, and UFOs*', essential reading for any budding ghost hunter.

We snuck up the back way onto Stony Road via the old cement works so as not to be noticed by the residents of Stony Street. We clambered over the tumbled-down brick wall and through the weed-choked garden. In the dark, the 'Welcome Home George' house looked even stranger. The house was not large, two-up-two-down, not like some mansion in a Hammer film. We were approaching it from the back and without the writing to hold our attention we concentrated more on the house itself. I wondered why the council had not done anything about the place or if the next door neighbours had complained. Up close it looked even more filthy and dilapidated than before. Surely, the dampness of the house must be creeping through the wall of the building next door and causing problems?

We pushed aside what was left of the door and, switching on our torches, entered the remains of the kitchen. There was an old mildewed table, ragged curtains and a rusty sink filled with shards of damp plaster. We looked into the dark cupboards to find only nasty smells and a dead spider. We moved into the living room. An old settee, rank with decay dominated the room. There was a rotting carpet where not even rats scurried. Equally pungent leather chairs lay toppled. The ceiling was covered in a dark wet patch, and sagged slightly. A slight breeze stirred the curtains in the glassless window letting in silver moonlight. No one spoke.

We headed for the stairs and began to climb. David was ahead of us and pushed open the bathroom door. A rusted bath half filled with rain that had fallen through the roof was against once wall. The sink and tiled floor was caked with pigeon droppings. David motioned us over and gleefully pointed out a dead rat floating in the broken toilet much to the revulsion of the girls. Back in the hall, a door to one of the bedrooms was open while the other was shut. David opened the latter and entered, with the rest of us behind him.

As he swung the door open something tall and white seemed to rise up flapping. In my brief view I got the idea of a slender ragged form reaching for us with spindly arms; it seemed to have no face. David screamed. Instinctively I took a snap with my camera. David, who was so close to the thing that it was almost touching him, seemed to go into a blind panic. He tossed me and the others aside with a fear-augmented strength that belied his small size, and fled. But in his panicked state he ran not for the stairs but for the other bedroom.

The ceiling above that second bedroom must have been in a very bad state and letting in more rainwater than anywhere else in the house. There was no bed and the floorboards had almost rotted through. They couldn't even support someone as small as David. I saw him fall and heard the crack as the floor gave way, followed almost instantly by a louder crack. David was still alive when I saw him, when I looked over the edge of the ragged hole that had opened up. He had fallen on the old table that had splintered under him. Several pieces were protruding from his body. He had a pleading look on his face, and was reaching out to me.

We ran out of the house screaming for help. A woman came out of the house next door.

There was a special assembly at Camp Hill Secondary School to remember David and to warn other children about the dangers of messing around in derelict houses.

It's funny but none of us ever mentioned David again, it was as if he had never existed. Of course, that event put an end to the Nuneaton Ghost Club. I somehow managed to keep hold of that instamatic photo I took. It showed an old sheet suspended from part of a splintered joist. A breeze had made it billow up.

The council boarded up the doors and windows of the last house on Stony Road but they didn't pull it down. Sometime later I found out the truth about the 'Welcome Home George' sign. It was for George Evans, a man who had been a Desert Rat in WWII. His mates had painted it for him as he came home from the war. He wasn't killed and his wife and family lived on in the house for years before moving out to find somewhere bigger. He still has relatives in Nuneaton.

The story of the crying war widow was an urban myth probably made up by kids years before I ever heard it. There was no ghost in the 'Welcome Home George' house. I said 'was' because now there are new stories. Gone is the weeping woman. Now the kids in the playground whisper stories about a tiny figure in the dark that reaches out with begging arms and pleading eyes.

That house is haunted, everyone knows that.

COLD SNAP

Beautifully illuminated, Durham Cathedral rose out of the darkness like some fairy-tale citadel above a sea of mist. Below the colourful, if somewhat garish, Christmas illuminations twinkled and winked in streets and houses. The view from the railway carriage was quite breathtaking to most onlookers but to Russell Arkwright it just formed a knot in his stomach. He stepped down onto the platform clutching his small hold all, his breath forming a series of tiny ghosts that danced away into the sharp, cold night air. It had been a long trip up from London and for every moment of it Russell had wondered if he was doing the right thing. Sixty-two years it had been since he set eyes on Durham and it still felt like too soon. He shuddered and hugged himself against the cold.

As he began to cross the platform, something caught his eye. A discarded newspaper on a bench. It was a copy of the *Durham Times*, a photograph of a gap-toothed urchin grinning out from the front cover. He bent to pick it up.

'ANOTHER CHILD LOST IN THE WEAR' the headline proclaimed. Russell scanned the story with mounting dread. Lines jumped out at him. 'Alfie Randle, 10, missing, believed drowned in the River Wear at Durham.' 'Third child lost in the river this winter.' 'Police divers find no trace.'

He realised that he couldn't stay and turned back, but the train was already pulling out of the station. Now he had no choice, this had been the last train. He looked down at the paper in his hands.

"It's still happening," he whispered.

Survivor's guilt, the psychologist had called it, whatever that meant. Why should he feel guilty about surviving? Lucky maybe, but not guilty. What had happened on Christmas morning 1948, had stayed with him all his life. Bad dreams that seemed to get worse with age. They had cost him his marriage and his health. He held off going to see a psychiatrist until last year. Perhaps it was his age. Most folk of Russell's generation associated psychiatrists with the stigma of madness. In the 1940s and '50s the 'mad' were locked away in county institutions and quietly forgotten about. But he was 72 now and long retired. He felt he had little to worry about.

The doctor on Harley Street had suggested hypnotherapy, a regression to the events of that morning so long ago. Facing and conquering the fear that had tormented him for most of his life. The fear he had blotted from his memory. It was nothing unusual he had been told. Thousands of people had experienced traumatic events that the conscious mind had blotted out. The suppressed memories resurfaced as bad dreams. It was a commonplace complaint and easily treatable. Nothing to be worried about. Nothing at all.

He had recalled some of the events unaided. Meeting with his friends on that crisp, bright morning. They had all asked for the same thing, ice skates. The Wear froze deep in those days. Not like today when you hardly get a winter. Back in the 1940s he recalled snow drifts six feet deep. The thaw didn't start till the end of March. Durham was a wonderland for kids then; hills to sledge down, snowmen to build, snowball fights to have. Best of all was the Wear froze so well that men rode horses and carts along it. One year they built a big bonfire on it.

But the thought of whizzing over the frozen water was so exciting. He'd seen ice skaters at the pictures and a few of the better-off folk in Durham actually had skates. Russell had looked on in envy at them as they sped by. Now he had a pair of skates of his own.

His mates met him by the river, Larry, Brian, Tim, Cyril, each proudly showing off a new pair of ice skates. There was a deep wooded gully ideal for practicing. They had wasted no time in putting on their skates and unsteadily tottering out onto the frozen river. It was hard at first. Even standing was difficult. All five of them toppled down again and again, bruising knees and elbows. Thankfully it was early on and no one was about to see them make fools of themselves. Like riding a bike, it came in time. The boys helped each other and soon they were sailing across they ice, grinning and rosy cheeked.

Russell recalled a noise that he thought was a gunshot. He imagined someone out shooting pheasants or woodcock. Then the noise came again followed by and awful rending sound like nails on a blackboard magnified a thousand times. Looking back he saw huge cracks forming in the ice. How could ice so thick, as strong as steel crack like that? The surface of the Wear lurched crazily tipping him to one side. All around him his mates were tumbling and sliding as the ice was torn apart. A thick fog was billowing in. Moments before the air had been crystal clear. The fog smelt strange. It was acrid and burnt his nose and throat as he breathed it in. It made him feel sick and dizzy.

He heard Cyril screaming and a splashing sound. Trying to peer through the thick fog, he thought he saw Larry tumble into the freezing water. Russell staggered to his feet and made for the bank in a series of crazy floundering hops. The skates, so prized earlier were a hindrance and he frantically fumbled with the laces to get them off then leapt from chunk to chunk of sundered ice. Behind him there was more splashing and a screaming that was cut short. He couldn't tell if it was Tim or Brian calling out. All he recalled was somehow scrambling up the bank and collapsing. A couple walking their dogs had found him. He woke up in hospital suffering from hypothermia.

The family had moved away from Durham after that. His dad was lucky, he had an elder brother who worked on the parks department in Crawley who got him a job. Ruth, his sister was born five years later.

Moving down south had not meant Russell could escape the memories of that morning. The dreams started not long after. They were always the same, a re-playing of that fateful day, but in greater clarity. He saw the faces of his friends pleading for help as they went under. He tried to grasp their hands with frozen fingers as they vanished into the dark, icy water. He could not save a single one, despite their pleas, despite how hard he pulled at the floundering arms.

He was surprised at how young the hypnotherapist was. He had expected some shock-haired, bow-tied stereotype, but Dr. Mullard was young enough to be his son, no more than 35. He'd seen a hypnotist at Butlin's Holiday camp as a boy. The man had made audience members do and say ridiculous things. He was still nervous.

But there were no swinging fob watches or commanding stares. He and Dr. Mullard had just talked for a while; pleasantries at first and then the specifics of his problem. Lying back on the couch he found it easier to relax than he had at first thought. Dr. Mullard's voice seemed to put him at ease as he tried to mentally travel back to that day so long ago. It was easier than he had thought it would be, letting down his defenses, breeching his cerebral resistance. Perhaps it wasn't the soft, reassuring voice of Dr. Mullard; perhaps he had just grown tired of fighting it.

Soon he was back there, on the ice, the wind in his hair and face as he sped faster and faster across the gleaming surface. Around him his friends spun and twirled, abandoning themselves to the joy of the moment. Strange to be out on the Wear after fearing water for so long. He had avoided lakes and rivers after what had happened. Even crossing a river on a train or in a car or bus made him shudder. The sea had horrified him and he had never been abroad. Holidays were spent in the countryside not at the seaside. But now he was elated and excited once more, panting with boyish exertion as the white landscape blurred.

Then the revelry was split by *that* noise, that booming retort of the ice sheet shattering. The world pitched crazily as he fell. Looking back he saw his friends tumbling in all directions. He also saw something he hadn't recalled consciously before. He saw the fog but it wasn't rolling in like fog was supposed to. It seemed to be rising up directly from the split in the ice, rising up from the river itself. Was it gas from the decaying matter on the river bed? It seemed to be under pressure as it came whooshing and hissing up in a great plume, almost like film he had seen of geezers. It smelt odd; sickly sweet and stung his eyes. Soon it was rolling across the ice obscuring his view. The screams began.

In his mind, Russell re-lived scrambling across the splitting ice. Cyril was already in the water and reaching out for help. Following the cries, Russell found him and grabbed his hands. Maybe if he could save just one of his friends this time around the dreams would end.

He began to haul the sodden, shivering boy out of the water. He was wet and heavy. The slippery surface made it all the more difficult but he heaved again and Cyril began to rise from the water. Then he was jerked violently back, torn from Russell's grip by something of phenomenal strength pulling against him. Was it the undercurrent of the Wear? In a second, Cyril was wrenched underwater and vanished.

Russell looked round desperately for the others. He saw Tim thrashing weakly twenty-feet away and stumbled over to him on the moving ice. Once more he grasped his friend's arms; once more he was yanked away before he could even scream.

A yell from behind him made him turn in time to see Larry scrambling up onto a raft of ice through the strange, stinging fog. Suddenly it pitched to one side as if it had been struck from beneath, tossing the blue, trembling boy into the dark waters of the Wear. He did not rise again.

Brian was actually in the river, in one of the widening channels that opened up as the separate pieces of ice drifted away. There was something else in the water with him. He remembered for the first time in 62 years. There were lights under the water, two of them. They looked like the headlamps on the old-fashioned cars you got back then but they were *under* the water, near the bottom of the Wear. They rose up and the boy seemed to be *sucked* down into the depths.

The sickening fog was making his head swim. He pulled desperately at the laces on his skates, cursing their length and his proficiency at tying knots. Through the fog he saw the twin lights beneath the surface. They seemed to turn his way and approach the chunk of ice on which he was lying. Abandoning his skates, he ran blindly into the fog, leaping from chunk to wobbling chunk of ice. Fear gave him strength and speed. Soon he was shambling through the shallows near the bank. He felt the bow wave of something huge behind him as he clawed at frozen grass and rushes. He glanced back once.

He awoke on the couch in screaming hysteria, his mind recoiling and blanking out the last image.

He did not return for a second session.

The dreams got worse after that. Those weird lights, whatever they had been, now seemed to dominate his nightmares. Finally, he had made his mind up to exorcise his daemons by returning to Durham to the River Wear.

Ruth had lived all her adult life here, having married a local man she met on holiday. They were not a close family. Russell and Ruth had exchanged cards at Christmas and on birthdays. She occasionally came down to London. Her husband Harry, over a decade her senior, had died that summer. They had no children and he thought she could do with the comfort. He was the only family she had now. He could kill two birds with one stone. He climbed down the steps, slick with frost, and made his way to the taxi rank. Ruth was waiting at the door of the little house. They hugged awkwardly.

"Good journey?" she enquired.

"Nine hours on a train is never good."

"Never mind, there is some tea on and something a bit stronger for you when you've unpacked."

The decorations at Ruth's house were minimal. Russell was thankful for that small mercy. He hated decorations. Loud, crass and tacky. A physical personification of a time of year he loathed. A large photo of Harry stood upon the television. Russell had only met him a few times but he had been a good man and treated his sister well.

Ruth was a good cook and he ate well at supper. Lamb and blackberry pie, an old recipe he had not tasted in years. Mulled wine followed with sticky toffee pudding.

Russell and Ruth exchanged gifts shortly after the old grandfather clock, that was once their father's, had struck twelve. He had told her that he would be up at the crack of dawn for a walk. He gave her a porcelain Labrador. She gave him a tie and gloves. Brother and sister hardly knew one another.

Strangely, he slept very well that night. For once, no nightmares. Maybe this was the best course of action. Facing one's fears and exorcising them once and for all. When he awoke it was with a feeling of finality.

He left the house quietly so as not to wake Ruth. The sun was just crawling over the horizon spreading its ruddy light across the bleak landscape. It was frosty but there was no snow, not like there had been back then. No one had risen yet. No excited children scrambling around the streets. Russell wondered if kids still had snowball fights or built snowmen (on the rare occasions that there was snow). They were probably too busy with their video games, growing fat and pasty in front of a flickering screen.

Soon he was wandering through the naked trees, the frozen grass crunching underfoot. Then the Wear came into view, silvery white and frozen. The ice didn't look as thick or as strong as it had when he was a boy. He felt himself shaking as he slowly approached the bank.

"Come on, you've got this far. No point in turning back now," he told himself.

The silence was deafening. Russell thought he could have been in the wilds of eastern Siberia, rather than in the boundaries of a small city. There was no one here, nothing stirred. It was just him and the silver Wear, like the trail of some gargantuan snail.

His throat was dry as he stood on the bank and looked at the frozen water. He knew that the ice was not thick enough to support him these days. It was thin enough in places for him to see the dark waters moving silently below it. He recalled the newspaper, the lost boy. He had not been the first.

After the hypnotherapy failed he had done some searching online. Computers were more or less a mystery to him, but the lady in the library had been so helpful. It seemed that every year people vanished on in the Wear. Not just children, but adults as well. Not just in winter either, all year round. Some were drownings, accidents that happen in all bodies of water. But there seemed to be a significant amount of cases where no body was ever found. The Wear was not like any other river. There was something wrong with the Wear.

Swallowing and trembling, he forced himself to wander along the bank as the sun slowly pulled itself higher in the sky. The silence was broken by rooks calling in the distance. Turning, he saw them rise up from the rookery in an untidy black cloud.

As he looked back at the Wear, his eyes were drawn to a section where the thinning ice became transparent. The endless cold, ceaseless flow seemed to have a pull. His eyes and brain began to form shapes below, underwater simulacra constructed of shadow, weed and mud. It seemed something huge was moving sluggishly through the river. It looked like the trunk of some ancient oak, thick and gnarled. But no tree could be so long. The shape's length seemed unending and horribly flexible. Even as he watched, it seemed to be turning back on itself. An illusion of moving water and bad memories, nothing more. Yet then he saw the lights. Two shining orbs like car headlights moving under the Wear. The same lights Dr. Mullard's session had drawn out of his memories. They seemed to pause every so often and swing from side to side like twin, underwater searchlights.

Horrified and fascinated, Russell watched from the bank. The lights seemed to be associated with the long, thick shape he had taken to be a trick of the eye. They seemed to be attached to one end of it. A rivulet of liquid fear oozed slowly down his back as he realised that what he was looking at were *eyes*. The body was like some mammoth snake. No snake could possibly be so huge. A coil arched and the fragile ice fell apart in shards. Geysers of fog shot up, billowing out of the water.

The thing heaved itself up, black slime from the Wear's muddy bed sloughing away to show horny green scales. Only a tiny portion of a body that extended beyond view had breeched. His mind recoiled at the thought of the sheer size of whatever this was slithering through the waters of the River Wear.

Then, with and awful sucking sound, a massive, wedge shaped head reared up. It was the size of a car, with eyes glowing like some deep-sea fish that never saw the light of day. The jaws swung open showing row after row of murderous teeth. Between them a red, forked tongue as long as a couch flickered tasting the air.

Another lost memory rose. A rhyme chanted by children in his playground so very long ago.

> "But the worm got fat an' grewed an' grewed,
> An' grewed an aaful size;
> He'd greet big teeth, a greet big gob,
> An' greet big goggly eyes."

The Lambton Worm, the creature that mothers still told their children of when they wanted to scare some obedience into them. The great reptile that had terrorised the area in the 1400s until slain by Sir John Lambton, wearing a suit of spiked armour. Russell realised then that the stories were lies. No one and nothing could slay the worm. It was the spirit of the Wear itself made flesh and fang and scale. *Genius loci* in the form of a serpent dragon, now risen hungry from its sleep. The vile, acrid fog was the worm's breath, gushing from its nostrils in twin jets.

Fold after fold of its coils humped up from the river as the jaws rose before the transfixed man. The great glowing eyes transfixed him like a rabbit before a stoat. For a moment, the worm paused. Did he see a look of recognition before the final snap?

![STILL ON THE TRACK OF UNKNOWN ANIMALS](logo: THE CENTRE FOR FORTEAN ZOOLOGY www.cfz.org.uk)

STILL ON THE TRACK OF UNKNOWN ANIMALS

The Centre for Fortean Zoology, or CFZ, is a non profit-making organisation founded in 1992 with the aim of being a clearing house for information, and coordinating research into mystery animals around the world.

We also study out of place animals, rare and aberrant animal behaviour, and Zooform Phenomena; little-understood "things" that appear to be animals, but which are in fact nothing of the sort, and not even alive (at least in the way we understand the term).

Not only are we the biggest organisation of our type in the world, but - or so we like to think - we are the best. We are certainly the only truly global cryptozoological research organisation, and we carry out our investigations using a strictly scientific set of guidelines. We are expanding all the time and looking to recruit new members to help us in our research into mysterious animals and strange creatures across the globe.

Why should you join us? Because, if you are genuinely interested in trying to solve the last great mysteries of Mother Nature, there is nobody better than us with whom to do it.

Members get a four-issue subscription to our journal *Animals & Men*. Each issue contains nearly 100 pages packed with news, articles, letters, research papers, field reports, and even a gossip column! The magazine is Royal Octavo in format with a full colour cover. You also have access to one of the world's largest collections of resource material dealing with cryptozoology and allied disciplines, and people from the CFZ membership regularly take part in fieldwork and expeditions around the world.

The CFZ is managed by a three-man board of trustees, with a non-profit making trust registered with HM Government Stamp Office. The board of trustees is supported by a Permanent Directorate of full and part-time staff, and advised by a Consultancy Board of specialists - many of whom are world-renowned experts in their particular field. We have regional representatives across the UK, the USA, and many other parts of the world, and are affiliated with other organisations whose aims and protocols mirror our own.

You'll find that the people at the CFZ are friendly and approachable. We have a thriving forum on the website which is the hub of an ever-growing electronic community. You will soon find your feet. Many members of the CFZ Permanent Directorate started off as ordinary members, and now work full-time chasing monsters around the world.

Write to us, e-mail us, or telephone us. The list of future projects on the website is not exhaustive. If you have a good idea for an investigation, please tell us. We may well be able to help.

We are always looking for volunteers to join us. If you see a project that interests you, do not hesitate to get in touch with us. Under certain circumstances we can help provide funding for your trip. If you look on the future projects section of the website, you can see some of the projects that we have pencilled in for the next few years.

In 2003 and 2004 we sent three-man expeditions to Sumatra looking for Orang-Pendek - a semi-legendary bipedal ape. The same three went to Mongolia in 2005. All three members started off merely subscribers to the CFZ magazine. Next time it could be you!

We have no magic sources of income. All our funds come from donations, membership fees, and sales of our publications and merchandise. We are always looking for corporate sponsorship, and other sources of revenue. If you have any ideas for fund-raising please let us know.

However, unlike other cryptozoological organisations in the past, we do not live in an intellectual ivory tower. We are not afraid to get our hands dirty, and furthermore we are not one of those organisations where the membership have to raise money so that a privileged few can go on expensive foreign trips. Our research teams, both in the UK and abroad, consist of a mixture of experienced and inexperienced personnel. We are truly a community, and work on the premise that the benefits of CFZ membership are open to all.

Reports of our investigations are published on our website as soon as they are available. Preliminary reports are posted within days of the project finishing.

Each year we publish a 200 page yearbook containing research papers and expedition reports too long to be printed in the journal. We freely circulate our information to anybody who asks for it.

We have a thriving YouTube channel, CFZtv, which has well over two hundred self-made documentaries, lecture appearances, and episodes of our monthly webTV show. We have a daily online magazine, which has over a million hits each year.

Each year since 2000 we have held our annual convention - the Weird Weekend. It is three days of lectures, workshops, and excursions. But most importantly it is a chance for members of the CFZ to meet each other, and to talk with the members of the permanent directorate in a relaxed and informal setting and preferably with a pint of beer in one hand. Since 2006 - the Weird Weekend has been bigger and better and held on the third weekend in August in the idyllic rural location of Woolsery in North Devon.

Since relocating to North Devon in 2005 we have become ever more closely involved with other community organisations, and we hope that this trend will continue. We have also worked closely with Police Forces across the UK as consultants for animal mutilation cases, and we intend to forge closer links with the coastguard and other community services. We want to work closely with those who regularly travel into the Bristol Channel, so that if the recent trend of exotic animal visitors to our coastal waters continues, we can be out there as soon as possible.

Apart from having been the only Fortean Zoological organisation in the world to have consistently published material on all aspects of the subject for over a decade, we have achieved the following concrete results:

• Disproved the myth relating to the headless so-called sea-serpent carcass of Durgan beach in Cornwall 1975
• Disproved the story of the 1988 puma skull of

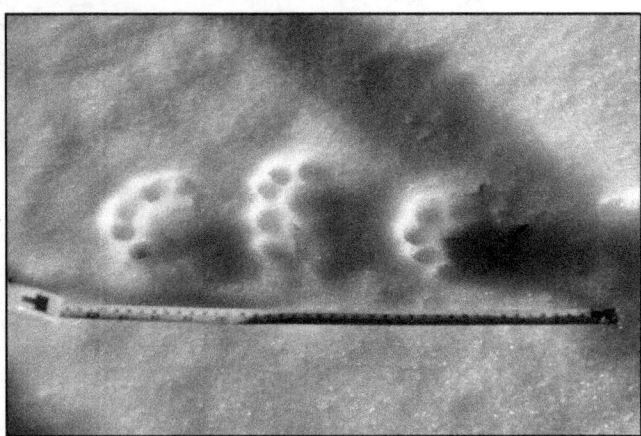

Lustleigh Cleave

- Carried out the only in-depth research ever into the mythos of the Cornish Owlman.
- Made the first records of a tropical species of lamprey
- Made the first records of a luminous cave gnat larva in Thailand
- Discovered a possible new species of British mammal - the beech marten
- In 1994-6 carried out the first archival fortean zoological survey of Hong Kong
- In the year 2000, CFZ theories were confirmed when a new species of lizard was added to the British List
- Identified the monster of Martin Mere in Lancashire as a giant wels catfish
- Expanded the known range of Armitage's skink in the Gambia by 80%
- Obtained photographic evidence of the remains of Europe's largest known pike
- Carried out the first ever in-depth study of the ninki-nanka
- Carried out the first attempt to breed Puerto Rican cave snails in captivity
- Were the first European explorers to visit the `lost valley` in Sumatra
- Published the first ever evidence for a new tribe of pygmies in Guyana
- Published the first evidence for a new species of caiman in Guyana
- Filmed unknown creatures

on a monster-haunted lake in Ireland for the first time

• Had a sighting of orang pendek in Sumatra in 2009

• Found leopard hair, subsequently identified by DNA analysis, from rural North Devon in 2010

• Brought back hairs which appear to be from an unknown primate in Sumatra

• Published some of the best evidence ever for the almasty in southern Russia

CFZ Expeditions and Investigations include:

• 1998 Puerto Rico, Florida, Mexico (Chupacabras)
• 1999 Nevada (Bigfoot)
• 2000 Thailand (Naga)
• 2002 Martin Mere (Giant catfish)
• 2002 Cleveland (Wallaby mutilation)

- 2003 Bolam Lake (BHM Reports)
- 2003 Sumatra (Orang Pendek)
- 2003 Texas (Bigfoot; giant snapping turtles)
- 2004 Sumatra (Orang Pendek; cigau, a sabre-toothed cat)
- 2004 Illinois (Black panthers; cicada swarm)
- 2004 Texas (Mystery blue dog)
- Loch Morar (Monster)
- 2004 Puerto Rico (Chupacabras; carnivorous cave snails)
- 2005 Belize (Affiliate expedition for hairy dwarfs)
- 2005 Loch Ness (Monster)
- 2005 Mongolia (Allghoi Khorkhoi aka Mongolian death worm)

- 2006 Gambia (Gambo - Gambian sea monster , Ninki Nanka and Armitage's skink
- 2006 Llangorse Lake (Giant pike, giant eels)
- 2006 Windermere (Giant eels)
- 2007 Coniston Water (Giant eels)
- 2007 Guyana (Giant anaconda, didi, water tiger)
- 2008 Russia (Almasty)
- 2009 Sumatra (Orang pendek)
- 2009 Republic of Ireland (Lake Monster)
- 2010 Texas (Blue Dogs)
- 2010 India (Mande Burung)
- 2011 Sumatra(Orang-pendek)

For details of current membership fees, current expeditions and investigations, and voluntary posts within the CFZ that need your help, please do not hesitate to contact us.

The Centre for Fortean Zoology,
Myrtle Cottage,
Woolfardisworthy,
Bideford, North Devon
EX39 5QR

Telephone 01237 431413
Fax+44 (0)7006-074-925
eMail info@cfz.org.uk

Websites:

www.cfz.org.uk
www.weirdweekend.org

HOW TO START A PUBLISHING EMPIRE

Unlike most mainstream publishers, we have a non-commercial remit, and our mission statement claims that "we publish books because they deserve to be published, not because we think that we can make money out of them". Our motto is the Latin Tag *Pro bona causa facimus* (we do it for good reason), a slogan taken from a children's book *The Case of the Silver Egg* by the late Desmond Skirrow.

WIKIPEDIA: "The first book published was in 1988. *Take this Brother may it Serve you Well* was a guide to Beatles bootlegs by Jonathan Downes. It sold quite well, but was hampered by very poor production values, being photocopied, and held together by a plastic clip binder. In 1988 A5 clip binders were hard to get hold of, so the publishers took A4 binders and cut them in half with a hacksaw. It now reaches surprisingly high prices second hand.

The production quality improved slightly over the years, and after 1999 all the books produced were ringbound with laminated colour covers. In 2004, however, they signed an agreement with Lightning Source, and all books are now produced perfect bound, with full colour covers."

Until 2010 all our books, the majority of which are/were on the subject of mystery animals and allied disciplines, were published by `CFZ Press`, the publishing arm of the Centre for Fortean Zoology (CFZ), and we urged our readers and followers to draw a discreet veil over the books that we published that were completely off topic to the CFZ.

However, in 2010 we decided that enough was enough and launched a second imprint, `Fortean Words` which aims to cover a wide range of non animal-related esoteric subjects. Other imprints will be launched as and when we feel like it, however the basic ethos of the company remains the same: Our job is to publish books and magazines that we feel are worth publishing, whether or not they are going to sell. Money is, after all - as my dear old Mama once told me - a rather vulgar subject, and she would be rolling in her grave if she thought that her eldest son was somehow in `trade`.

Luckily, so far our tastes have turned out not to be that rarified after all, and we have sold far more books than anyone ever thought that we would, so there is a moral in there somewhere…

Jon Downes,
Woolsery, North Devon
July 2010

CFZ PRESS

Other Books in Print

ORANG PENDEK: Sumatra's Forgotten Ape by Richard Freeman
THE MYSTERY ANIMALS OF THE BRITISH ISLES: London by Neil Arnold
CFZ EXPEDITION REPORT: India 2010 by Richard Freeman *et al*
The Cryptid Creatures of Florida by Scott Marlow
Dead of Night by Lee Walker
The Mystery Animals of the British Isles: The Northern Isles by Glen Vaudrey
THE MYSTERY ANIMALS OF THE BRTISH ISLES: Gloucestershire and Worcestershire by
Paul Williams
When Bigfoot Attacks by Michael Newton
Weird Waters – The Mystery Animals of Scandinavia: Lake and Sea Monsters by Lars Thomas
The Inhumanoids by Barton Nunnelly
Monstrum! A Wizard's Tale by Tony "Doc" Shiels
CFZ Yearbook 2011 edited by Jonathan Downes
Karl Shuker's Alien Zoo by Shuker, Dr Karl P.N
Tetrapod Zoology Book One by Naish, Dr Darren
The Mystery Animals of Ireland by Gary Cunningham and Ronan Coghlan
Monsters of Texas by Gerhard, Ken
The Great Yokai Encyclopaedia by Freeman, Richard
NEW HORIZONS: Animals & Men issues 16-20 Collected Editions Vol. 4
by Downes, Jonathan
A Daintree Diary -
Tales from Travels to the Daintree Rainforest in tropical north Queensland, Australia
by Portman, Carl
Strangely Strange but Oddly Normal by Roberts, Andy
Centre for Fortean Zoology Yearbook 2010 by Downes, Jonathan
Predator Deathmatch by Molloy, Nick
Star Steeds and other Dreams by Shuker, Karl
CHINA: A Yellow Peril? by Muirhead, Richard

Mystery Animals of the British Isles: The Western Isles by Vaudrey, Glen

Giant Snakes - Unravelling the coils of mystery by Newton, Michael

Mystery Animals of the British Isles: Kent by Arnold, Neil

Centre for Fortean Zoology Yearbook 2009 by Downes, Jonathan

CFZ EXPEDITION REPORT: Russia 2008 by Richard Freeman *et al*, Shuker, Karl (fwd)

Dinosaurs and other Prehistoric Animals on Stamps - A Worldwide catalogue by Shuker, Karl P. N

Dr Shuker's Casebook by Shuker, Karl P.N

The Island of Paradise - chupacabra UFO crash retrievals, and accelerated evolution on the island of Puerto Rico by Downes, Jonathan

The Mystery Animals of the British Isles: Northumberland and Tyneside by Hallowell, Michael J

Centre for Fortean Zoology Yearbook 1997 by Downes, Jonathan (Ed)

Centre for Fortean Zoology Yearbook 2002 by Downes, Jonathan (Ed)

Centre for Fortean Zoology Yearbook 2000/1 by Downes, Jonathan (Ed)

Centre for Fortean Zoology Yearbook 1998 by Downes, Jonathan (Ed)

Centre for Fortean Zoology Yearbook 2003 by Downes, Jonathan (Ed)

In the wake of Bernard Heuvelmans by Woodley, Michael A

CFZ EXPEDITION REPORT: Guyana 2007 by Richard Freeman *et al*, Shuker, Karl (fwd)

Centre for Fortean Zoology Yearbook 1999 by Downes, Jonathan (Ed)

Big Cats in Britain Yearbook 2008 by Fraser, Mark (Ed)

Centre for Fortean Zoology Yearbook 1996 by Downes, Jonathan (Ed)

THE CALL OF THE WILD - Animals & Men issues 11-15 Collected Editions Vol. 3 by Downes, Jonathan (ed)

Ethna's Journal by Downes, C N

Centre for Fortean Zoology Yearbook 2008 by Downes, J (Ed)

DARK DORSET -Calendar Custome by Newland, Robert J

Extraordinary Animals Revisited by Shuker, Karl

MAN-MONKEY - In Search of the British Bigfoot by Redfern, Nick

Dark Dorset Tales of Mystery, Wonder and Terror by Newland, Robert J and Mark North

Big Cats Loose in Britain by Matthews, Marcus

MONSTER! - The A-Z of Zooform Phenomena by Arnold, Neil

The Centre for Fortean Zoology 2004 Yearbook by Downes, Jonathan (Ed)

The Centre for Fortean Zoology 2007 Yearbook by Downes, Jonathan (Ed)

CAT FLAPS! Northern Mystery Cats by Roberts, Andy

Big Cats in Britain Yearbook 2007 by Fraser, Mark (Ed)

BIG BIRD! - Modern sightings of Flying Monsters by Gerhard, Ken

THE NUMBER OF THE BEAST - Animals & Men issues 6-10 Collected Editions Vol. 1 by Downes, Jonathan (Ed)

IN THE BEGINNING - Animals & Men issues 1-5 Collected Editions Vol. 1 by Downes, Jonathan

STRENGTH THROUGH KOI - They saved Hitler's Koi and other stories by Downes, Jonathan

The Smaller Mystery Carnivores of the Westcountry by Downes, Jonathan

CFZ EXPEDITION REPORT: Gambia 2006 by Richard Freeman *et al*, Shuker, Karl (fwd)

The Owlman and Others by Jonathan Downes

The Blackdown Mystery by Downes, Jonathan
Big Cats in Britain Yearbook 2006 by Fraser, Mark (Ed)
Fragrant Harbours - Distant Rivers by Downes, John T
Only Fools and Goatsuckers by Downes, Jonathan
Monster of the Mere by Jonathan Downes
Dragons:More than a Myth by Freeman, Richard Alan
Granfer's Bible Stories by Downes, John Tweddell
Monster Hunter by Downes, Jonathan

Fortean Words

The Centre for Fortean Zoology has for several years led the field in Fortean publishing. CFZ Press is the only publishing company specialising in books on monsters and mystery animals. CFZ Press has published more books on this subject than any other company in history and has attracted such well known authors as Andy Roberts, Nick Redfern, Michael Newton, Dr Karl Shuker, Neil Arnold, Dr Darren Naish, Jon Downes, Ken Gerhard and Richard Freeman.

Now CFZ Press are launching a new imprint. Fortean Words is a new line of books dealing with Fortean subjects other than cryptozoology, which is - after all - the subject the CFZ are best known for. Fortean Words is being launched with a spectacular multi-volume series called *Haunted Skies* which covers British UFO sightings between 1940 and 2010. Former policeman John Hanson and his long-suffering partner Dawn Holloway have compiled a peerless library of sighting reports, many that have not been made public before.

Other books include a look at the Berwyn Mountains UFO case by renowned Fortean Andy Roberts and a series of forthcoming books by transatlantic researcher Nick Redfern. CFZ Press are dedicated to maintaining the fine quality of their works with Fortean Words. New authors tackling new subjects will always be encouraged, and we hope that our books will continue to be as ground-breaking and popular as ever.

Haunted Skies Volume One 1940-1959 by John Hanson and Dawn Holloway
Haunted Skies Volume Two 1960-1965 by John Hanson and Dawn Holloway
Haunted Skies Volume Three 1965-1967 by John Hanson and Dawn Holloway
Haunted Skies Volume Four 1968-1971 by John Hanson and Dawn Holloway
Grave Concerns by Kai Roberts

Police and the Paranormal by Andy Owens
Dead of Night by Lee Walker
Space Girl Dead on Spaghetti Junction - an anthology by Nick Redfern
I Fort the Lore - an anthology by Paul Screeton
UFO Down - the Berwyn Mountains UFO Crash by Andy Roberts

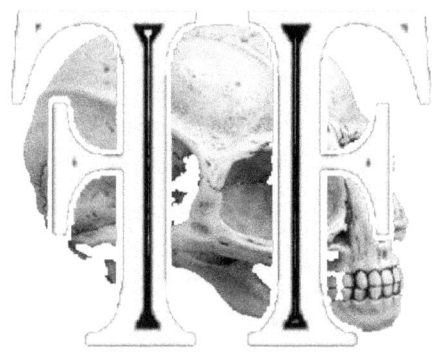

Fortean Fiction

J ust before Christmas 2011, we launched our third imprint, this time dedicated to - let's see if you guessed it from the title - fictional books with a Fortean or cryptozoological theme. We have published a few fictional books in the past, but now think that because of our rising reputation as publishers of quality Forteana, that a dedicated fiction imprint was the order of the day.

We launched with four titles:

Green Unpleasant Land by Richard Freeman
Left Behind by Harriet Wadham
Dark Ness by Tabitca Cope
Snap! By Steven Bredice